The Last Bl

JD Kirk lives in the north of Scotland with his wife, two children, and a number of sturdy umbrellas. He loves the Highlands, crime thrillers, and cats.

Also by JD Kirk

DCI Logan Crime Thrillers

JD KIRK

THE LAST BLOODY STRAW

CANELO CRIME

First published in the United Kingdom in 2020 by Zertex Crime

This edition published in the United Kingdom in 2024 by

Canelo
Unit 9, 5th Floor
Cargo Works, 1–2 Hatfields
London SE1 9PG
United Kingdom

A CIP catalogue record for this book is available from the British Library.

Paperback ISBN 978 1 80436 819 0

Look for more great books at www.canelo.co

Printed and bound in Great Britain by Clays Ltd, Elcograf S.p.A.

1

For all of us looking for an escape from these strange and difficult times we find ourselves in. Stay safe.

Chapter 1

The final evening of Iona Wallace's life started well enough. A couple of drinks in the house, the last of the oven chips—plenty of salt and vinegar—and a quick wash of the nether-regions over the bathroom sink, because you never knew your luck.

The weather had seen to it that the ferries were off more than they were on lately, but there might still be the odd tourist looking to have some fun. God knew, the island was in short supply of anything else that might pass for entertainment.

After a wee skoosh of perfume in all the wrong places, she wrestled herself into a dress. It was a figure-hugging burgundy number that matched her favourite shade of lipstick, which was about the only thing the dress had going for it these days.

She'd bought it a decade ago in Inverness. It hadn't been figure-hugging then. Nor, she suspected, was it ever designed to be.

Iona checked her cleavage, twisting and bending at the waist to survey it from every possible angle. Perfect. Sure, it was taking more and more scaffolding to keep it that way, but to the casual observer, she looked as young as she ever had.

Her reflection met her eye in the mirror.

Aye, right.

When she stepped outside, the cold grabbed her lungs and twisted, ejecting twin snorts of steam from her nostrils, and instantly cutting through her carefully cultivated alcohol fuzz.

'Jesus fuck!'

She pulled her coat tighter around her shoulders, hugging herself through it. The fur collar, once thick and luxurious, was now a sparse, paltry thing. She'd found it in a charity shop longer ago than she'd care to remember, and it had served as an important part of her armour ever since.

The identity of the animal that the fur had once belonged to had been a mystery back then, and was even more so now. Most people guessed mink. When they did, Iona would just wink and smile enigmatically, confirming nothing, and denying even less.

It was half a mile to the pub if you went by the track, a good bit less if you cut across the field. Her boots were reasonably sensible—between the island terrain and her back, heels were out of the question these days—but with the rain they'd been having of late, the field would be a marsh.

She shut the cottage's front door with a clunk that rattled the windows in their frames. There was no need to lock it. Not out here.

'You'll keep an eye on the place, won't you, Archie?' Iona cackled into the darkness. Fifty yards across the field, the pale moonlight picked out the eyeless hollows of a crudely-formed face.

Lighting the last cigarette from her crumpled pack, Iona took a draw, savoured the swirl of smoke as it warmed her lungs, then set off down the track under the empty-eyed gaze of the scarecrow.

–

'Christ. What's she doing here?'

Isaac Young found himself taking cover behind the double-doors of the pub, the sight of his mother stumbling from table to table freezing the blood in his veins more effectively than the cold wind blowing in off the water could ever hope to.

A hand slipped into his, fingers interlocking like they were a custom fit, built to be together. His fiancée, Louise, offered him the most convincingly authentic smile she could muster and gave his hand a squeeze.

2

'It'll be fine. It's a Tuesday night, and it's hardly party central in here. She probably won't stay long.'

Isaac exhaled slowly. 'Aye. She might get a lumber,' he said. He returned the smile, but it was even less genuine than the one Louise had plastered on. The pain in his eyes almost made her recoil.

Through the glass of the door, Isaac watched his mum draping herself over the bar, cleavage aimed squarely at the Australian barman, eyelids fluttering.

'Jesus, he's younger than me,' Isaac muttered.

'We can go somewhere else,' Louise suggested. 'There's always…' She ran through her mental list of available options. 'Home.'

Isaac was tempted. She could see it on his face, and in the way the tension in his shoulders eased off.

But then he shook his head.

'We came out for a drink. We're having a drink,' he said, then he pushed open the door, and they both stepped inside.

The warmth of the place reached out to welcome them, the fire blazing in the grate a Siren-call from the other side of the wood-panelled room.

There were half a dozen other people gathered near the fire. Most of them were local, and so made a point of not catching Isaac's eye, sparing all concerned from that moment of embarrassment.

A fella in his forties looked up from where he'd been studying a map at the corner table. He wasn't native to the island, and the big backpack propped up on the seat beside him suggested he had no intention of becoming one.

Nevertheless, he gave the newcomers a nod and a smile, tentatively attempting to initiate a conversation that neither of them had any interest in being part of.

'What you having?' Isaac asked Louise, his gaze still fixed on his mother's back. She was wearing that ugly fur coat and the burgundy dress that was too young for a woman half her age and a third her size.

'Bottle of Fraoch,' Louise said. 'Sure you don't want me to—?'

'It's fine,' Isaac said, already approaching the bar.

He took up a spot as far from his mother as it was possible to get. The bar was small and curved, though, so the distance between them was no distance at all.

The barman, Bruce, noticed him first, relief spreading across his face like a fast-acting rash as he extracted himself from the conversation with Iona and came striding over to Isaac, a slurred, 'Ah, fuck off, then,' following behind him.

'Evening, mate. What can I get for you?' asked Bruce, his Australian accent so thick as to almost be a parody of itself.

'Pint of cider and a bottle of Fraoch,' Isaac said. He'd gone from glaring at his mother to studiously avoiding meeting her eye. It was coming, of course—there was no escaping that—but he was happy to delay it for as long as he could.

Bruce's big forehead furrowed behind the curtains of his blond hair. 'Cider and…?'

'Fraoch,' Isaac repeated. He pointed to the fridge at the back of the bar. 'The heather ale.'

'Right. Gotcha. Sorry. Still getting the hang of the lingo,' Bruce beamed, reaching for a pint glass.

'Zac!'

Isaac took a slow breath through his nose. Here it came.

'Mum.'

She shambled closer, one arm in constant contact with the bar, like it was playing a vital part in her remaining upright.

'Ditched the bitch for the night, have you?' Iona asked. She grinned, showing a smudge of lipstick on her teeth. Each of her eyes seemed to be blinking independently of the other, and the wafts of her breath had probably pushed Isaac over the drink-drive limit before he'd touched a drop.

'Louise's over there,' Isaac replied, pointing to one of the tables by the fire.

Iona turned and spent a few seconds trying to focus, before she raised a hand and gave a little wave. Louise's reply was a curt nod, then a questioning look at Isaac that he dismissed with a shake of his head.

'Shite, aye, so she is,' Iona said, turning back to her son. 'You still…?'

'Yes. And we're happy.'

Iona pulled a face that suggested she couldn't possibly comprehend how, then shrugged and showed the lipstick on her teeth again. 'Buy your mum a drink.'

'I think you've had enough.'

She laughed at that. He didn't.

'Funny. Like your dad.'

Isaac blocked his mother's hand before she could reach up to stroke his hair. He'd been ready for it. For the insincerity of it. Of her.

'Come on. One drink. For your old mum.'

'Four-eighty, mate.'

Mother and son both turned as the drinks were set down. Bruce looked between them, settling in the end on Isaac.

'Or… sorry, did you want something else?'

Isaac fished in his pocket and pulled out a handful of coins. 'No,' he said, counting out the exact amount and handing it over. 'No, that's everything.'

The words were shouted at his back, each one louder and packed with more venom than the one before.

'Fucking selfish little *twat*!'

The pub was all but silent as Isaac took his seat, the only sound the crackling and popping of the logs on the fire, and the faint droning of the background music.

'You know what I gave up for you? What I fucking sacrificed?'

Louise answered on Isaac's behalf. 'Yes, everyone's very aware of what you sacrificed, Iona. Nothing.'

'The fuck's it got to do with you?' Iona snarled. She released her grip on the bar and stumbled, untethered, towards the group knotted around the fire. 'You snooty fucking jumped-up fucking… fucking… cow.'

Chair legs scraped on the rough wooden floor. One of the men who had been sitting staring into their drink straightened to his full, impressive height. His voice was slow and methodical, like each word was having to be thought about in advance.

'I think you should go.'

Iona almost collided with him, only stopping herself by placing a hand on his broad chest. It felt solid beneath his thick checked shirt.

'Dudley. You don't get it,' she spat. 'You don't know what the bitch is like.'

'You want to say that to my face?' Louise snapped.

'Gladly. If this big fucking… retard gets out of my way.'

Half a dozen heads turned her way.

'Hey, now!'

'That's enough of that.'

Iona looked across the angry faces glaring up at her. Her neighbours. Her 'friends'. What was it to do with them? What was it to do with anyone?

She turned away from them, and the backpacker in the corner was too slow in looking down.

'Haw. You,' she called over to him. 'Want to buy me a drink?'

The tourist raised his head just long enough to give it a shake.

Iona shifted her weight, creaking her leather boots. She adjusted her cleavage before trying again.

'You want to come back to my place?'

'Jesus Christ,' Isaac muttered, choking down a sip of his pint.

'Uh, no,' said the tourist. 'Thank you.'

'What are you? A poof or something?' Iona demanded, her face twisting into a scowl. She turned on the spot, arms out, presenting herself to the rest of the bar. 'Anyone else up for a go? Hmm? Buy us a drink and I'm all yours.'

Louise bounced to her feet, her knee clonking against the table and rocking the drinks in the glasses. She dodged past Dudley and slammed both hands against Iona's shoulders, sending her staggering clumsily towards the door.

'Oh, just fuck off, will you?' Louise spat. 'Look at you! Look at the state of you! You're an embarrassment, Iona. You're a complete fucking horror show, and you need to go. Seriously. Go.'

Iona stood by the door, her chest heaving, her face reddening with rage or shame or some rich blend of the two.

For several seconds, both women just stared at one another in the near-silence. Then, with a shifting of her gaze, Iona looked to Isaac. To her son.

'Are you going to let this bitch talk to me like that?'

Isaac looked up from his drink, just briefly. Just once.

'Go home, Mum,' he said. 'Just go home.'

–

The world lurched sickeningly, the slick, sodden ground contorting beneath her bare feet as if it were alive. She stumbled on through the dark, pain radiating from the wound on her head, blood nipping at eyes already blinded by the darkness.

She could hear the footsteps behind her. A little slower than her own, but more controlled. Less frantic. Gaining. Always gaining.

'Leave me alone!' she screamed into the chasing void.

Only the wet thacking of those footsteps replied. Stable. Steady.

Inevitable.

Her fur coat trailed behind her through the mud, flapping from one arm. Her shoes were gone. Her dress was torn. The alcohol and the head wound were working together to spin the world in looping circles around her, and she had no idea where she was running to. No idea where she was going.

Anywhere but here. Anywhere but now. Anywhere. Somewhere. Please, God, let her get somewhere.

The ground rolled like the deck of a ship in a storm. Thrown sideways, she caught sight of a figure standing in the darkness and grabbed for its outstretched arms, eyes pleading, mouth already babbling a cry for help.

'P-please, help me! Help me!'

The crudely stitched mouth couldn't have replied, even if it had wanted to. The empty, eyeless gaze of a hessian sack peered down at her, like Christ gazing down from the cross.

A breeze swirled around them, fluttering the scarecrow's ragged clothes, and almost disguising the slap–slap–slap of wet footsteps approaching.

Almost.

'Please, don't,' she whispered, still clinging to the scarecrow like it might yet leap to her defence.

The footsteps stopped. A weapon raised.

And Iona Wallace died, screaming in the dark.

Chapter 2

DCI Jack Logan regarded the man in the chair like one might regard a big daud of shite on a clean kitchen worktop. The big daud of shite in question smirked up at him from behind his expensive desk, his Italian leather seat creaking over and over as he rocked it incrementally back and forth.

'I would like to say I was expecting you, my friend. But this would be a lie, yes?'

Bosco Maximuke held his hands out in a welcoming gesture and ratcheted his smirk up a notch or two. 'Still. Is nice surprise. To what am I owing this pleasure?'

Logan didn't return the smile. He had no interest in exchanging pleasantries with the podgy Russian bastard. This was anything but a social call.

Not that Bosco had any real intention of making nice, either. Logan could feel Valdis, the largest and most Neanderthal-like of Bosco's small army of henchmen, looming a pace or two behind him. He could hear the faint whistle of the man's breathing, hear the rustling of his gloved fingers as they curled into fists over and over and over again. Classic intimidation strategy.

Aye, good luck with that.

Logan shot a glance over to the corner of the room, where Bosco's daughter was tapping away on an iPad, a set of *Pokémon* headphones clamped over her ears.

'In-service day,' Bosco said, reading the detective's mind. 'I swear, I should've been teacher. So much time off.'

'Teachers work in-service days,' the girl said, without turning.

'Oh. Well. Good,' Bosco said, after a moment's thought. 'This is what my taxes pay for. This and...' He gave a dismissive wave in Logan's direction. '...you people, of course.'

Clasping his hands on the desk in front of him, the Russian leaned forward. 'Please, my friend, speak freely,' he told the DCI. 'What brings you here to my workplace? Have you come to scratch my back, or are you hoping for me to scratch yours?'

'Neither, actually,' Logan replied. 'I met some friends of yours recently. Or... associates, maybe. Sandy and Maureen Gillespie. Down near Fort William.'

Bosco puffed out his acne-scarred cheeks, his smile fixed in place. 'Never heard of them.'

'See, I think you have,' Logan argued. 'I think you knew them well. I think you and they had a business relationship going on, Bosco. A thriving business relationship.'

'Oh! They were in building trade?' the Russian asked, with an air of innocence that didn't remotely suit him.

'The other business,' Logan said. 'And I think it turned sour after one of their guys went and got himself killed, when he was supposed to be bringing in a shipment of merchandise from abroad.'

He took a hand from his coat pocket and jabbed a finger in the Russian's direction. 'Your shipment. Your merchandise.'

The floor of the Portakabin office creaked as Valdis shifted his weight. Bosco shot him a look, and Logan could swear he felt the henchman's internal struggle as he fought to contain himself.

'I, of course, have no idea what you mean, Detective Chief Inspector,' Bosco said. 'I resent any suggestion that I may be mixed up in any... how would you say? Criminal activity. If this is what you are suggesting.'

'Do us both a favour and cut the shite, Bosco. I know you were funnelling your gear through the Gillespies,' Logan said, his voice dropping into a guttural growl. He jabbed a thumb over his shoulder. 'And I know that you—or, more likely, this big streak o' pish—killed Maureen.'

'Oh, and how would you know such a thing?' Bosco asked.

'Sandy,' said Logan, and the word seemed to hang there in the air between them. 'Sandy told us everything.'

Bosco stopped rocking in his chair. The creaking of Valdis's gloves fell silent, too, and the only sound in the office was the tapping and swiping of Olivia's fingers on the iPad screen, and the faint tshk, tshk, tshk, of music playing over her headphones.

Eventually, the Russian cleared his throat. His smile, which had all but died away, returned, bringing reinforcements with it. 'Oh. Did he, now?'

Logan said nothing.

Damn it.

So much for that plan.

'No, I think he did not. I think if this "Sandy" you speak of had told you the things you say he told you, then you would not be standing here in my office alone. You would not be—what is word? Fishing. You would have cars, and vans. Helicopters, maybe. You would have idiots in uniform scurrying around, poking their noses in. Poke, poke. Pry, pry.'

Bosco rolled his chair back and stood up. The shirt he was wearing probably cost more than Logan made in a week, but the Russian's squat, bloated frame did it no favours at all.

Logan watched in silence as Bosco unfastened his gold cuff-links and began to roll up the shirt sleeves with slow, calculated precision.

'You know what I think, old friend? I think that nobody knows you are here. I think you are here on personal vendetta. I think you are looking for someone to blame for death of… policewoman. What was her name again?'

Logan bristled. Deep in the pockets of his coat, his hands became fists.

'Caitlyn? This is right, yes? Caitlyn… silly Scottish name…' Bosco clicked his fingers, like the name was dancing around on the tip of his tongue. 'McQuarrel?'

'Detective Sergeant McQuarrie,' Logan said. 'And yes.'

Bosco finished rolling up his sleeves and raised an eyebrow. 'Yes?'

'You're right. Nobody knows I'm here. Honestly? I don't care if you were supplying the Gillespies. Not really. That'll all come out in the wash sooner or later. That's CID's job, no' mine.'

He took a half-step forward so he was towering over the desk, and the man standing behind it.

'But yes, Bosco, I'd very much like to blame someone for the death of DS McQuarrie. Don't get me wrong, Sandy Gillespie pulled the trigger, and I'm going to make damn sure that he spends every waking moment of his miserable life deeply regretting that decision.'

Taking his hands from his pockets, Logan leaned down. He placed his knuckles on the desk and rested his weight on them, like a silverback gorilla demonstrating its dominance.

'But I also hold the individual who drove him to pull that trigger equally responsible,' he continued. His voice was flat and measured. No nonsense. Matter-of-fact. 'I also blame the person who got him so scared, so wound up, that he shot one of my officers dead. You see, *that* person? That's the one I'm gunning for now, Bosco.'

He gave that a moment to sink in, before standing up straight.

'And, let me be very clear when I say that I will stop at nothing to bring that bastard down. I'll dedicate my life to it, if I have to. Whatever protections he's built around himself, whatever wee empire he thinks he lords it over, I will burn it all to the ground with him inside it, and I will dance on the fucking ashes. Is that understood?'

For a moment, Bosco almost looked concerned, but then he nodded sympathetically. 'I understand, my friend. I do. It was tragic loss. We were all very cut up when we heard about her having her guts blown out.'

Bosco made the sound of a gunshot, then clutched at his stomach before beaming broadly over Logan's shoulder. 'Weren't we, Valdis?'

'Heartbroken,' agreed Valdis. His accent was thicker and less polished than Bosco's. The voice came from closer than Logan had expected. A pace. Half a pace, maybe. No distance at all.

'You know what else upsets me?' Bosco continued. He was peering down at his metal desk organiser, fingers dancing above an assortment of pens and pencils.

He finally selected a metal fountain pen, removed the lid, and tapped his finger gingerly against the pointed tip. He hissed as it drew blood, then gave the fingertip a quick suck before continuing.

'Your arrogance. Your stupidity. You are suggesting that I am big bad guy. That I am evil villain, but you come barging in here making accusations. Making your threats. In front of my employees. In front of my family.'

He gestured to Olivia, who was still glued to her iPad, paying them no heed whatsoever.

'You have no evidence. No proof,' Bosco said.

Logan heard the clunk of the door being locked behind him.

'No back-up. No support. No-one who knows where you are.'

Bosco's smile broadened, showing his yellowing teeth.

'Death of the woman cop has made you forgetful. Careless, maybe,' the Russian continued. 'You forget that I know things, my friend. That I have scratched your back in past. Do your bosses know this? Your subordinates? I think not. What would they say? What would they think of you? What would they do to the great Detective Chief Inspector Jack Logan if they knew what you really are?'

Bosco rolled his chair in all the way under his desk, and untucked his shirt from his belt. Freed from this constraint, his stomach flopped out over the top of his belt. One of the bottom buttons had come undone, revealing a diamond of hairy flesh.

'I think maybe you need reminder of who is in charge here, yes?' Bosco said. 'I think we must do you favour, and jog your memory.'

Logan sensed the looming presence of Valdis behind him again. He felt the heat of the man's breath on the nape of his neck, breathed in the stink of it. He watched as Bosco turned the pen over and over in his hands, the pointed nib glinting in the office's artificial lighting.

He knew what was coming next. Of course he did. He'd known from the moment he'd set foot inside the office. From the moment he'd made his excuses to get out of the station that afternoon.

From before then, even. When he'd woken up that morning. When he'd stood at Caitlyn's graveside. When he'd sat at the back of the church watching her parents crying in the front row.

When he'd seen the hole in Sandy Gillespie's front door, and the spray of blood on the path.

Yes, that was it. Then. That was when he'd known this moment was coming. That was when he knew he'd be standing here. Now. In this room.

'You not going to send her out of the room first?' Logan asked, indicating Bosco's daughter with a nod. 'She doesn't need to see this.'

'Forgive me, old friend, but I do not think you are right man to give parenting advice. Anyway, I disagree. One day, this will all be hers,' Bosco said, gesturing around at the world in general. 'She must get used to the business of doing business sooner or later. Yes? Why not today?'

'You sure that's wise? I mean, how old is she?' Logan asked.

Bosco's smile was swept away by an indignant sneer. 'None of your fucking business. That is how old,' he snapped, then he gave a wave of his hand, and Logan felt a burst of movement behind him.

He was ready as the bastard made a grab for him. A half-step back, a sudden jerk of the head, and Valdis's nose exploded against the back of Logan's skull. The detective followed it up with an elbow to the henchman's solar plexus, then turned and capped it all off with a particularly satisfying knee to the balls.

Satisfying for him, at least. Less so for Valdis, judging by the way he buckled in the middle and dropped to the floor, choking on snot, tears, and a not inconsiderable amount of blood.

Bosco stared, open-mouthed, as Logan rounded on him. He tried to retreat, but there was nothing but wall behind him, leaving nowhere for him to go.

He yelped in fright as Logan lunged across the desk and grabbed him by the shirt, cried out in shock as the pen was ripped from his grasp and his hand was slammed onto the desktop.

Logan raised the pen, nib pointing downwards. Bosco's face came alive with panic.

'No, no, please, no! My daughter! My daughter is here!'

'Come on, Bosco. Got to get her used to the business of doing business, sooner or later, eh?' Logan spat, his grip tightening on the pen's metal casing. 'Why not today?'

He brought the pen down hard. Bosco screamed—a high-pitched squeal like a pig going to slaughter—as the pointed nib tore through the web of flesh between forefinger and thumb, and was embedded into the desktop below.

'You… fuck! Crazy fuck!' the Russian sobbed.

Logan turned and looked over his shoulder at Olivia, who was gazing at them in rapt fascination.

'You. Outside,' he told her. 'Now.'

The girl's brow furrowed in complaint. 'Aw, but I want to—'

'Just do as you're told, all right?' Logan instructed.

She looked between the detective and her father for a few moments, then tutted and picked up her iPad.

'Fine,' she muttered, stepping over Valdis on her way to the door.

She stopped there and shot a look back at her father. Her expression wasn't one of concern, more a sort of mild irritation.

'Should I, like, call the police or something?'

'Fuck, no!' Bosco hissed. He swallowed, steadying his voice. 'I mean… no. We are… chatting. Is all. Having conversation. Yes?'

Olivia rolled her eyes. 'Fine. If you die, it's your own stupid fault,' she said, then she opened the door so wide it thumped the foetal Valdis on the back of the head, and left.

'Apple doesn't fall far from the tree with that one, eh, Bosco?' Logan said, once the door had slammed closed behind the girl. 'I'll have to keep my eye on her when she's older.'

He twisted the pen, then yanked it free. Blood seeped from Bosco's wound, pooling over the paperwork that lay scattered across the desk.

'Now,' Logan growled, leaning closer to the whimpering Russian. 'What was that you were saying about being in charge?'

–

Logan's phone rang just as he shut the car door. He tapped the ignition button and let the Volvo's Bluetooth connect. The words, 'Yon Arsehole', flashed up on the radio screen. Logan sighed before tapping the green phone icon.

'Detective Constable Neish,' he said. 'What can I do for you?'

Tyler's voice sounded uncharacteristically rich and deep over the car's speaker system, yet somehow still retained the fingernails–down–a–blackboard effect it usually had on Logan.

'All right, boss? Where are you?'

'Ach, just out and about,' Logan said. 'Nowhere exciting.'

He glanced in his wing mirror as a flash of blue light caught his eye. Tyler started to reply, but the screaming of passing sirens made it impossible for Logan to hear him.

'What was that?' the DC asked, once the racket had thundered by.

'Fire engine,' Logan said, reaching for his seatbelt.

He watched the big red vehicle take a corner, headed for the growing column of grey–black smoke rising a couple of streets away.

'There a fire, or something?' Tyler asked.

'Naw, they probably just fancied a wee day out,' Logan replied. He rolled his eyes at the silence that followed. 'Aye, son, there's a fire. Now, what do you want?'

'Oh. Aye,' Tyler said, remembering his reason for calling. 'We've had a shout. Body found on one of the islands.'

'Which one?'

'Eh, a woman, I think. Forties. There's not a lot of info through yet.'

Logan's brow furrowed. As with most conversations involving Tyler, he could feel a low-level headache developing behind his eyes.

'I hope that was a joke, son. Which island, I mean, no' which body.'

'Oh. Haha. Aye. Just kidding, boss,' Tyler said, but Logan had been in the job long enough to know bullshit when he heard it.

There was a rustling of papers down the line before Tyler spoke again.

'Canna, boss. Heard of it?'

'Of course I've bloody heard of it,' Logan said.

'Right. Aye,' Tyler said, in a tone that suggested he hadn't. 'Ferries are off with the weather, so they're choppering us over.'

Logan grunted and put the car into gear. 'Christ, Ben'll be like a kid at Christmas,' he remarked.

'No, boss. DI Forde and Hamza are both on their way back from Dundee. Won't arrive in the office for a couple of hours. They're not heading over yet.'

Logan stiffened in his seat. 'Right. Then who's all going?'

Even down the phone, he could hear the DC grin.

'Just me and you, boss.'

Logan's response was mercifully drowned out by the wailing of another passing siren.

'Was that another one? Big fire, is it, boss?'

'Aye, pretty substantial,' Logan said. He shot a glance at the column of smoke and allowed himself a grim smile. 'If I do say so myself.'

Chapter 3

The only part of DC Neish that was currently whiter than his knuckles was his face. It had taken on a greyish hue soon after take-off in Inverness, and in the forty-five minutes that followed had paled to the point of near translucence.

His eyes were shut, and Logan could hear him groan over his headphones whenever the helicopter ascended, descended, turned, or otherwise made any sort of movement whatsoever.

A light sheen of sweat glistened on Tyler's forehead. Light danced across it whenever his head bobbed around. Which, given the current turbulence, was constantly.

'Mayday! Mayday!'

Tyler's eyes snapped open. Somehow, his face managed to turn a full shade whiter.

'What? Fuck! What's wrong?' he yelped, eyes fixed desperately on the DCI.

Logan looked up from his phone. Despite the headset comm-system, he still had to raise his voice to be heard over the thrumming of the rotor blades overhead.

'Hmm? Oh. Sorry. There's nothing. I'm just planning my holidays for next year. I'm thinking of taking the Mayday weekend.'

'Aye. Funny. Good one, boss,' Tyler croaked, closing his eyes and settling his head back against the seat.

He was sitting behind the pilot, a stern-looking older man who had barely spoken a word to them since the pick-up, and who looked entirely unimpressed by Logan's attempt at humour.

Not as unimpressed as DC Neish looked, granted—not by a long shot—but unimpressed all the same.

Logan sat up front, watching the water roll by below them. Rain lashed at the windscreen, and the pilot's lack of conversation was probably down to how hard he was concentrating on fighting against the wind and keeping them in the air.

'We nearly there yet?' Tyler asked, not for the first time.

The pilot gestured ahead. 'That's it,' he muttered. Which, for him, was positively chatty.

Tyler risked opening an eye and leaned over so he could see between the front seats. An island rose out of the storm a mile or so ahead. From this distance, it looked wild and unwelcoming, but Tyler had never been more grateful to see anywhere in his life.

'Is it your first time in a chopper, or something?' Logan asked.

Tyler shook his head. 'No. First time in this weather, though.'

Right on cue, a gust of wind buffeted the helicopter, forcing the pilot to wrestle with the stick.

It hadn't been too bad in Inverness. A few spots of rain. A bit of a breeze. Practically tropical for the area.

Ten minutes into the flight, though, everything had taken a turn for the worse. Since then, it had seemed like the gods themselves had been conspiring to turn the helicopter back. They'd gone through every possible type of precipitation, from rain to hail and back again, all hammered into them by gale-force winds.

'Aye, it's a bit of a rough one, right enough,' Logan said. He shrugged. 'Still, on the bright side, at least we're not in the same chopper as Geoff and his lot.'

Geoff Palmer and the rest of the Scene of Crime team had set off for Canna almost as soon as the call had been received. Apparently, they were hoping to beat the weather front that was rapidly moving in.

'What are they flying in? A fucking time machine?' Logan had asked, after just the briefest of looks at the weather map.

There was no chance of them getting to the scene before the storm hit, but if it meant not having to spend the better part of an hour cooped up with Palmer, Logan was all in favour of them trying.

The helicopter began its descent without any warning. It was far less smooth than even Logan would've liked, and the contents of his stomach sloshed unpleasantly upwards as he heard a whimper from Tyler crackling in his ears.

'Soon be on the ground, son,' he said.

Tyler swallowed. 'Cheers, boss.'

'Whether we'll be in one piece or not,' the DCI continued. 'That's another question…'

–

'They could've at least given it a clear-out first,' Tyler grumbled. He had been inside the Land Rover for less than five seconds, and was already complaining.

It was, Logan feared, going to be a very long trip.

'I mean, look at this.'

Tyler lifted a partially crumpled Red Bull can from the passenger footwell. A smattering of ash around the hole on top told them someone had been using it as an ashtray.

'There's loads of empty crisp bags on the floor, too,' Tyler continued. 'Did nobody tell them we were coming?'

Fewer than fifty people lived on the island—not enough for a full-time police presence—and the only available vehicle was an ancient National Trust for Scotland Land Rover that had probably seen more welders than the Clyde shipyards.

'You could always walk,' Logan suggested. 'It's only a couple of miles.'

Tyler peered out through the blurry windscreen. The wipers were going at full-tilt, but it was very much a losing battle. When the wind wasn't angrily slamming itself against the Land Rover, it was whistling in through a thousand tiny gaps, filling the vehicle with the kind of air that fogged the inside of all the windows.

Tyler tossed the Red Bull can onto the back seat, where it joined half a dozen others.

'Nah, you're all right,' he said, kicking aside the carpet of litter to make room for his feet. 'I'm sure I'll cope.'

'What a trooper,' Logan remarked. He cranked the key until the engine coughed into life, then studied the controls on the dash. 'Now, where the hell's the blower on this thing?'

—

Twenty minutes of partially-blinded directionless driving down dirt tracks later, Logan and Tyler finally arrived at the scene.

They parked the Land Rover at the edge of a field where several members of the SOC team were struggling to fasten down a tent under the direction of Geoff Palmer.

They were too far away to be able to hear what Palmer was saying, but from the way he was stomping and flailing his arms around, it was clear he wasn't having an enjoyable time.

Another helicopter, larger than the one they'd flown in, stood at the far end of the field. They could just make out the pilot sitting watching on from the cockpit and occasionally sipping from a Thermos flask.

Logan cursed himself. Tea. Why hadn't he thought of that?

'We should probably give them a hand,' Tyler said, as the SOC team grappled with the writhing sheet of white canvas.

'We probably should, aye,' Logan agreed.

Neither man moved.

Across the field, one corner of the tent was whipped up into the air, and Geoff Palmer literally jumped up and down on the spot in rage.

'God. He's having a hell of a time of it,' Logan remarked.

'Terrible, boss.'

They sat observing in silence. The Land Rover groaned in a sudden gust of wind.

Outside, Palmer raised his face to the sky and shouted loudly enough for them to hear it, if not make out any of the actual words.

'Aye. Just terrible,' said Logan. He indicated the folder in Tyler's lap. 'The victim. How long did the report say she's been missing for?'

Tyler consulted the printout through the transparent plastic. 'Last seen five nights ago in the local pub. Nobody's heard from her since then.'

Logan nodded. 'They're going to get bugger all evidence from the scene anyway, then,' he said. His seat squeaked as he settled himself back into it. 'Might as well give it another few minutes.'

Chapter 4

Palmer didn't hold back when Logan and Tyler joined them inside the tent.

'Oh, look who finally decide to show their faces,' he spat. 'Thanks for the assist, lads. Good of you to help out.'

'Ach, come on now, Geoff. You lot know what you're doing. We'd only have got in the way,' Logan said. 'Besides, someone had to film it for YouTube.'

The circle of Geoff's face that was visible within the folds of the white paper hood contorted in displeasure. Behind him, the rest of the team bustled around, already taking their photographs and measurements.

'New member of the team?' asked Logan, nodding past them to the far end of the tent.

A scarecrow slouched there, knocked onto an awkward angle, like something had crashed into it. Despite the angle, the top of its head almost touched the canvas roof of the tent. Down at its feet, a person-sized lump was covered by a sheet that was already going damp around the edges.

The ground was a quagmire of mud and wet grass. By all accounts, it had been raining pretty constantly for the past week, and if the victim had been here since she went missing—and the cloyingly sweet smell of decay that was starting to pollute the tent suggested she had—then the chances of getting anything useful from the scene were low.

Still, much as Logan hated to admit it, Palmer's lot had a better chance than most. Palmer himself was a horrible bastard, but he and his team knew their way around a murder scene.

'What have we got?' Logan asked.

'What have we got?' Palmer parroted. 'A body, a scarecrow, and two massive pains in my arse, that's what we've got.'

He looked both detectives up and down, making his point very clear.

'If you want more than that, you'll have to wait. Maybe if you'd given us a hand to get the tent set up, we'd be further along, but for now, that's all you're getting.'

'Aye. Right. Very good,' said Logan, who had tuned Palmer out midway through the man's first sentence, when it was obvious he wasn't going to prove himself useful.

Picking his way carefully over to the body in his paper boots, he took a pencil from his pocket and lifted the edge of the sheet.

'Do you mind?' Palmer snapped.

Logan glanced up at him. Palmer's angry red face was a swollen circle surrounded by the white hood of his suit.

'Jesus, Geoff. You look like the Japanese flag. Take a breath, man,' the DCI said, then he turned his attention back to the lifeless shape beneath the sheet. 'Head injury,' he observed. 'Looks like it would've bled a lot, but the rain's washed most of it off. Plenty on her coat, though. Still looks pretty superficial, though. Not deep.'

He squatted down, taking a closer look. A deep red welt ran across the victim's throat, a line of bruising cushioning it on either side.

'Strangled, by the looks of it. Thin rope or wire.' He shot Geoff a look. 'Keep an eye out for it.'

Palmer tutted, then raised his voice, addressing the rest of the team. 'Hear that, everyone? Since we're all here, the Detective Chief Inspector would like us to look out for a murder weapon. Add that to your To-Do lists, will you?'

There was a murmur of half-laughter from the others, and Palmer drew Logan a filthy look. 'Anything else you'd like us to look out for, Jack? Clues, maybe? Evidence of some description?'

'Aye, very good,' Logan muttered.

'I tell you, it's a good thing you're here, or we'd be fumbling about in the dark with our thumbs up our arses, trying to figure out what to do next.'

Logan gave Palmer a cool, protracted stare that suggested the point had been made, and it would be in everyone's best interests if he shut his mouth and got back to work.

Palmer shook his head, mumbled, 'Keep a bloody eye out for it,' but then turned away before Logan's stare bored a hole right through his skull.

After a brief check to make sure Tyler was writing down his observations, Logan turned back to the corpse.

She was in her mid-forties, by the looks of her. Roughly around Logan's age. Her eyes were open, the red fractures on the whites of her eyeballs supporting the strangulation theory.

There was a small mole, like a beauty spot, on her left cheek. She would've been a looker back in the day, but the years had taken their toll on her complexion.

Being murdered almost certainly hadn't helped, either.

Logan's brow furrowed. He craned his neck so he was looking at the victim's face straight-on.

'See something, boss?' asked Tyler, his pencil hovering over his notepad.

'What did you say her name was?' Logan asked, not looking up.

'I didn't. I don't think so, anyway,' the DC replied. He wiped the rain off his plastic folder with a sleeve, and consulted his notes. 'It's, eh... Wallace,' he said, angling the printout towards one of the lights the SOC team had set-up. 'First name...'

'Iona?'

Tyler looked up from his folder. 'Eh, aye. Aye. How'd you know that?'

'Formerly Iona Kerr,' Logan said. He let the sheet drop back into place, then stood up. He sighed. It was a heavy, weary thing that came from somewhere deep inside him. 'That there's the lassie who took my virginity.'

Logan sat in the Land Rover, watching Tyler trampling around in the rain as he tried to get a signal on his phone.

After leaving the SOC team to do their stuff, they'd driven to the most south-westerly point on the island, in the hope of picking up a network bar or two. Judging by the convoluted interpretative dance Tyler was in the process of performing, Logan reckoned their odds were not good.

He flicked on the wipers, clearing the screen. Across the water, the Isle of Rum rose darkly through a bank of grey mist. To most folk on the mainland, Rum was the very definition of 'the arse end of nowhere'.

Canna was a step further still. It was right at the arse end of the arse end of nowhere. In fact, if the arse end of nowhere sprouted a tail, Canna would be clinging for dear life to the tip.

It was probably nice enough, Logan thought. Given that his only experience of it to date was pishing rain, a Land Rover almost as old as he was, and the body of a former fling lying rotting in a field, it was unlikely to make his list of top places to visit.

Iona Kerr. Jesus. That was a name he hadn't thought of in a long time.

He'd first met her in Primary School, where her name had provided countless hours of mirth.

Iona Kerr.

Oh, really? What colour is it? How fast does it go? Can you gie us a lift hame in it?

That sort of thing.

They were in different classes and social groups in high school, and hadn't really spoken to each other until the night of the fourth year school disco, when they'd reconnected in the most literal of senses.

That would make them, what? Fifteen or sixteen when they'd done the deed. A clumsy, late-night fumble in an unfamiliar close in the east end of Glasgow that had painted neither of them in a particularly good light, and which they never spoke of to each other again.

Her big brother had gotten wind of it a few weeks after it had happened. Him and a couple of his mates had leathered seven shades out of Logan. They'd given him his first broken nose of what was, over the decades since, to be many.

Still. Absolutely worth it, though.

The family had moved away a couple of months later. Iona's old man was a minister, or a priest, or something, Logan dimly recalled. Strict old bugger, always a bit too eager with the belt, by all accounts.

The mother wasn't on the scene, hadn't been for a few years. Logan had never known why. A lot of folk locally reckoned that was why Iona had ended up the way she was. Loud. Reckless.

Desperate.

He'd wondered about her occasionally in the weeks and months that had followed her leaving. Until, one day, he hadn't. One day, she was just no longer occupying any space in his head.

Until today.

'Getting wilder out there, boss,' said Tyler, breathlessly ejecting the words as he pulled open the passenger door.

Seizing its chance, the wind swirled in around the footwell, whipping half a dozen crisp bags and an empty Jaffa Cakes box out of the car and into the air.

Tyler grabbed for them, frantically snatching and grasping like a contestant on *The Crystal Maze*. He came away empty-handed, and Logan could only tut his disapproval as the wind carried the litter towards the water that crashed against the rocks at the island's edge.

'Well, that's a turtle dead,' Logan remarked, as the crisp bags alighted on the tide. 'Good work, son.'

'I tried to grab them,' Tyler protested, sheepishly clambering into the car and pulling the door closed.

Logan nodded. 'Aye. And breathtaking it was to watch, too. Like a gazelle having a seizure.'

Tyler pulled on his seatbelt, hands shaking from the cold. Logan nudged up the heating a few degrees. Not too far, obviously. No point spoiling the lad.

'I'm guessing from your performance out front that you didn't get a signal.'

'Not a thing, boss,' Tyler said. 'Didn't even flicker.'

Logan nodded. No surprise. 'Aye. That figures,' he said, staring blankly out through the rain-blurred windscreen ahead.

'You all right?' Tyler asked.

Logan blinked and turned to the junior officer. 'What? What do you mean? Aye. Why?'

'Just... you know. The victim. Iona,' Tyler said, shifting uncomfortably in his already uncomfortable seat. 'You and her. Your relationship, and all that.'

Logan let out a derisory grunt. 'We had a drunken teenage fumble. She wasn't exactly the love of my life.'

'Aye. No. I know,' Tyler said. 'It's just... if you need to talk, or anything...'

'I'm pretty sure I'll cope, son,' Logan said, cutting him off. 'I don't need an agony aunt. What I need is a competent—no, a *vaguely* competent—police officer to assist in this investigation.'

He turned the key in the ignition, and the Land Rover's engine reluctantly turned over on the third try.

'But since I don't have one of them available at the moment, you'll have to stand in,' Logan concluded. He checked his watch. 'Right, we've got a couple of hours before Palmer finishes up. What's say we go meet the locals?'

Chapter 5

Canna's main, and in many regards *only,* street ran from the ferry terminal, past a shop, a café, and a pub, then meandered off into the wilderness never to be seen again.

As much through old habits as any sort of strategy, it was outside the pub where Logan elected to pull up in the Land Rover, smoke farting in great grey puffs from the vehicle's rattling exhaust.

The pub was housed in a whitewashed old stone building. Its name, 'Canna Come Inn,' was painted on a wooden board above the door.

'Quality,' Tyler remarked, when he saw the sign, although Logan couldn't tell if he was being sarcastic or not.

There were no other cars parked along the road, and a solitary older woman stood watering a basket of flowers that hung from an arm fixed to a street light a little further along from where they'd parked.

Were it anywhere else in the world, Logan would've said the place was deserted. For here, though, it was practically rush hour.

Still, at least the rain was off. For now.

Tyler's phone gave a bleep, and he quickly fumbled in his pocket for it. A text displayed on the screen, letting him know he had three voicemails. He flicked his gaze up to the notification bar at the top of the screen in time to see the single signal bar become an empty triangle once more.

'Bastard,' he muttered. 'Missed it.'

Logan checked his own phone. No signal. No messages. No missed calls.

No point.

He switched it off to save the battery, then shoved it back in his inside coat pocket.

Truth be told, it was almost a relief to be out of signal. Given the barrage of anonymous phone calls he'd been receiving lately, he wasn't going to complain too much about being out of reach.

Besides, Detective Superintendent Hoon was bound to be gunning for him soon. The longer he could delay that particular conversation, the better.

'Right. Let's go see what we can find out,' he said, jabbing the button that unfastened his seatbelt.

They had both barely opened the doors before the woman with the watering can came tearing up the pavement towards them.

'Hey. No, no! You can't park that there!'

Logan stepped out, very deliberately closed his door, and produced his warrant card as the woman rushed up, brandishing the watering can like an offensive weapon.

She wasn't as old as she'd looked at a distance. What he'd taken as wrinkles seemed to just be her default resting face—mouth puckered up, eyes narrowed in suspicion.

'Police,' Logan said.

'I don't care if you're the Queen of bloody Sheba, you can't park there,' the woman insisted. 'It's an obstruction.'

Logan and Tyler looked along the street in both directions. There didn't seem to be a whole lot of anything to obstruct.

The DCI's instinct was to point out that there were no yellow lines or 'No Parking' signs, and to tell the woman to ram her objection up her hoop, but it was a tight-knit community, and he suspected it wouldn't do to get on the wrong side of this one.

'Of course. We'll get it shifted,' he said, in a display of diplomacy that drew a faint gasp of surprise from DC Neish.

'Right. Yes. I should think so,' the woman replied, none of the fight going out of her.

'Where do you suggest we stick it?' Logan asked, even though he could think of a few places. One in particular.

'There's a parking spot further down,' she said, a little waspishly. A quick jerk of a hand indicated a painted white box a dozen yards along the same road. If the car was an obstruction in its current spot, it would be no less of one over there.

It took all Logan's self-control to toss Tyler the keys. 'Shift it, will you, DC Neish? Like Mrs...?'

'Bryden,' the woman sniffed. 'Joy Bryden.'

Joy. Logan almost laughed. Her parents must've been sorely disappointed.

'Chair of the Community Council,' she added. Logan wasn't in the least bit surprised by this information, but still felt a shudder of dread ripple through him from head to toe.

How many Community Council meetings had he spoken at over the years? How many times had he been forced to field questions so banal and inane that just a modicum of common sense and five-seconds thinking time would've negated their need to be asked?

Once you took murderers, rapists, and all that lot out of the equation, the only thing Logan despised more than the average Community Council chairperson was a member of the tabloid press. And, truth be told, it was quite a close-run thing.

'Of course you are,' he said, smiling at the woman in a way that showed far too many of his teeth.

He joined her on the pavement while Tyler climbed into the driver's seat of the Land Rover. Logan watched him adjust the position of the seat and the angle of the mirrors before telling him to 'stop pissing about', in no uncertain terms.

'It's literally driving two car-lengths down the hill. We could've just taken off the handbrake and let it roll down,' he concluded, but Tyler was already over-revving the engine, and pointing at his ear to suggest he couldn't hear what the DCI was saying.

Logan and Joy both stepped into the pub doorway as a haze of blue-black smoke came hissing from the exhaust, and the Land Rover creaked off down the incline towards the designated parking space.

'You'll be here about the body,' Joy said. Her nostrils flared, like she didn't approve of that sort of thing. *Bodies.* 'It's Iona Wallace, I hear.'

The way she said the name made a little light blink on inside Logan's head. He got the sense that Joy probably didn't like very many people, but from the tone she took and the way her mouth turned down at the corners, she'd disliked Iona more than most.

Logan could see it. The Iona he remembered would've been the complete antithesis to the sour-faced specimen standing before him now. The average Community Council wouldn't last five minutes in the same room as the Iona Kerr of old.

'Did you know her?' Logan asked. Stupid question on an island whose entire population could fit on one double-decker bus, but he wanted to gauge her reaction.

'Of course I knew her. Everyone knew her. Everyone knows everyone,' Joy replied. 'But her, especially.'

'What do you mean by that?'

'Let's just say, her own business was rarely her own business. She'd enough dirty laundry to start her own launderette, that one. If you find anyone with a good word to say about her, you'll be doing well. And they'll be lying,' Joy said.

She sniffed and pulled her jacket tighter around herself. It was an expensive waterproof number. Probably a necessity of island life, if the wind was anything to go by.

'Not that I'm one to talk ill of the dead,' she added, clearly as an afterthought. 'And it's all poor Abraham needs at his age.'

Logan raised an eyebrow, but didn't need to ask the question.

'Her father. The minister. Years of trouble she's given him. Years of it. He's been very tolerant, considering, and how does she thank him?'

'Well, Mrs Bryden, I highly doubt she got herself murdered on purpose...'

Joy's ears visibly pricked up. Logan bit down on his tongue, but far too late.

'So it is murder, then? I'd heard a rumour, but I didn't want to say anything. I'm no' one for gossip.'

That, Logan thought, was very hard to believe.

'We're still investigating. We'll know more when the forensics team has finished up and a full post-mortem has been carried out.'

He glanced around and lowered his voice. 'But between you and me, Joy? Just between us? Aye. I think she was murdered. I think she was murdered, and I think there's a very good chance that whoever did it is still here on the island.'

Joy stepped in closer, enjoying being part of the detective's inner circle. 'I mean, that would make sense. The ferries haven't been running for days. I haven't seen any other boats coming and going, not with the gales.'

She put a hand to her chest to steady herself, then squinted up and down the street, like she might spot the killer lurking there behind one of the windows.

'You'll keep your eyes open for us?' Logan asked.

'Of course. I'm Secretary of the Neighbourhood Watch,' Joy told him. 'I'll rally the troops, find out if anyone has seen or heard anything.'

'Aye. You do that,' Logan told her.

From experience, this could go one of two ways. Either it would keep her out of his hair until the case was all wrapped up, or he had just opened himself to a regular bombardment of irrelevant information and gossip.

Still, if it meant getting her on-side, it could only make his life easier in the long run. The smaller the community, the more power the Community Council tended to wield, and communities didn't come much smaller than this one.

'Hey! No!' Joy shouted, derailing Logan's train of thought. She glowered angrily at Tyler, who was walking back from where he'd parked the Land Rover.

He stopped walking and looked at Logan in alarm when Joy started marching towards him, gesturing down the hill to where he'd parked.

'Not *that* white box. That's the disabled space,' she bellowed. 'What are you? Blind, as well as stupid?'

Logan sighed through his gritted teeth. *On-side.*

Aye, right.

Chapter 6

The pub's front doors were shut tight, and no amount of hammering was drawing the attention of anyone inside.

Joy Bryden had personally supervised Tyler as he'd moved the car forward six feet into the adjoining space to the one he'd parked in, guiding him with shouted commands, indecipherable hand gestures, and an assortment of disapproving looks.

That done, she'd nodded curtly at Logan, before crossing the road and vanishing into an alleyway between two whitewashed houses.

'She's a bit scary, eh?' Tyler observed, once he was confident she was well out of earshot.

'She's a slightly built Community Council leader in her late-fifties,' Logan pointed out. He blew out his cheeks and shuddered. 'So, aye. Bloody terrifying.'

He thumped a fist on the pub's wooden doors again, then glanced up at the darkened upstairs windows.

'Notice anything strange about her?' he asked, shooting Tyler a brief look.

'Eh… like what?'

Logan tutted. 'That's what I'm asking you. Did you notice anything?'

'She's got issues with parking?' Tyler guessed.

'I'd imagine she's got issues, full stop,' Logan replied. He watched the DC for a few more seconds, giving him time to offer something else. Hoping that he would.

'I don't know then, boss,' Tyler was forced to admit.

Logan made no attempt to hide his disappointment. 'Jesus. It's been raining solidly for several days, has it not?'

'Think so, aye.'

Logan nodded past him, to where a hanging basket creaked back and forth on the breeze.

'So, what was she doing out watering the flowers?'

Before they could dwell too much on this, there was a loud clack from the other side of the doors, as a bolt was slid aside.

One of the doors opened a crack, offering a tall, narrow glimpse of a grey-haired man with a moustache and glasses. His eyes were sunken deep into a skull that looked a half-size too small—an effect not helped by the thickness of the lenses in his NHS style frames.

'We're not open yet,' he said. There was a rasp to his voice that implied he was a heavy smoker. Or, could he be upset? 'Opening at five tonight.'

He started to close the door, but the judicious positioning of Logan's right foot stopped it shutting all the way. He held up his warrant card.

'Detective Chief Inspector Jack Logan, Major Investigations Team.'

The man on the other side of the door blinked several times in quick succession. He looked from the ID to each of the detectives in turn, then back again.

It took him three full circuits of this before he said anything. 'The police?'

'Aye. That's right. The police,' Logan said. He gave Tyler a nudge, and the DC presented his own identification.

'Mind if we come in, sir?' Tyler said. 'Ask you a few questions?'

'Questions? Me?' the man asked through the gap. 'What for?'

'We're investigating... an unexplained death,' Logan told him. 'We're just trying to get a feel for the place.'

He returned his ID to his pocket, and arranged his features in a way that made it very clear they weren't going anywhere except inside.

'We won't take up too much of your time,' he said. 'I appreciate you're probably very busy.'

The man gave a little groan below his breath, then let the door swing open. He was wrapped in a faded brown dressing-gown, the letters 'RM' embroidered inexpertly on the left breast. Below the dressing-gown was an old grey t-shirt patterned down the front with a multi-coloured assortment of food stains.

There was a smell of alcohol about him. Not the usual pub smell that Logan had subconsciously been bracing himself for, but some stale, stagnant variant that came seeping from the pores of the man standing in the narrow wood-panelled corridor beyond the front doors.

'Right. You'd best come in, then,' he told them, shuffling around on his bare feet.

He motioned to a door marked 'Private' that led off from the corridor, and winced at the thought of what lay behind it.

'I'd take you up to the flat but, well, I need to give it a tidy,' he said.

There was another set of double-doors behind him. Unlike those out front, these were mostly made of textured glass, with curved brass handles and matching kick plates down at the bottom.

'We can go through to the bar, though, if you like?' the man suggested, then he shook his head like he was admonishing himself, and lunged for Logan with a hand extended. 'Sorry, sorry. I'm Roddy. MacKay. Roddy Mac, they call me. I'm the landlord. This… this is my place. My pub.'

He looked down and reacted in surprise, like he'd suddenly realised what he was wearing.

'But then, you know that, don't you?' he said, self-consciously retying the belt of the dressing-gown around his narrow waist. 'Of course, you know. Of course, you do. That's why you're here. Why you've come.'

Logan felt Tyler's gaze slide in his direction, but ignored it.

'I don't follow, Mr MacKay,' the DCI said.

'Well, this was it, wasn't it?' Roddy said. 'Here. The pub. This was it.'

'This was what?' Logan pressed.

'This was the place Iona was last seen alive.'

Roddy shoved his hands in his dressing-gown pockets, but not before Logan saw how badly they were shaking.

'I didn't see her. The night she died, I mean. I was upstairs.'

He flinched, realising his error almost as soon as the words had left his mouth.

He wasn't the only one.

'We don't know what night she died, Mr MacKay,' Logan said.

Roddy's face reddened behind his silver-grey moustache. For a moment, his mouth just flapped open and closed like a fish out of water, before words began to babble out.

'No. I mean, yes. I mean, I know. But... the night she... the last night she was here, I mean. The night she disappeared. That's the one I was... I didn't see her. I was—'

'Upstairs. Aye. You mentioned,' said Logan. He gave the door that led to the flat a very calculated once-over, before turning back to the landlord. 'To be honest, we were really just hoping to grab a cup of tea and use your phone, Mr MacKay. But, since we're on the subject, why don't we step into the bar? And you can tell us everything you know about the night Iona Wallace went missing.'

There was a knock at the front door, which still stood ajar. Roddy practically sagged with relief when the door was nudged open from outside, and a young Asian woman with her hair tied up in a bun smiled nervously at the towering detective in the hallway.

She couldn't have been older than twenty-two or twenty-three. There was something vaguely familiar about her, although Logan couldn't quite place where he'd seen her before.

'Uh, hi,' she said, shuffling on the front step. 'Hoped I might find you here.'

'All right?' asked Tyler. The way he was frowning suggested he was struggling to work out who she was, too.

It was only when she jabbed a thumb back over her shoulder and said, 'Geoff wants to see you,' that both men realised she was a member of the SOC team.

It was the first time either of them had seen her without a paper hood and a mask covering her head and half her face.

Her eyes were a dark walnut brown, and the smile she was plastering on her face had formed little dimples in her cheeks. There was a glow about her that suggested she'd run all the way here to find them.

Young, fit, and attractive, then. No doubt Geoff himself had taken a keen interest in her recruitment. They didn't call him 'Sex Pest Palmer' for nothing. The poor girl probably spent half her day fending him off with a shitty stick.

'Storm's coming in,' she said. 'Chopper wants to get going. We're done at the site, and going to take the body back to Inverness. I'm Samira, by the way. Hi.'

'Hi. You're packing up already?' asked Tyler. 'Bit quick that, isn't it?'

'Site's badly compromised,' she replied. 'We've got what we can.'

'Which is…?' asked Logan.

The young woman gave an embarrassed sort of shrug. 'Not much, I'm afraid.'

'Great,' said Logan, his chest heaving with a sigh. Half-turning, he pinned Roddy to the spot with a steely glare. 'Don't go too far, Mr MacKay,' he warned. 'We'll be back to have that chat.'

–

The Land Rover bounced up the track leading to the field, Logan behind the wheel, the SOC lassie in the front passenger seat, and Tyler relegated to the back.

'It's a complete shithole back here,' DC Neish had been quick to point out, and the soundtrack for most of the journey had been the rustling of crisp packets, the rattling of empty cans, and a low-level muttering about basic standards of hygiene.

'There they are. Looks like they're about loaded up,' Samira said, indicating the helicopter that sat crouching in the field, its blades rotating lazily like it was stretching itself awake.

The tent had been folded down and packed away, and the body was presumably already on board the chopper, along with most of the team. Geoff stood by the side door, watching a younger guy cordon off a ten-feet by ten-feet square of field.

Right at the centre of it, the lop-sided scarecrow stood with its arms outstretched, its rough canvas face turned in the Land Rover's direction.

Logan steered them towards the layby near the edge of the field, where they'd watched the farce with the tent earlier. He had just pulled on the handbrake when Tyler let out a sudden yelp of panic.

'There's a fucking mouse in here!'

Logan's chair groaned as he turned and looked into the back. Tyler was already out of his seat belt, and grabbing for the door handle.

'What?'

'There's a mouse! An actual mouse! The cheeky wee bastard ran right over my hand!'

He shuddered in revulsion, then tugged on the handle, but the door refused to open.

'Fuck's sake! Who put the child lock on?' he cried, rattling the handle over and over again. 'Come on, let us out, boss.'

'Calm down. It's just a mouse, no' a rat,' Logan said. He sucked in his bottom lip. 'Unless… maybe it *is* a rat. Big hairy bugger of a thing. Full of disease.'

He looked across at Samira in the passenger seat, his face a picture of concern. 'God, would that not be terrible?'

'I'll climb through, boss,' Tyler warned. 'I mean it, I'll climb right over you, if that's what it comes to.'

Logan shook his head. 'Jesus. Pull yourself together, Detective Constable. All this fuss over a wee…'

He fixed his gaze on Tyler's shoulder, his eyes widening. 'Christ. Aye. It's a big brute of a thing, right enough.'

Tyler contorted, swiping at his shoulder, and was halfway towards a panic attack when he spotted the smirk on the DCI's face, and realised he'd been had.

'Sorry,' Logan said, opening his door and squelching down onto the muddy grass. 'Couldn't resist.'

–

When Samira had said the SOC team didn't have much, she wasn't lying. She may actually have been exaggerating. 'Not much' was a step-up from what they did have, which was practically nothing at all.

'Given the conditions onsite, anything I can give you is pretty much just speculation,' Palmer told Logan, while Samira helped load the final few boxes into the chopper.

A bank of truly murderous-looking cloud was moving in from the west, and the pilot was starting to get antsy. He was keen to get off—a sentiment Palmer himself shared, judging by how quickly he was talking.

'It's likely she was killed here, although given the condition of her clothing I can't rule out her being dragged through the mud. There has been a lot of animal activity around the site, both before and after she was here. Them, probably.'

He pointed to a flock of sheep scattered across one of the low hills that rose up just beyond the crumbling wall that marked the far edge of the field.

'Whoever found her wasn't canny about keeping their distance, either. At least two people. Looks like they attended the body, then either paced around waiting for help to arrive, or maybe had themselves a wee ceilidh. Either way, their prints have obliterated whatever else was below. Although, I doubt we'd have got much even if they hadn't been around.'

'Who found her?' Logan asked.

Palmer tutted and shrugged. 'The bloody hell should I know?'

There was a knocking on the helicopter's windscreen, and the pilot made a show of tapping his watch.

'We need to get off,' Palmer said.

Logan blocked his route to the chopper. 'Wait. That's it? There's nothing else?'

'Oh! No! We found you an eyewitness,' Palmer said.

Tyler looked up from where he'd been writing in his notepad. 'Aye?'

Palmer indicated the partially toppled scarecrow with a nod. 'He's the strong, silent type, but I'm sure you two can talk him into giving a statement!'

Logan's expression made it very clear that he did not appreciate Palmer's attempt at humour. It made it clear, in fact, that he did not appreciate Palmer's very existence.

'It's a puddle of mud and sheep shit. What did you expect us to find?' the SOC boss asked. 'Dr Maguire might get something from the body, but... come on, Jack. There are, what? Fifty adults on the island? Nobody's been or gone in days.'

He backed towards the helicopter, his mouth wrenching into a sneering smile. 'A couple of bright lads like you? With your experience, Jack, and his...' He gestured at Tyler, racked his brains for a moment, then shrugged. 'Whatever it is he brings to the table. Just how hard can it be?'

Chapter 7

Logan stood just beyond the cordon tape, eyeballing the ground as a fine drizzle dampened everything that wasn't already soaked through.

He was hoping he might spot something that Palmer's team had missed, although he knew that the likelihood of that happening was slim.

Palmer was right. It was a puddle of mud and sheep shit. Even the indent where the body had been lying had now been almost completely smoothed away by the rain. The site was so far beyond compromised that even if they'd found a written confession, it was unlikely to be admissible as evidence.

'What's the scarecrow for?' Tyler asked.

'Scaring crows. I'd have thought that was pretty self-explanatory,' Logan replied without looking up.

There was a soft squelch as Tyler picked his way forward through the mud until he was standing at the DCI's side by the cordon tape. The scarecrow looked sturdy and well-made, its straw body and workman-like clothing holding together well, despite the ravages of the recent weather.

'No. I know what scarecrows are for, boss. I meant, what's this one particular scarecrow for?'

Logan looked at the mud-pit around them. It was a field in name only. Beyond a few clumps of waist-high weeds, nothing grew here, and almost certainly hadn't for a number of years.

'What's it guarding?' Tyler pressed.

'Huh. Good question,' Logan said, somewhat begrudgingly. 'Why's it here? The mud's no' exactly worth protecting, and he doesn't look all that old.'

He met the hollow gaze of the scarecrow, ran his hand through his hair, then tapped on Tyler's breast pocket, where he kept his notebook. 'Write it down. Probably nothing, but... good spot. Well done.'

'Cheers, boss,' Tyler chirped, pleased with himself. He whistled below his breath as he made a note in his book, then flipped it closed and returned it to his pocket.

A line of shadow was creeping closer across the field, mirroring the progress of the vast dark clouds above. Tyler regarded it with growing concern.

'Looks like it's going to get rough soon. Maybe we should go hole up somewhere until it passes?' he suggested. 'We could go back to the pub, talk to your dressing-gown fella. Should probably phone the office, too, see if they've sorted us out somewhere to stay.'

Logan gave a non-committal sort of grunt, then paced around the outside of the cordon tape, checking out the scarecrow from every available angle. It was, as far as he could tell, just a bog-standard scarecrow. Palmer's team would've gone over it when they were searching the site, so if it had any secrets to give up, it would've already handed them over.

And yet, Tyler had got his mind racing. Why was it here? What was the point? And how come Iona Wallace's body had been found right there in front of it?

'Aye. I'll get it out of you yet,' Logan muttered.

'Sorry, boss?'

'Nothing. Doesn't matter,' the DCI replied. He took the keys from his pocket and used them to point in the direction of an old thatched cottage that squatted on a low hill just beyond the field's edge. 'That must be Iona's house. Let's go get inside and check it out before the storm hits.'

Tyler didn't need telling twice. He trudged, splashed, and skidded back in the direction of the Land Rover, with Logan following behind.

And the scarecrow watched them, every step of the way.

–

DCI Logan and DC Neish entered the house wearing gloves and shoe protectors. Given the vicinity to the crime scene, SOC would usually have given the place a going-over, but their rush to get the body back before the storm cut them off had meant it would have to wait for another day.

The door was unlocked. Not really a surprise way out here, where everyone knew everyone, and crime was a thing that happened to people on the mainland.

From outside, the cottage was quaint, if a bit run-down. The few single-glazed windows that weren't cracked were desperately in need of a power washing, and while Logan would never claim to be an expert on roof thatching, he was reasonably certain it was never meant to look quite like that.

The stone walls were solid, though, despite no-doubt having been there for generations. An attempt had been made to brighten up the garden at one point, with half-sized whisky barrels used as planters for flowers by the front door and along both sides of the narrow path.

Whatever had been planted in them was long-dead, though, the compost now crusted with moss and a selection of short, stubby weeds.

Inside, the situation was much the same. There was potential for it to be a lovely wee place, from the exposed beams of the ceiling, to the rustic-looking log burner set back in a stone fireplace, topped with a driftwood mantelpiece.

But it was all so grimy and grim. The windows were as filthy on the inside as they were on the outside, and rings of damp were congregating between the ceiling beams.

46

An area of several square feet around the log burner was caked in ash and soot, with footprints trampling various paths through it and across the threadbare carpet.

The kitchen sat at one end of the living area, a mishmash of different units, half of them with grubby curtains instead of doors. The sink was stacked high with dirty dishes. Judging by the smell, and the colour of the water they were half-submerged in, they'd been that way for some time.

But it was the general odour of the place that was most overwhelming. The twin aromas of tobacco and cannabis permeated every fibre of the cottage, right down to the stone that made up the walls.

Ashtrays sat in various spots around the room—on the arm of the chair, on the mantelpiece, and two on the kitchen worktops—each one overflowing worse than the one before.

Clothes lay scattered on the floor and across the tired old sofa that slouched indignantly in the far corner of the room, like a teenager who'd stormed off in the huff.

'I like what she did with the place,' Tyler remarked, picking up a lacy black bra with the end of his pen and examining it like it was some alien specimen. 'Really homely.'

It was chaotic. A bloody shambles. It told him that Iona hadn't changed much in the years since he'd known her. If he'd been asked to describe how he pictured her living, it would've been almost exactly this.

'Any idea what we're looking for?' Tyler asked. He'd returned the bra to where he'd found it draped across a cheap plastic kettle and was now poking around in a cutlery drawer.

'No' really,' Logan admitted. He hadn't moved from the middle of the room since they'd entered, and was slowly turning on the spot, taking the place in. 'We want to build up a picture of her last few days. See if anything jumps out. Notebooks. Mobile phone and laptop, if she had them. Letters.'

Tyler snorted. 'No one sends letters these days, boss,' he said, closing the cutlery drawer and crossing to the fridge.

'Aye, well, maybe they do out here. Keep your eyes peeled, anyway.'

Outside, the storm was building. The wind had started to whistle in through gaps in the roof and the windows, and there was a steady drip-drip-drip from somewhere above the worst of the damp stains.

'You look in here. I'll check the bedroom and bathroom,' Logan instructed.

'Right you are, boss. One thing I will say about her...' Tyler opened the fridge door all the way, revealing shelves filled with cans of cheap cider and lager. 'She liked a drink.'

'Aye. She did that, all right,' Logan confirmed, recalling the girl he used to know. 'Now, get going. I want us done and out of here, sharpish. I don't know about you, but I'm bloody starving.'

Leaving Tyler to search the living room and kitchen area, Logan headed through an open door that led to a hallway which would've been a squeeze for two full-sized adults. Three other doors ran off from the hall, two of them open, the other closed.

He could see a bathroom and bedroom behind the two open doors, and a quick check behind the third revealed a cupboard containing an old vacuum cleaner, an ironing board, and about three months' worth of ironing spilling out of a plastic basket.

Closing that door, Logan opted to check the bathroom first.

It was freezing. That was the first thing he noticed. It was right at the back corner of the house, and the wind was busy chilling both outside walls. There was no heater that he could see, although an ancient towel rail that was no longer wired into the wall had probably doubled as one at some point.

There wasn't much else to report. Another ashtray was balanced on the edge of the chipped and stained bath, half a hand-rolled cigarette propped up in one of the grooves.

Logan picked it up in his gloved fingers and sniffed the end. The smell of cannabis was unmistakable.

A check of the bathroom cabinet revealed mostly painkillers, some antihistamines, and a couple of near-empty containers of thrush cream. The tube of toothpaste, by comparison, was almost new, and the only toothbrush he could find was mostly hidden behind the half-used blister strips of paracetamol, ibuprofen, and...hello.

Reaching into the cabinet, Logan took out a small stack of blister strips that didn't fit in with the others. There were five strips, each containing four tablets—twenty in total.

Each tablet was diamond-shaped and pale blue. Distinctive enough that he recognised them at once. They were a common find during shakedowns back in Glasgow.

Viagra.

He angled one of the packs to the light, checking the dosage printed on the pills. A hundred milligrams. Max strength, he thought, but he'd have to double-check.

What was a single woman living alone doing with five packs of a male impotence drug? Selling them? Maybe. An insurance policy in case some late-night hook-up couldn't fulfil their end of the bargain? Very possibly.

Logan returned them to the cabinet and jotted down a note in his pad. Then, after a further check of all the likely hiding spots in the bathroom, he left the room and headed to the one across the hall.

Compared to Iona's bedroom, the rest of the house was positively presentable. It had seemed like half of her clothes had been strewn across the living room, but that was a fraction of what lay in piles around the bedroom, hung on hooks from the curtain rail, or sat teetering on the short, wooden poles at the end of the unmade double bed.

'Jesus.'

'All right, boss?' Tyler called through to him.

'Aye. Just marvelling at what a clarty bastard she was,' Logan replied.

He tried to ignore the mess, and concentrate instead on anything that might help with the case. It was difficult to know where to start.

The arrangement of the covers and pillows on the bed suggested only one person had slept there recently. Looking closely at the exposed sheets revealed a rainbow of different stains, which he'd have to get forensics to look at.

Some of them he could dismiss as food stains. Others either suggested that Iona had enjoyed a highly active sex life in recent weeks, or that she hadn't washed the sheets in a very long time. Again, hopefully, forensics could tell him more.

There was a phone charger plugged in by the bed, which suggested she must have a mobile somewhere. Logan checked in the bedside drawers, but found no phone. He did find several other 'devices', though, all battery-operated, and all different sizes—if broadly similar in shape.

Beneath the bed was a clutter of more clothes, several pairs of shoes, and a couple of cardboard boxes. With a bit of effort, Logan managed to reach both boxes, and pulled them out to check inside.

The first box was filled with old video cassette tapes. There were fifteen of them in all, at least six of which had variations on the theme of Tom Cruise staring smokily out from the cover.

The rest were a mix of various trashy horrors, a couple of 80s rom-coms, and *G.I. Jane*, starring Demi Moore. Logan opened a few of the boxes, checked the tapes corresponded with the covers, and then set the box aside.

The second box was older and more battered. It had a removable lid that was taped down on one side, so it moved as if on a hinge.

Flipping it open, Logan let out a little grunt of satisfaction. In it, there were a dozen or more diaries, the year hand-written on some of the earlier ones, and embossed in gold on the two most recent, which covered the years 2013 and 2016. Not current, then, and not continuous, but recent enough that they might reveal something about her relationships with the other people on the island.

A quick flick through confirmed that she'd written entries on at least a handful of the dates, which made the box an important find. If luck was on their side, the identity of the killer might be written somewhere on those pages.

'Aye,' Logan muttered, folding the lid back into place. 'We can but hope.'

–

When Logan returned to the living area, cardboard box under one arm, he found Tyler on all-fours in front of the couch, using the torch on his phone to peer into the gap beneath it.

'What've you got?' the DCI asked, as Tyler carefully slid a hand into the narrow space.

'One sec...'

After a bit of squirming, Tyler removed his hand, the blade of a knife pinned beneath the tip of one finger.

The blade was long, curved at the end, with a serrated edge running down its back. The handle was a rubberised grip, with a black metal hilt to protect the hand of anyone wielding the weapon.

'Jesus. That's a serious blade,' Tyler remarked.

'Hunting knife.'

'Aye, but what the fuck's she hunting? Bigfoot?'

Logan considered the knife, its position beneath the couch, and the couch's relative position to the front door. 'For self-defence, maybe?'

'Hardly handily placed for an emergency, boss,' Tyler said. 'I've been trying to fish the bastard out for the past five minutes.'

Logan regarded him impassively. 'Couldn't you have tilted the couch back?'

Tyler opened his mouth to reply to this, hesitated, then sighed and said, 'Shite, aye.'

'Bag it up,' Logan instructed, indicating the knife. He patted the box under his arm. 'Found some old diaries. Don't expect to get much, but good background.'

'Maybe you'll be mentioned in them, boss,' Tyler teased. He took an evidence bag from his pocket and carefully dropped the knife inside. 'Although, did they have pen and paper back then, or was it all chisels and slate?'

'Aye, good to see you're still as witty as ever, son,' Logan said. 'By which I mean, not at all.'

He set the box on the floor beside the door, took the knife from Tyler, and placed it on top, then turned and surveyed the room again. The wind was howling through the gaps in the windows now, and the dripping above the ceiling was now a steady pitter-patter of trickling water.

'Right, let's give the place one more going over, then get the hell out of here before the bloody roof comes down.'

Chapter 8

Roddy MacKay was nowhere to be seen when Logan and Tyler returned, dripping wet and windswept, to the Canna Come Inn. The pub was open, though, and a tall, blond-haired man with a chiselled jaw smiled at them from behind the bar, showing the most perfectly aligned, impeccably white teeth either of the detectives had ever seen.

'G'day,' he said, in an accent that was straight out of Ramsay Street.

He had a bungee-cord braid around his wrist, fastened with a clasp made from a polished shell, and wore a shark's tooth on a leather strap around his neck. If the man wasn't a surfer, Logan reckoned, then he had missed his life's calling.

'How can I help you gents?' he asked, reaching under the bar and producing a couple of laminated menus. 'You after a bite to eat?'

'Aye. Maybe,' Logan said, taking both menus. 'We're looking for Mr MacKay. We were having a chat with him earlier, but got called away.'

'Oh! Right! You must be the cops!' the barman said. 'Roddy said you'd be in. I'm Bruce.'

'Of course you are,' said Logan. He glanced around at the empty pub. A back door stood open, an arrow on the wall informing anyone who might be interested that this was the way to the beer garden.

Given that the sky was in the process of falling, and the rain was rattling off the ground like bullets, it was unlikely anyone would be out there enjoying the fresh air now.

'Is Mr MacKay around?' asked Tyler, half-looking at Bruce, and half-eyeing up the menus that Logan was still keeping a firm hold of.

'Nah, he nipped out. Said he'd be back... actually, I don't know when he'll be back. I mean, he did say, but I was only half-listening,' Bruce told them. 'He said to get you boys a bite to eat, though. On the house.'

'Very kind of him. But we couldn't accept that,' Logan said.

'He says it's no problem. Honestly.'

'No, I mean we literally can't accept that,' Logan told him. 'Wouldn't want anyone to suggest that Mr MacKay was bribing us with a couple of juicy steaks.'

Bruce blinked a few times, like he didn't quite understand. 'We don't do steaks,' he said, which was up there with the most disappointing things Logan had heard all day.

Tyler was practically salivating beside him, so Logan slid one of the menus onto the bar in front of him. 'Mind if we use your phone, Bruce?'

'Ah, defo. Fire on,' Bruce said, indicating the payphone sitting down at the far end of the bar, near the door leading to the beer garden. 'You got on the Wi-Fi all right, though, yeah?'

Tyler looked up from the menu, a hand already slipping into his jacket pocket. 'The pub's got Wi-Fi?'

Bruce grinned at both of them, his forehead furrowing a little like he wasn't sure if DC Neish was joking.

'Nah. Whole island, mate. Complete coverage, end to end. All free. It's a bloody marvel.'

Logan turned his head towards the pub's windows, like he might be able to catch a glimpse of the wireless internet signal bouncing around out there.

'The whole island has free Wi-Fi?'

'Yeah, I reckon,' Bruce said.

'You reckon? You mean you don't know?' Logan asked him.

Tyler shook his head. 'That's just what they say, isn't it? It's the way they talk.'

Logan scowled at the younger detective. 'So, does it have Wi-Fi or not?'

Tyler thumbed his screen, then held it up for Logan to see. The words, 'Canna Community Network' filled a couple of lines on the screen. As Logan watched, a little tick appeared beside it, and Tyler's phone ding-d-ding-dinged as a couple of emails and a Facebook notification all arrived at the same time.

'Looks like it, boss,' Tyler confirmed. 'Fast, too.'

'Community Council put it in, I think. They got a grant, or a loan, or whatever. From the Government, I think. Everyone was pretty stoked,' Bruce explained. 'The phone signal is pretty bad out here, but the internet's slick. I think it uses satellites. Or maybe tunnels? Undersea wires, or something, I mean.'

'We can use the Wi-Fi for VOIP calls,' Tyler suggested.

Logan took out his phone and regarded it as if it had suddenly morphed into a piece of tech from the distant future. 'We can what?'

'Voice Over IP. If we download Skype—or, no, WhatsApp—then we can use that to send messages, make calls and—' Tyler began, but Logan handed him the phone and gave a dismissive wave designed to shut him up.

'Aye, well. I'll let you handle that, then,' he said, finally taking a look at the menu he was holding. 'While I order us up some grub.'

Detective Inspector Ben Forde shot a sideways glance at the office door as he flopped into his chair and rolled it closer to his cluttered desk. He had a haunted look about him, like he'd just been confronted by the grim reality of his own mortality.

Which wasn't a million miles away from the truth.

'The DS didn't sound best pleased, sir,' said a junior detective sitting at a neighbouring desk. His voice was little more than a whisper, like he was afraid the walls had ears.

'Aye. Well, you can say that again, Hamza,' Ben muttered. He puffed out his cheeks, tore his eyes from the door, and offered a wafer-thin smile to Detective Constable Khaled. Hamza, for his part, bounced it right back with added sympathy.

After more years on the force than he had any inclination to count, it took a lot to rattle Ben's cage. The past ten minutes with Detective Superintendent Hoon, however, hadn't so much rattled his cage as hurled it against a brick wall and then furiously stamped it to bits.

'I mean, I always go in there expecting him to rip me a new arsehole, but it's like Swiss bloody cheese today. Something's got him wound up worse than usual,' Ben said.

He checked the door again, then rolled his chair a little closer to Hamza's, so he could drop his voice even further.

'Usually, there are at least a couple of non-swear words scattered here and there amongst the barrage of abuse. The occasional oasis of clean language. But that? That was just relentless from the get-go. I mean, there were swear words in there I've never even heard of, and I like to think of myself as a fairly educated man when it comes to that sort of thing.'

Reaching for his shirt pocket, he took out his notebook and flicked through a few pages. 'I even wrote one down. Hang on…'

Hamza took a sip from his mug of tea while he waited for the DI to find the right page.

'Right. Here we are. At one point, he said I was a "scumbering fuckstick",' Ben announced. He looked up from his pad, his expression suggesting he was a little hurt, but mostly confused. 'I mean, what's that when it's at home?'

'Well—'

'The "scumbering" bit, I mean. I can figure out the "fuckstick".' He pointed down at his pad. '"Jeb end". That's another one. I mean, I've heard of a knob end. I wouldn't have minded knob end. Bell end, even. But *jeb end*? What's a jeb?'

Hamza bit his lip, fighting hard to contain the urge to laugh. 'Aye, sounds like he was off on one, sir,' he said. 'What's got him so riled up this time?'

'Oh, Christ, don't ask me. Would you believe, I stand there and take all that dog's abuse, and I'm still none the wiser as to what the problem is? Something to do with Logan, though. Hoon's gunning for him. Probably just as well he's tucked away on Canna. Short of the dark side of the bloody moon, a remote island's probably the safest place for him.'

He rolled his chair back to his own desk, picked up his mug, and was unable to hide his disappointment when he found it was empty.

'Any word from him yet?' he asked, depositing the mug back down with a sullen clunk.

'SOC team landed forty minutes ago. Body's off to Raigmore for the PM,' Hamza said. 'But no, nothing yet from the boss.'

Ben rummaged in his desk drawer until he found a packet of Polo mints. They were a poor substitute for a hot cup of tea, but making a fresh brew would mean leaving the safety of the office, and he didn't want to risk bumping into Hoon again.

Where the hell was DC Neish when you needed him?

'You ever been to Canna, Hamza?' Ben asked.

'Can't say I have, sir, no,' said Hamza.

DC Khaled had been brought up in the east. The *far* east.

Aberdeen, to be precise. Anything west of Inverness and south of Dundee was generally something of a mystery to him.

Ben wrinkled his nose. 'You're not missing much. I mean, it's nice enough, don't get me wrong. And if rocks or sheep are your thing, then you'll be like a pig in shit. But, it's not big. No' exactly well equipped. I'd be very surprised if they can even get a mobile signal all the way out—'

The phone on Ben's desk rang. He pounced on it quickly, grabbing for the receiver before Hoon could get wind of it.

'Detective Inspector Ben…' he began, then an echoey voice down the line cut him off.

'Benjamin.'

Ben lowered both his head and his voice, cupping a hand around the phone's mouthpiece like he was sharing some big secret with it. 'Jack. It's yourself. Your ears must've been burning. Hamza and I were just talking about you.'

'Aye? All nice things, I hope,' came the voice down the line.

'Nicer than the stuff Hoon was saying, that's for sure. It's fair to say he was being less complimentary about you than we were. He's gunning for you. Wants you to get in touch, pronto. What have you done to piss him off this time?'

'No idea,' Logan said, but Ben knew him well enough to know a lie when he heard it.

'Right. Good. Fair enough, then,' Ben replied. 'On an entirely unrelated note, I hear Bosco Construction had a fire on the premises earlier this morning. One of the Portakabins went up like a match.'

'Did it, indeed? I hadn't heard a thing,' Logan replied. 'One of the downsides of being stuck in a storm in the arse end of nowhere, I suppose.'

'Suppose so,' Ben said. 'Well, if I see Bosco, I'll pass on your condolences.'

'Aye. Do that,' said Logan. 'That'd be lovely. Now, has Hamza sorted us out somewhere to kip yet?'

'Hang on, I'll put you on speaker,' said Ben, setting the phone on the desk between himself and DC Khaled. 'But keep your voice down. Hoon's bastard-sense is no doubt already tingling.'

'All right, sir?' said Hamza, once Ben had tapped the loudspeaker icon on the phone's screen. 'Enjoying your quality time with Tyler?'

'God, aye. It's like all my Christmases have come at once,' Logan replied. 'You get us somewhere to stay?'

'Uh, yeah. I did.'

There was a slight change to the tone of Logan's voice. A subtle sort of wariness creeping in around the edges.

'What's wrong with it?' he asked.

'Nothing, sir. It's a nice wee B&B. It's the only B&B on the island, actually. It's not big. They've only got two rooms.'

'We only need two rooms.'

Hamza's chair gave a soft groan as he shifted his weight back a little, putting more distance between himself and the phone, like he was worried it might suddenly make a grab for him.

'That's the thing, sir. One's already taken.'

There was silence from the handset. Hamza stole a look at DI Forde. It was Ben's turn to be struggling to contain his laughter.

'What?' Logan finally asked.

'The other room's taken, sir. There's only one available. It's a twin, though, so... there's that.'

Despite his many years of investigation experience, it seemed to be taking a long time for Logan to process what Hamza was telling him. Either that, or he was simply refusing to believe it.

'What are you saying here, DC Khaled? *Exactly*?' the DCI asked. 'You're telling me that... what?'

Ben cleared his throat. 'Hello, Jack? It's me. Ben.'

'You've both got different voices, Ben, I know it's you,' Logan snapped.

'Right. Aye. Well, I think what Hamza's saying is that, despite his best efforts—and he worked hard on this, I saw it myself. Despite those best efforts, he has only been able to secure you a twin room for tonight.'

Another burst of silence from the other end of the line. Hamza and Ben exchanged looks, and both men found themselves struggling to hold it together.

'Well, where's Tyler going to...?' Logan began.

And then, it happened. Then, the penny dropped.

'Wait a minute! Wait just a fucking minute. Are you saying...? I'm no' sharing a room with this bawbag.'

Tyler's voice echoed tinnily in the background.

'Are we sharing a room, boss?'

'No, we bloody well are not!' Logan barked at him. His voice became clearer as he turned back to the phone. 'There must be something else.'

'There's…' Hamza coughed, concealing a chuckle that he hadn't managed to contain in time. 'Sorry. There's not, sir. There's the caravan park, but it's shut until summer. The other guest at the B&B is due to move on as soon as the weather lifts, so I've pre-booked that room for when he does, but until then…'

He wasn't sure how to finish that sentence without getting shouted at, so just let it trail away into silence.

Ben was quick to take up the mantle. 'Think of it as a chance to get to know each other better, Jack,' he said. 'Think of it as bonding time.'

'I'll bond the toe of my boot to his arse if I've to put up with him all night,' Logan replied. 'And why would I want to get to know him better? Have you met him? I'd like to get to know him *less*, if anything.'

'You know I'm standing right here, boss, aye?' Tyler asked.

'Yes, Detective Constable. I know. I can sense you looming behind me like the spectre of fucking Death,' Logan snarled. 'Away and sit down, for Christ's sake. You're making the place look untidy.'

Ben bit hard on one of his knuckles. Hamza buried his face in the crook of his elbow, his shoulders heaving.

'Are you pair laughing?' demanded the voice from the phone.

'Us? No,' Ben said, the words squeaking out of him like air escaping from a balloon.

'You'd bloody better not be,' Logan warned them.

And then, it all became too much, and Ben and Hamza both exploded with laughter so loud and uncontrolled, that they missed the entirety of the expletive-filled rant that came spitting at them through the speaker.

Chapter 9

Logan and Tyler stood in a small, fussily-decorated bedroom, staring in mute horror at a double bed.

The owners seemed nice enough. Patricia and Norman Dawson, originally from Beith in Ayrshire. They were a couple at opposite ends of their thirties, Patricia not much out of her twenties, Norman approaching forty. They'd seemed genuinely apologetic when explaining the shortage of rooms.

'It's Kevin, the other guest. He was meant to leave, but, well, the ferries,' Pat had explained, before launching into another round of apologies.

After a quick tour of the house—the shared bathroom, the dining area, and the lounge with its big bay windows currently looking out onto a wall of grey fog—they were given the key to the room and left to their own devices.

And here they were now. Standing there.

Right at the foot of the double bed.

'This can't be right, can it, boss?' Tyler asked. He'd seemed pretty amused about the sleeping situation until that point. Now, he looked almost as concerned as Logan felt. 'We can't be sharing a bed, can we?'

'I'll chainsaw the bastard down the middle, if I have to,' Logan said.

He dropped his bag by the door and had just turned to head back down the stairs when he heard the hurried thudding of racing footsteps.

Pat's head popped up above the gloss-painted bannister, her face red, her bob of brown hair practically standing on end.

'Sorry! Sorry! I thought Norman had split the bed into singles. He just told me he thought I'd done it!'

'Oh, thank God,' Tyler muttered, physically sagging with relief.

'Give me fifteen minutes, and I'll get it all sorted,' Pat said, squeezing past them. She had a small stack of sheets and single quilt-covers draped over her arms, and a screwdriver sticking out of her back pocket.

'You need a hand?' Logan asked, as she set the linen on an ancient-looking bureau, and reached for the screwdriver.

'No, I'm a dab hand these days,' Pat said, shooing them both towards the door. 'Away you go downstairs. Norman's got the kettle on, and I just made a carrot cake.'

Logan nodded graciously. 'Aye. Well,' he said. 'Now you're talking my language.'

–

After dishing out the tea and a couple of generous slices of carrot cake, Norman left the detectives alone in the lounge.

Like the rest of the house, it could generously be described as 'quaint' and less generously as 'horribly dated.'

The walls, with their swirling brown and cream floral print, felt like they were closing in on the mismatched leather couches and wingback chairs.

A small television was balanced on a bookcase in one corner, positioned so impractically that it would be almost impossible to see from all but one of the available seats, and even from that one, you'd have to hope nothing important was happening in the bottom left corner.

There were two big display units, all smooth, curved wood and scuffed glass. Inside one was a veritable safari-park of animal-themed ornaments, arranged in groups according to species.

The other case held stacks of old crockery. Teacups and saucers, mostly, and the occasional big plate. Logan couldn't say if they were valuable, but he could say, with some conviction, that they were a bloody eyesore.

Somewhere in the house, a cuckoo clock called out nine times. Logan wanted to throttle it by the fourth.

He didn't know enough about Pat and Norman to make the call yet, but he had a feeling they didn't really fit with the style of the house. The cups and plates the detectives had been given with their tea and cake were plain, unfussy things. A world away from the dated clutter of the rest of the place.

'Jesus, that's hard,' Tyler remarked, attempting to settle himself down in one of the wingback chairs. 'I thought what it lacked in looks it might make up for in comfort, but nope. Does it fuck.'

He got back up again and joined Logan by the big bay window, face to face with the storm. It screeched and battered against the other side of the glass, like a monster trying to force its way inside.

Logan sipped his tea, unblinking and uncowed by it, and enjoyed a bite from his slab of cake. They'd grabbed dinner in the pub—a couple of toasties, and some underwhelming chips—but the cake was undoubtedly the culinary highlight of the day.

'Forecast says it's supposed to ease off overnight,' Tyler said, indicating the weather with a tilt of his cup. 'Still going to be grim, but not as bad as this.'

Grim. It was how Logan always imagined life out on the islands. A relentless parade of drudgery beneath an overcast sky. Backbreaking labour on too-salty soil. A life spent squinting in the wind.

The rain raged against the window, doing nothing to change his mind.

'Right, where are we?' Logan asked, turning his back on the storm. 'What have we got?'

He took a seat on one of the couches, and Tyler returned unenthusiastically to the wingback. The DC had spent most of the evening emailing and messaging back and forth with Hamza, who was co-ordinating with SOC and Pathology.

The hope was that, between them, they could build up an early picture. What they'd actually pulled together wasn't so much a picture as a child–like scribble, and Tyler had been dreading the moment he had to deliver his report.

He took a bite of his cake, washed it down with a gulp of tea, then swiped at his phone until he found his notes.

'Right, boss. Iona Wallace, aged forty-six. Formerly Iona Kerr.'

'Aye, I know that bit,' Logan said.

'Moved to the island with her father and older brother back in—'

Logan raised a hand, silencing him. 'And that bit. What else?'

Tyler glanced up from his phone, then swiped the screen with a thumb a few times, scrolling through a lot of text he'd typed out that, now he came to look at it, didn't actually say very much.

'Uh, her dad's the minister. Abraham Kerr. He's with the Wee Free church.'

'Jesus. Don't beat around the bush. Give me the headlines, son. Has cause of death been confirmed?'

'Not yet, boss. Dr Maguire's still on the post–mortem, last I heard. You reckoned strangulation though, didn't you?'

'Aye, but hard as this may be for you to believe, I've been wrong in the past,' Logan said. 'Very occasionally. So I'd like an expert opinion to confirm.'

His eyes went to Tyler's phone. 'Can we Skype on this connection?'

Tyler's brow furrowed. 'What, each other?'

'No! Why the f--?' Logan pinched the bridge of his nose, muttered quietly, then shook his head. 'Why would you and I Skype each other? We're sitting in the same room. Off the island, I mean. Can I Skype, I don't know, Dr Maguire, for example?'

A smirk tugged at the corners of Tyler's mouth. 'Ah. Gotcha. Aye. No bother, boss. Connection's good. You'll be grand. I installed WhatsApp for you, too, if that's easier.'

'Skype will be fine,' Logan said. He knew how to use Skype. Vaguely. He had enough on his mind without worrying about some new bloody technology.

He shifted his weight on the couch, making the leather creak beneath him. 'I'll do that later, then, when you're not lugging in. Where are we at with getting back-up? Not that there's anywhere for them to stay, mind you.'

'Can't do much until the weather clears a bit,' Tyler said. 'DI Forde said he'll get a team of Uniforms across on the ferry as soon as it's back up and running, but no saying when that'll be.'

'That's fine, but I don't want any other ferries running until we give the say-so. We don't want anyone leaving before we've had a chance to speak to them,' Logan said.

'Shouldn't take us that long, boss. Population's only forty-seven, Hamza tells me.'

'Is that before or after someone murdered Iona?'

Tyler hesitated. 'Forty-six,' he corrected. 'And are we sure it's definitely murder, aye?'

'Well, unless she clonked herself on the coupon and then throttled herself to death, I'd say so,' Logan replied.

'She couldn't have hanged herself? The way the body was lying at the foot of that scarecrow, I just wondered...'

Logan shook his head. 'Briefly contemplated it myself, but it doesn't fit. If she did away with herself, where's the rope? Not enough height on the scarecrow, either. To get enough weight on her neck, she'd have to have lifted her feet off the ground and kept them there until she choked to death.'

'Suppose. She'd have had to have been determined.'

'She'd have had to have been a bloody miracle worker,' Logan retorted. 'Before she died, she'd have passed out. I'd have liked to see her keeping her legs up then.'

He took another mouthful of tea, rolled it around, then swallowed it. 'No. She was murdered. And right now, we're in the fortunate position of having a finite number of possible suspects. Forty-six people, take away... what? Ten or so kids, probably. She was found in a pretty remote location, and it'd have taken some strength to throttle her, so rule out the older folk, and we've probably got twenty or so possibilities.'

'Assuming whoever killed her didn't get off the island before she was found, boss.'

'Ferries haven't been running. Private boats are a possibility, but someone will have seen something, so at least we'll know,' Logan said. 'Right now, though, let's work on the basis that the killer's still on the island, and concentrate on catching the bastard before they can get their arse off it.'

Tyler stifled a yawn that prompted Logan to check his watch. Twenty to ten. No point getting stuck into anything more tonight.

'Tomorrow, we'll start the house calls. I want to speak to Iona's father, find out who her friends are, and build up a picture of the last night she was seen alive. We'll have to find somewhere to set up an Incident Room, or at least to do more formal interviews, if it comes to that. Ask Pat and Norman, or get on Google Maps. See if there's anywhere that might fit. A school, maybe.'

He clicked his fingers, a thought occurring to him. 'I bet the Community Council has got an office somewhere. If so, we can use that.'

'I'll get on it, boss,' Tyler said. He yawned again, and there was no holding this one back. 'Sorry, long day,' he said, once it had passed. 'I was pitching in with CID on some of the donkey work for the Gillespie case from early this morning.'

Logan regarded the DC with surprise. 'Were you?'

Tyler fiddled with the handle of his mug, then poked a couple of crumbs around on his plate, not quite looking up. 'Caitlyn's case, isn't it? Just want to help make sure the bastard goes down.'

'Aye. Well,' Logan said. It was the only words that were really needed. 'Go and get your head down. We can carry on in the morning. With a bit of luck, we'll have it all wrapped up by lunchtime.'

'Cheers, boss,' Tyler said. 'I'll maybe just give Sinead a ring first. See how she's doing.'

'Tell her I said hello,' Logan said. 'And remind her that she could do much better for herself.'

'Will do,' Tyler said. He set his cup on his plate, looked around for somewhere to put them that wasn't cluttered with bowls, vases, and assorted other nonsense, then just placed them on the floor next to his chair.

He was almost at the door when Logan called to him.

'Oh, and Tyler?'

'Yes, boss?'

'If you snore, I swear to God, I will smother you with a pillow.'

Tyler grinned. 'No promises, but I'll see what I can do.'

When he was gone, Logan swallowed the now nearly cold remnants of his tea, winced at the taste of it, and crossed to the window. It was dark now, but the way the window shook in its frame made it clear that the storm was still raging away.

Logan saw himself reflected in the window. His face heaved and moved, like his flesh was alive and squirming beneath his skin. An optical illusion caused by the rainwater running down the outside of the pane. But still, it did nothing to boost his confidence as he smoothed down his hair, adjusted his shirt collar, then took out his phone and tapped on the big blue icon that opened the Skype app.

Chapter 10

Shona Maguire was not midway through the process of cutting up a corpse when she answered. This was always a pleasant surprise.

She wasn't even in the hospital, unless the staff areas had been given a complete redesign since he'd last been in.

Shona was half-sitting, half-reclining on a couch, the colour of which could only be described as 'organ purple'. She had on an oversized checked shirt, her hair was hanging loosely around her shoulders, and she was a good two-thirds of the way through a generously-sized glass of red wine.

On the wall behind her were three framed movie posters: *Ghostbusters 2, Gremlins 2,* and *The Empire Strikes Back.* A satin gold scarf was pinned to the wall beneath them with the words, 'Rock On, Tommy!' emblazoned across it in faded black print.

There was another framed picture to the right of the posters, only half in shot. It was a photograph, and showed a grinning Shona with an arm around what looked like one of the Doctor Whos. One of the originals, Logan thought, not the new lot.

At the bottom of Logan's screen, right at the very edge of the camera's frame, the top of a Chow Mein-flavoured Pot Noodle rose into view like an obelisk. The thin metal handle of a fork stuck out of the top like a tiny lightning rod.

'I wondered when you were going to call,' Shona said, her Irish lilt drifting from the phone's speaker like music. 'You're cutting it fine. I was getting ready to head to bed.'

Logan swallowed, coughed, and cleared his throat, all in one movement.

'Jesus, are you choking?' Shona asked, leaning forward in concern.

'What? No. No. I'm fine,' Logan assured her. 'Sorry to call so late. I thought you'd still be... you know.'

'Elbow deep in a chest cavity? Nah, she's on ice until tomorrow. Had an OD and a car accident earlier. Worked too many hours, so they made me go home.'

'Ah right,' Logan said. He fumbled around for the right words. God, why wasn't he better at this? 'Rough day, then?'

Shona shrugged. 'Pretty standard, really. You? I hear you got a burl in a helicopter. That must've been exciting.'

'"No" quite the word I'd have used to describe it,' Logan said. 'And now I'm stuck sharing a room with DC Neish.'

'Is he the good-looking one?' Shona asked, smirking behind her wine glass.

'No, *I'm* the good-looking one. He's the glaikit one with the stupid hair.'

She laughed at that, and Logan was almost annoyed by how grateful he felt for it.

Shona leaned forward again, squinting at the camera. She was using her laptop, presumably, propped up on a table to give a wider angle of the room.

'Where even are you? The nineteen-hundreds?' she asked.

Logan looked over his shoulder at the dated furniture and yellowed wallpaper. 'Aye, something like that,' he said.

He wanted to say more to her. To just chat for a while. Enjoy this moment of connection with her, just the two of them there on their wee screens.

Unfortunately, he'd completely run out of things to say, and so he defaulted back to what he knew best.

'So, when do you think you'll get a look at the body?'

'Officially? About half-eight tomorrow morning,' Shona said. 'Unofficially?'

She reached out of shot and returned with an A4 notebook.

'I already had a quick peek and did some swabs. I'll start getting results from those tomorrow. This is all subject to change, and the body wasn't in great condition, but I'm putting cause of death most likely as asphyxiation caused by strangulation. Definitely murder. Someone standing behind her with a wire of some sort, I'd say. Either substantially taller than her, or she was kneeling. The wire wasn't sharp, but fairly thin and pulled tight, so it cut into the flesh. You know your phone charging cable? Something like that. Slightly thinner, maybe, but touch and go.'

'There was a head wound,' Logan said. A teasing smile started to form at the corners of Shona's mouth, and he jumped in before she could say anything. 'You know, in case you hadn't noticed.'

'Actually, now that you mention it, I think I did spot something along those lines,' she said. 'Not fatal, though. Not even all that serious. Bled a lot, but these things do. Would've been distressing, though. Probably blinded her temporarily. All in all, it wouldn't have been a very pleasant final few minutes.'

'They very rarely are,' Logan said. 'Any ideas on when she died?'

'Few days ago. I'd have to check the weather and temperature records to get a better idea of decomposition rate, but she's obviously been somewhere wet. The skin on her fingers is what I'd expect to find on someone who drowned.'

'She was in a big muddy puddle, and it's been pishing down,' Logan told her.

'Sounds about right. I'd estimate tail end of Tuesday, first half of Wednesday, but call that an educated guess until I've had a chance to look at her properly.'

'That fits. Tuesday was the last night anyone saw her alive. As far as we know at this stage, anyway.'

'Close-knit community, and not a big place. Chances are, if she was still alive after that, someone would have seen her,' Shona reasoned. 'And decomposition would rule out her being alive even by Wednesday evening, so you've got a decently small window.'

'Aye. It's looking like the Tuesday night, right enough.'

Logan shuffled his feet on the lounge's awful carpet for a few moments, before continuing. 'I knew her. The victim, I mean. Way back. We were in school together.'

Shona stopped swirling her glass and sat it down on the table in front of her. 'Oh. God. I'm sorry. I didn't know. Were you close?'

'Eh, no. Not really,' Logan said, skirting around the edges of the truth. *Not often,* would've been more accurate. 'She moved away when we were in high school. Hadn't really thought about her until I saw her under the sheet today.'

'Still, though,' Shona said. 'Must've been a shock.'

'Ach, yes and no. From what I remember of her, it was only a matter of time before she got on the wrong side of some bad bastard. But, aye, I've a bit of a personal stake in this one. I'd like to nail whoever did it, pronto. So, anything you can get me tomorrow...'

'Yeah, well, sure, you can count on me, Jack,' Shona told him.

'Aye,' he said, with a nod and a smile. 'Aye. I know.'

He cleared his throat again. Christ, his mouth was dry. He wished he hadn't polished off the last of the tea before the call. He wasn't prepared. Not properly. Now probably wasn't the time.

Although, it was rare that they were having a conversation that wasn't taking place above the remains of a murder victim, so maybe now was as good a time as any.

Sod it. He was going in.

'So, listen, I was thinking. I know we've made plans before, and something's come up, so we've never really... you know? I mean, we spoke about maybe... before, I mean. We'd discussed the idea that...'

He forced himself to shut his mouth, cutting off that awful bloody babble before it could go any further. On-screen, Shona was watching him in silence, her expression giving nothing away.

'I suppose, what I mean is, will we just do it?' he said, then his eyes widened in horror as he heard the words out loud. 'Have dinner, I mean! Dinner. Not, not... I wasn't saying... just, we could have dinner. I'd like to take you to dinner. Somewhere nice.'

Logan's mouth was racing ahead of his brain, which was currently fixating on what a weird word 'dinner' was. He'd said it so often in such a short space of time, it had lost all sense of meaning. Was it even a word?

Shona still hadn't replied, and Logan's instinct for self-preservation quickly kicked in.

'Somewhere nice-ish, I mean. Nowhere crazy. A kebab, or something. I'm no' made of money!' he said.

She was still saying nothing. Logan held his phone a little further away and squinted at the display.

'Hello?'

He tapped the screen. Shona's face remained completely frozen. The timer in the bottom corner that had been ticking up the minutes, ticked no longer.

'You are bloody kidding me,' Logan muttered, then a movement from behind him made him turn.

Norman was leaning into the lounge from the hall, offering up an apologetic smile.

'Sorry, forgot to say, the internet goes down at ten,' he explained. 'Cost-saving. It's back on at eight.'

'Sunday,' called Pat from elsewhere in the house.

'Oh, aye. Tomorrow's Sunday, so it won't be back on until after twelve. Reverend Kerr insisted.'

'Did he?' Logan sighed. He looked back at the screen in time to see Shona replaced by the Skype logo. 'Well, who am I to argue with a man of the cloth?'

'Aye. Well. Sorry, again,' Norman said. He started to leave, then leaned back in. 'Would you like a glass of wine, or something?'

72

'No, thank you,' Logan said, the response coming on auto-pilot.

'Whisky? Gin? We've a nice Lochaber one we haven't tried yet.'

Logan shook his head. 'You're fine. Honest.'

Through the ceiling above him, he heard the muffled rumble of a snore. He picked up his cup and plate.

'But I wouldn't say no to another cup of tea, if you're making one.'

Chapter 11

When Norman returned with the tea—and, to Logan's delight, another slice of cake—the detective took the opportunity to gather some background on Iona, and her relationship with the others on the island.

The relationship could generously be described as 'not great,' it transpired. Norman seemed reluctant to speak ill of the dead, but with a bit of reading between the lines, Logan got a picture of a woman who had turned almost everyone against her.

'It was the drink that was her downfall,' Norman said. 'I mean, so they tell me. She's been here a lot longer than we have. All we've ever seen her as is a bit... desperate. No offence to her, or anything,' he added, shooting a glance skyward. 'She was never far from drama, put it that way. And usually of her own making.'

'Some things never change,' Logan remarked.

Norman raised his eyebrows and tilted his head, like he hadn't quite heard. 'Sorry?'

'Doesn't matter. Her dad's on the island. What about the brother?'

Norman shook his head. 'Didn't know she had one. She's got a son, though. Grown-up now. Isaac. Isaac Young. Goes by his father's surname. He's got a house here with his girlfriend. Don't think his grandfather approves, unmarried couple living in sin, and all that, but then I don't think the Reverend approves of very much, really.' He shivered. 'Certainly not central heating, judging by the temperature in that bloody church of a morning.'

'The boy. Isaac. What was his relationship like with his mother?'

'Oh, I'm not sure… I wouldn't really know,' Norman said, but the uncomfortable look on his face told Logan enough.

'And Isaac's father? Is he around?'

'No. Lives in England somewhere, I think. Never known him to come out here. Probably doesn't like the idea of running into Iona.' Norman smiled thinly. 'I suppose there's no chance of that now, mind you.'

He had been sitting forward in the same chair Tyler had sat in earlier, but now leaned back and gazed through his reflection in the window at the darkness outside. The wind and rain had abated a little, so it was now just low-level background noise, and not the attention-demanding racket it had previously been.

'Murdered. I still can't believe it,' Norman remarked. 'I mean, we came here to get away from that sort of thing. Drugs and crime. Wee neds chucking stones at your windows. That's why we bought this place. Get away from it all. Somewhere you can leave your doors open, and not have to worry about who might be watching you coming and going.'

He blew out his cheeks and rubbed the arms of the chair with the flat of his hands. 'So, *murder*? An actual murder? I still can't believe it.'

'Any thoughts on who might've done it?' Logan asked, prompting a shocked look from Norman. 'Off the record, I mean. Just between you and me. I promise, I'm not going to go arrest someone on your say-so. Just thought you might have some personal insight, being local.'

'Oh, we're not local. Not by a long shot,' Norman said, deflecting the question. 'You've to be here at least three genera-tions before you can call yourself local. We've barely been here a year and a half. If we said we were local, we'd be bloody crucified!'

He clocked the way Logan was looking at him, and hurriedly clarified. 'Metaphorically. There's nobody I'd put down as violent. I mean, obviously it seems that there is, but... there's no-one I know who's capable of...'

He shook his head, visibly appalled by the very thought of it. 'So, no, Mr Logan. Sorry. I don't have any thoughts on who might have killed Iona.'

He stood up, collected Logan's empty cup and plate, then gave a nod. 'But I really hope you find them.'

Chapter 12

Logan found himself on page ninety-seven.

He hadn't been ready to face a night lying awake listening to Tyler snoring, and so had settled down beside an ugly lamp in the otherwise darkened lounge with the box of diaries they'd taken from Iona's house.

Logically, he should've started with the most recent, but he told himself it was important to build up a more long-term picture of the victim's life, and had gone straight for the one most likely to contain reference to their not-so-secret liaison.

It wasn't a diary, exactly, just an old school jotter Iona must've nicked from a class supply cupboard. She'd written 'The Secret Diary of Iona Kerr' on the front in bubble writing and shaded it with coloured pencils. Under it, in brackets, was another name, *Desiree Shanelle*, which didn't ring any bells for the detective. A pen name, clearly. Some teenage escapist fantasy.

The rest of the cover was decorated with little cartoon animals, the personalities shining off the page. She was good. Or had been, at least.

He'd looked through many diaries, private letters, and personal effects over the years. It was all part of the job. And yet, he found himself glancing cagily around before he opened the cover of this particular journal, and began scanning the pages for his name.

And there he was. Page ninety-seven.

'Jack Logan is a total knob.'

This wasn't the reference he'd been expecting, and he quickly read the rest of the entry, his frown deepening as he followed the whirling, twirling handwriting down the page.

They were in third-year at the time of the diary entry. Roughly six months before their post-disco get-together.

Logan had no recollection of it himself, but according to the diary, some sixth-year lads had been giving her grief after school, and she'd asked him if she could walk home with him.

He'd said no.

A weight formed low down in his stomach as he read the rest of the entry. Read the abuse she'd taken. Read how they'd pawed at her, ground themselves against her, before shoving her down the steps at the back of the Co-op and leaving here there in a dirty puddle.

Her old man had gone ballistic at the state of her uniform when she'd finally got home. Leathered seven bells out of her. Made her pray for forgiveness kneeling in her underwear on the cold kitchen floor.

And all because of him. All because he'd told her no. All because, for whatever stupid reason, he'd told her he wouldn't walk home with her.

'Aye,' he grunted, turning the page in shame. 'What a total knob.'

He wasn't mentioned again until the night of the disco. Even then, it was barely a cameo appearance, and not worth writing home about.

'Shagged Jack Logan,' it read. 'What was I thinking?!?'

There was a wee drawing of a girl next to it that Logan took to be Iona herself. She was holding her head in her hands.

It was, he thought, the single most damning review of his sexual performance he'd ever been privy to. He supposed he should be grateful that she hadn't used a star rating system.

Over in seconds. No stars. Wouldnae ride again.

Somewhere in the house, the cuckoo called midnight.

Skimming through the rest of the book, Logan got a clear impression of an unhappy home life, mostly caused by her

78

father's temper and strict religious bent. Iona had it bad, but her older brother, Jacob, got it far worse.

Logan remembered the sight of Jacob coming marching along the road towards him that night, his face twisted by rage into something monstrous. He'd had a couple of mates with him, but he wouldn't have needed them. Not with anger like that driving him on.

Logan had assumed at the time that all that rage was because of him. Now, though, he could see where it had really come from. Aye, it had been directed Logan's way that night, but it had been fuelled by years of violence and abuse from a father who punished frequently and, from what Logan could gather, loved rarely, if ever.

After sealing the book in an evidence bag, Logan wrote the details on the plastic label, and placed it back in the box.

He was reaching for the most recent diary when he heard footsteps shuffling softly along the hall. Someone was creeping about downstairs.

He could rule out Tyler, who was still snoring his head off on the other side of the ceiling.

Easing himself up out of the chair, Logan made his way quietly towards the door of the lounge. The top lights were out in the hall, but a couple of particularly hideous wall lamps were casting a thin, watery sort of glow across the walls.

A floorboard creaked. A shadow moved. Logan stepped out into the hallway, and a man in an orange cagoule screamed in fright.

'Shh. Jesus!' Logan hissed. 'People are sleeping.'

'Wh–who are you?' the man asked in a shrill whisper. His accent was south of England. Refined by years of expensive private education, the detective guessed.

'I was about to ask you the same thing,' Logan replied. 'Detective Chief Inspector Jack Logan. Mind telling me what you're doing sneaking about this house?'

A light came on at the top of the stairs, and footsteps hurried down. Pat practically jumped the last few steps, a sturdy-looking shoe clutched in one hand like a weapon.

Her relief when she saw the men in the hallway was immediate and palpable.

'Oh. God. It's just you two.'

'You know this gentleman?' Logan asked.

Pat smiled and nodded. 'That's Mr Tillerson.'

'Kevin,' the man added.

'He's the other guest,' Pat explained. 'The one in the double.'

'I've been stuck. With the weather,' Kevin said. He held up a pack of cigarettes. 'I was just nipping outside for a quick puff before I turn in.'

'Everything all right down there?'

That was Norman calling. Safely from the top of the stairs, Logan noted, and not down here in the thick of it with his wife.

Pat looked quizzically at the shoe she was carrying, like she couldn't remember picking it up. 'Aye. All fine,' she replied, backing up to the stairs. She smiled apologetically at her guests. 'Sorry. I'll leave you to it.'

Both men listened to her footsteps as she made her way back up to bed. Kevin raised his eyebrows and pulled a 'well, then' sort of face that suggested he'd really like to go and have his smoke now.

Logan had his own ideas about that.

'You didn't happen to see Iona Wallace on the night she died, did you?' he asked.

'Uh, I don't think so. I'm not sure I know who that is.'

Logan nodded. 'Right. I see. It's just, I was in the pub today, and the barman there—Australian boy—gave us a list of people who were in there the night Iona was murdered. You were on it.'

'Oh! Yes! The woman in the pub! The loud one? Is that her?' Kevin asked. He was fiddling with a cigarette, rolling it between finger and thumb. 'Yes. Sorry, yes. I did see her.'

'Right, then,' Logan said. He moved aside and motioned into the lounge. 'Would you mind stepping into my office, Mr Tillerson? I think it'd be useful if you and I had a little chat.'

Chapter 13

Kevin Tillerson was a refreshing change from most of Logan's interview subjects. Despite the informality of the set-up—him on the couch, Logan sat higher on one of the wingbacks—Tillerson spent the entire conversation wide-eyed in terror, babbling out answers almost the moment that Logan had finished asking the questions.

They'd started easy. Background stuff. What had brought him to the island? Who was he travelling with? Where was he going, and where had he been. That sort of thing.

Logan hadn't written down most of the answers. He'd just scribbled a catch-all, 'post-divorce mid-life crisis,' and then steered the conversation onto more important matters.

Tillerson had become even more willing to talk at that point. With no loyalties to anyone on the island but himself, he was holding absolutely nothing back.

The daughter-in-law had really hated her, he thought. He hadn't caught her name, but there was definitely no love lost there.

The son? Well, he had seemed mostly embarrassed by her, but angry, too. A cold sort of anger. Deep-rooted. Enough to drive him to murder? Kevin wasn't sure, but he wasn't ruling it out.

She'd had a go at a big chap. Got quite cruel. Kevin couldn't say for sure if he'd had learning difficulties, but he wasn't ruling that out, either. *Worth having a word, anyway, I'd say. He certainly looked capable.*

'Between you and I, I got the impression she was about as welcome as a fart in a spacesuit,' Kevin said. 'To, uh, to quote one of your countrymen.'

Logan regarded him blankly.

'Billy Connolly, wasn't it? Fart in a spacesuit?'

'I wouldn't know,' Logan said. 'So, she wasn't there with friends?'

'Goodness, no. I got the impression she didn't have any. Not among that lot, anyway. You could feel the hostility when she walked in—or staggered in, more accurately. And then, when the son and daughter-in-law arrived... oof. I'd swear the temperature dropped half a dozen degrees. Which is impressive, given the place is constantly ruddy freezing.'

'How long was she there?'

'Before they arrived? Maybe an hour. Afterwards? Oh, I don't know. Five, ten minutes?' Tillerson recalled. 'She became quite abusive to, well, to everyone. The big lad, as I mentioned, but the rest of them, too. The daughter-in-law got right up in her face by the end, screaming at her to go. And, well, she did. I think she was out of money, personally. No one would buy her a drink, so off she went.'

Logan scribbled in his pad. 'And that was the last you saw her?'

Tillerson's eyes went to the pad, drawn there by the movement of the pencil.

'Hmm? Oh. Yes. Yes. That was the last I saw of her.'

'And what was the atmosphere like once she'd left?'

'Fine.'

'Fine? Can you elaborate?'

Tillerson shrugged. 'Uh, well, I was sitting by myself, so I wasn't involved in anyone's conversations, exactly, but everyone seemed to relax after that. Well, almost. The son and daughter-in-law looked pretty shaken, still, but they left themselves soon after.'

'They left? Together?'

'Yes. Yes, I think so. I didn't see them go, just looked up from my map at one point and they were gone.'

'And how soon was this after Iona went?'

Tillerson made a weighing motion with his hands. 'I'd be lying if I said I knew for certain, but... ten minutes? Thereabouts.'

He gave a little jump as the cuckoo clock called once.

'Goodness. Is that the time?' he asked. It was diplomatic, if not exactly subtle.

'Aye,' Logan said, flipping his notebook closed. 'Thank you for your help, Mr Tillerson.'

'Right. Yes. Of course. Happy to.'

Tillerson sprang to his feet, already opening the top of his cigarette packet. 'If there's anything else I can help with while I'm here, do let me know. It's a lovely island, and such a terrible thing to happen. The community must be...' He smiled grimly. 'Well. It's very sad.'

'It is,' Logan agreed. 'And thank you. If we need anything more, we'll be in touch.'

'Well, you'll certainly know where to find me! I think we're right next door,' Tillerson said. 'Oh! That's a point. I don't suppose you know if they take cards at this place, do you? Been here longer than expected, and running a bit low on cash. Not sure if there's a machine anywhere.'

'No idea,' Logan told him, safe in the knowledge that he wouldn't be the one paying the bill at the end of his stay.

Tillerson looked a little disappointed, but then shrugged. 'Ah well. It'll all work out, I'm sure. I can do a cheque, if it comes to it.'

He nodded a farewell. 'Goodnight, Mr Logan,' he said, his waterproof jacket rustling as he headed for the door. 'And good luck.'

If Logan slept, it was brief and fitful, although he was fairly certain he didn't sleep at all. Partly, that was down to his mind whirring over the details of the case, but mostly it was because of Detective Constable Neish's incessant bloody snoring.

He wouldn't have minded so much, if it had been constant. If the snoring had taken just one form, and stuck to it. It was the variation that was the problem. One minute, he'd been roaring like a buzzsaw, the next he'd be whistling tunelessly through both nostrils, or making a clicking sound like a bubble bursting at the back of his throat, or one of a dozen other noisy ejections his airway decided to form while he slept.

Logan had woken him up six times, each time more irate than the last. Tyler had apologised every time, then immediately fallen back asleep before launching into some previously unheard nasal concerto.

After that, Logan had decided there was no point in waking him again, and had tried to learn to live with the racket.

This had not gone well. The couple of times he'd come close to dropping off, that bastard of a cuckoo clock had jolted him awake again.

And so, with time on his hands, and a ceiling to stare at, Logan had gone through what little he knew of the case so far, and made plans for the following day.

Talking to the family was going to be the priority, of course. Tomorrow—or today, technically—was Sunday, and Abraham Kerr was due to be running his church service as usual. The murder of a child might put lesser ministers off their stride, but not him. Not that bastard. Logan was very much looking forward to their chat.

Same with the son and daughter-in-law. They'd argued with Iona the night she'd died. Sounded serious, too. That conversation was another priority.

Roddy MacKay hadn't shown his face at the pub again, so he was on Logan's hit-list, too. The 'big chap' Kevin had referred to would be worth a word, and then it would be a case of asking around, talking to anyone else that might be able to shed some light on her final movements, to see if anything interesting emerged.

Shona should hopefully be able to provide him with some more information by early afternoon, and now that the weather was easing off a bit he'd like to get back out to where the body was found.

He lifted his head off the pillow, a thought striking him. Who'd found the body? He didn't recall seeing or hearing a name anywhere. He'd have to check.

A lot to do, then. And only him and the noisy snorting bastard in the next bed to do it.

He checked his watch. Almost five. Probably no point even trying to rest now. It was a complete waste of time. He might as well get up and get cracking. Get a head start on the rest of the world.

'Early bird catches the killer,' he mumbled.

And then, with Tyler wheezing across the room, and the cuckoo clock sproinging into life downstairs, DCI Jack Logan finally surrendered to sleep.

Chapter 14

Breakfast was the stuff that dreams are made of. Perfectly poached eggs, crispy bacon, three fat sausages, and some of the best tattie scones Logan had ever tasted, all accompanied by the usual beans, mushrooms, hash browns, and a nice wee slice of Stornoway black pudding.

Even the toast, which Logan could usually take or leave, was something a bit special. Homemade bread, apparently. You could taste the difference.

Tyler had been halfway through his breakfast by the time Logan came down. The DC grinned as he chewed a piece of bacon.

'Aye aye. Sleeping Beauty awakes,' he'd remarked, pronging a bit of square sausage with a fork.

Logan had said nothing as he pulled out the chair opposite him and sat down. He had waited until Pat had come to take his order, in fact, before launching into a whispered-but-passionate tirade about 'some bastard snoring all bloody night!'

'Who? The boy next door?' Tyler had asked, prompting a substantially louder outburst from the DCI.

Over breakfast, Logan had filled the junior detective in on his discussion with Kevin Tillerson the night before, and recounted some of the details of the diary he'd read, being careful to leave out any mention of himself.

The focus was mostly on Iona's relationship with her father. While there was no reference to any sexual abuse, it was clear the old man was a violent bampot, and that both children had suffered regularly at his hands. Or, more regularly, his belt.

'Sounds like a piece of work,' Tyler said. He pointed with a fork to Logan's plate. 'You going to eat that tattie scone, boss?'

'Yes, I bloody am!' Logan said, fending the DC's fork off with his knife.

'Oh. Right, aye,' said Tyler, crestfallen. He picked up one of his toast crusts and dragged it through what was left of his baked beans. 'How'd you get on with Dr Maguire last night?'

Logan chose to ignore the smirk and the waggling of the eyebrows that accompanied the question. 'She hasn't had a proper look at the body yet. Definitely strangled, though, and she reckons Tuesday night, early hours of Wednesday, fits the time of death. She'll know more this morning.'

Logan stopped when he became aware of movement by the door that led through to the kitchen. Pat hovered there, clearly unsure whether she should come in or not. She smiled with relief when Logan beckoned her through.

'How was it?' she asked, looking from one detective to the other. 'Everything OK?'

'Bloody marvellous,' Logan told her.

'Great! Would you like anything else? More toast? Tea?'

'I wouldn't mind another of those tattie scones, if it's—' Tyler began, but Logan picked up the DC's plate and held both it and his own out for Pat to take.

'He's fine. We're grand. Thank you.'

'Sleep OK?' Pat asked, taking the plates.

'Out like a light,' Tyler said.

'Oh, I'm sure the whole house is aware of how well you slept,' Logan said, shooting him a sideways look.

'Cuckoo clock didn't keep you up, did it?' Pat asked.

'No. I mean, not really,' Logan said. 'It was mostly this bugger.'

'Lucky you. Took me months to stop hearing the bloody thing,' Pat said, rolling her eyes. 'We wanted to get rid—wanted to strip the place right back and modernise it, in fact—but we weren't allowed.'

Logan frowned. 'No' allowed? How d'you mean?'

'Well, I mean, yes, I suppose we were allowed. It was just…' Pat shook her head and pulled an amused little smile, like she knew how ridiculous what she was saying sounded. 'The Community Council, they suggested we leave it as it was. For posterity's sake, sort of thing. Joy—the council, I mean—made it quite clear that they wouldn't be impressed if we changed it. Even specified that bloody clock. Said the house was of "local historical interest" and that the locals liked it as it was. We didn't want to make ourselves unwelcome, so we decided to hang off on the refurbishment. Just until we'd settled in a bit.'

'Right. I see,' said Logan. He glanced around at the faded wallpaper and garish curtains. 'How long have you been in?'

'Year and a half,' Pat said. 'We've owned it a bit longer, but that's when we moved in. Joy stops by every so often to say hello. Although, she's really just checking to make sure we haven't started redecorating, I think.'

'Aye, we ran into her yesterday,' Logan said. 'She seems like she could be…'

'An interfering old arsehole?' Pat suggested.

'Well, I was going to say "stubborn", but aye. That, too,' Logan said. He stood up and took another look around the place. 'If it's any consolation, I quite like it.'

'Do you?' asked Pat, her eyebrows rising in surprise.

Logan shook his head. 'No.' He smiled, apologetically. 'No' really.'

–

The rain had died down into a light drizzle, so they started the morning with a trip back to the site where the body had been found.

The scarecrow seemed to grin down at them as they sloshed carefully through the mud, the indentations in the hessian sack of its face carefully positioned to form rudimentary features.

'What is it we're looking for now, boss?' Tyler asked, pulling his jacket tightly around himself.

The coat he'd brought hadn't been particularly waterproof, and Pat had insisted both men take one of Norman's Gore-Tex jackets before heading out. Tyler had gladly accepted, but Logan had kept hold of his own overcoat. It was a large, heavy woollen thing, and was good for cultivating a nicely intimidating presence.

Also, he liked the big pockets.

Logan approached the scarecrow, snapping his rubber gloves into place. He hadn't yet heard any more from Shona—it was just after nine, and she'd barely be back at it yet—but something she'd said last night had made him think the site was worth another look.

With his hands protected, he reached up and began running his hands along the scarecrow's arms, patting down the padded sleeves from shoulder to wrist.

'Shouldn't you read him his rights first, boss?' Tyler asked. 'Or is this some sort of personal interaction? Should I even be watching this?'

'Shut up and give me a bloody hand,' Logan barked.

Pulling on his own gloves, Tyler joined him by the scarecrow. He didn't have the height advantage of the DCI, so felt around the legs and lower torso on the left side, while Logan focused on the right.

'What we actually looking for, boss?'

'Wire,' Logan said. 'Iona was throttled with a length of wire. I thought this thing might be held together or tied to its stand with the same stuff.'

'Doesn't feel like it,' Tyler said, after another half-minute of searching. He glanced back over his shoulder at the road. 'I hope nobody drives past. We'll look like a right pair of weirdoes standing here touching up a scarecrow.'

'It's the islands,' Logan remarked, still prodding at the thing. 'This probably qualifies as a good night out.'

'Creepy bloody thing, isn't it?' Tyler said. 'Or have I just watched too many horror movies?'

'*Wizard of Oz* doesn't count as a horror movie, son,' Logan said. 'Don't try to make yourself sound like the big man.'

They searched until they were sure that they weren't going to find what they were looking for. The scarecrow was attached to its post with wire, but it was thick metal fence wire, that would've had to be bent into shape with tools. Not the sort of thing you could really strangle someone with, and it didn't match the description that Shona had provided.

So much for that idea.

Peeling off the gloves, they trudged back to the Land Rover, the wind nudging and shoving at them as it came whistling in off the water.

'Internet back on yet?' Logan asked, once they were safely installed back in the Land Rover. He turned over the engine and cranked up the heating. The vents emitted an acrid burning smell, but not a whole lot else.

'No. After twelve today, boss,' Tyler said, although he took out his phone and checked, just to be sure. 'I asked Pat when she was taking my brekkie order.'

'Oh, aye. They said last night.'

Logan checked the clock on the dash. The bottom row of the LED lines were permanently off, but there was enough left for him to piece the time together.

'Not too long, though. We'll see if Hamza's got anything for us when it's back up and running. Soon as you can, I want you to fire him over names of everyone we've spoken to. Have him run background. On the family, too, if he hasn't already. And pay attention to the daughter-in-law.'

'Will do, boss,' Tyler said. He rubbed his hands together, then held them in front of the heater, in the hope it might start spitting out hot air at some point in the not too distant future. 'What's the plan now?'

'Now?' Logan began. He took a breath, readying himself to say words he hadn't spoken in a very long time. 'Now, we're going to church.'

Chapter 15

'Anything back from them yet?' asked Ben, checking his watch for the fifth time since he'd entered the Incident Room.

He'd had a bash at putting together the Big Board, but without Logan and Tyler here, there didn't seem much point. Besides, that had been Caitlyn's area of expertise, and Ben's efforts looked positively amateurish by comparison.

Right now, it consisted of a few scribbled Post It notes, a Google Maps printout of Canna with a red X marking the location of the body, and not very much else.

'Not yet, sir, no,' said Hamza, after clicking 'refresh' on his email for the umpteenth time that morning. 'Tried getting Tyler on WhatsApp, but he's not showing as online.'

Ben grunted. 'Probably dead, then. Maybe Hoon caught up with them.'

'Preliminary pathology report's in, though. I was going to forward it over, but we've all been CC'd in, so it'll be in your inbox. There's an update from Geoff Palmer in there, too.'

'Anything exciting?'

'Potentially,' was all Hamza would say on the matter. 'Worth having a look.'

Ben clicked his mouse a few times, then gave it a shake, waking the computer from its slumber. Judging by the series of whirring and grinding noises it made, it wasn't impressed.

'Any word on the ferries?'

'Not due to start running today, sir, but they're eyeballing tomorrow as a possibility. Weather's supposed to get worse this afternoon, then improve from there. We should be able to get

93

a chopper over without too much bother, if you fancy a wee trip.'

From the look on Ben's face, he very clearly did not fancy a trip, wee or otherwise. 'Best if we head things up from here,' he said. 'No point in us all being stranded out there, is there?'

Hamza looked at his PC screen. The weather forecast for Canna for the rest of the week was laid out across it. There was a marked improvement by Sunday evening, but it was still due to be raining for most of the next seven days.

'Aye. That's true,' he agreed, picking up his mug of tea. 'It's a dirty, thankless job, but someone has to stay here and man the fort.'

The two men raised their mugs in a toast. 'We make a hell of a home team,' Ben said, and then they both jumped in fright when the door to the Incident Room was thrown wide, framing the hulking silhouette of Detective Superintendent Robert Hoon in the doorway.

Yesterday, while giving Ben the third degree, Hoon had looked angry. Furious. Apoplectic, even.

Today, though, he looked *evil*. Today, he looked inhuman. Steam practically blasted in great, billowing clouds from his nostrils as he jammed his hands against the door frame and pushed. Hamza and Ben both found their eyes drawn to the wood as it creaked and groaned in complaint.

'Have you heard from that fucker yet?' he hissed.

Taking his life in his hands, Ben played dumb. 'Which fucker are you referring to, sir?'

'You know full fucking well which fucker I'm fucking referring to! Logan!' Hoon jabbed a meaty finger in Hamza's direction. 'You've fucking spoken to him, haven't you? Haven't you?!'

Ben opened his mouth to speak, but Hoon was on it in a heartbeat. 'Keep your fucking mouth shut, Benjamin. Does it look like I was asking you, you Muppet-faced cockrash?'

Ben closed his mouth again, and made a mental note to write that one down later, assuming he survived the next few minutes.

94

Hamza's mouth flapped up and down like a ventriloquist's dummy with a faulty hinge. 'I, uh...'

'Let me make it very fucking easy for you, son. Let me simplify it for you,' Hoon growled, advancing into the office like a lion in search of prey. 'I know you fucking spoke to him. I know everything that goes on in this fucking place. See me? In this place? I'm God. I'm the Lord fucking Almighty. I'm everywhere. I'm all around. You can't go for a shite without me being there.

'So, I know you fucking spoke to him. That's not a subject that's open to fucking debate. What I want to know is, did you tell him that I'm looking for him? Did you tell him to take his bastarding thumb out of his puckered fucking ring and call me?'

Hoon leaned over Hamza's desk, his eyes practically bulging out of his head, like all the anger swelling inside him was trying to force its way out through the sockets.

'Did you say that to him, son?' Hoon asked. 'Did you tell him that from me?'

Hamza's chair squeaked. Or, it might have been Hamza himself. 'I, uh, I mean, not in so many words, sir, but aye. I passed the message on.'

'Oh, you did, did you?' asked Hoon, his mood lightening, his mouth forming something that was like a smile, but very much wasn't one. 'You passed the message on, did you?'

Ben knew full well what was coming, and started to speak. Hoon held up a finger for silence before the DI had got halfway through the first syllable.

'Benjamin. Please,' he said.

Then, when he was sure Ben wasn't going to continue, he placed both hands on Hamza's desk and leaned forward, forcing the DC to roll his chair back a few inches.

'So, tell me this, son,' he began. His voice was quiet, but it had lost the levity of a few seconds before. 'If you passed on the message—if you told him to call me—then why *the fuck* hasn't he?'

Hoon straightened, turning, threw his arms out to the side like a gladiator addressing a baying crowd. 'Eh? Can anyone tell me that? Benjamin? You were so fucking keen to say something a minute ago. Can you explain to me why Detective Chief Inspector Logan has ignored a direct fucking order from on high?'

'The, uh, the signal's not great,' Ben said.

'Do they have landlines?'

Ben squirmed under the heat of Hoon's glare.

'Um, aye. I think they—'

'Then what's the fucking problem?'

'Maybe... maybe the storm—' Hamza ventured, but Hoon spun on the spot and silenced him with a look.

'Your shot's over, son. Let the adults fucking speak now, eh?'

Ben stood up. 'Look, sir, it wasn't DC Khaled who spoke to Jack, it was me. I told him you wanted him to get in touch. Whether he did or not, that's not on us. He's a big boy, and can make his own decisions.'

'Oh, he's—'

'I wasn't finished, sir,' Ben said. The firmness in his tone caught Hoon by surprise, shutting him up.

Across at the other desk, Hamza quietly rolled his chair back another few inches.

'With all due respect, Detective Superintendent, DC Khaled here is a good officer. He's a valuable member of my team. You want to give me a bollocking? You want to scream, and shout, and call me a... a... Hamza?'

'Jeb-end, sir.'

'A jeb-end? Fine. Go for your life.' Ben stepped closer to the DSup, craning his neck to look up at him. 'But you do not come in here and take that approach with my officers. No' even if DC Neish is here. I won't have it. I'm pretty sure HR won't have it, and I know for a fact that the press would have a field day if they knew a senior officer was throwing around racist language like that.'

Hoon's eyebrows, which had been knotted together with fury, tightened further in confusion. 'What the fuck are you talking about? What racist…?'

The penny dropped.

'Oh. I see.'

Hoon drew himself up to his full height. Ben stood his ground. Hamza quietly wondered what the current jobs market was like.

When Hoon spoke, there was a note of amusement in it. 'I always did like you, Benjamin,' he said, then he wheeled around in a crisp about-turn and marched out of the Incident Room, bellowing, 'And get that fuckwit to phone me!' as he went.

Once the door had swung closed, Ben sunk back down into his chair like a punctured balloon.

'Cheers for that, sir,' said Hamza. 'I owe you one.'

'One? You owe me about three years of my bloody life,' Ben said, clutching at his heart. 'Twelve years military service, getting shot at and dealing with bloody IEDs in the Gulf, and it still doesn't prepare you for that bugger when he's off on one.'

'Didn't know you were in the army, sir,' Hamza said.

'Aye. Long time ago,' Ben replied. He reached a shaking hand for his mug, then motioned to the DC's PC with it. 'Now,' he said. 'Any word?'

Chapter 16

The internet signal returned halfway through the church service, sending Tyler's phone into a frenzy of pings and bleeps, and drawing him dirty looks from much of the congregation, and the old man standing at the head of it in particular.

The Reverend Abraham Kerr was a minister very much in the fire-and-brimstone mould. He hadn't yet addressed the death of his daughter, choosing instead to devote the first part of his sermon to the importance of fearing God. Not loving God, which Logan dimly recalled being generally encouraged at other services he'd been dragged along to in the past, but *fearing* him.

Fear of God, according to Reverend Kerr, was key. Fear, not love. That was the main thing. Those who didn't fear the Lord would find themselves in hot water come the Day of Judgement—a day which, going by the way the old man spoke about it—he felt couldn't come soon enough.

'Turn that thing off!' the reverend roared, his narrow eyes blazing righteous fury all the way from the front of the church to the back, where DC Neish was fumbling with his handset.

This was not actually all that impressive, each end of the church being only half a dozen pews away from the other.

Once Tyler had finally managed to switch his phone into silent mode, he cleared his throat, smoothed his hair, and shot a sideways look at the man beside him, who sat shaking his head in disgust.

'You're a disgrace,' Logan whispered, enjoying every moment of Tyler's embarrassment.

The sermon resumed. Fear this. Worship that. Do as you're told and, if you were very lucky, you might not end up having a hot poker rammed up the jacksy on the regular for the rest of eternity.

The usual.

Logan let it wash over him and indulged instead in one of his favourite pastimes: people watching.

Judging by the numbers, most of the island had turned out for the service. That might be unusual—they might've turned out to hear what the minister was going to say about the death of his daughter—but Logan suspected it was probably the norm.

He didn't know most of the congregation, but he recognised a few of its members. Pat and Norman from the B&B were there, sat in the second row from the back, like they weren't too sure of their place.

They'd smiled and waved at the detectives when they'd entered, before being frowned at by a stout woman with copper-coloured hair who sat a few feet along the same pew.

Joy, the Community Council chairwoman, had parked herself right down the front. She was really putting her back into the whole Sunday worship thing, and sang the dreary selection of hymns louder than anyone else.

Although not, it had to be said, particularly well.

Roddy MacKay from the pub was pretty much slap-bang in the middle—third row from the front, six from either end. He didn't seem to have come with anyone, and while Logan couldn't see his face, he shifted and fiddled like someone who was on edge, much to the chagrin of the well-dressed families on either side.

A couple down the front caught Logan's eye. They were sat off to the side, so he could make out at least part of their faces. He'd put them in their late twenties or early thirties, and while the woman was listening intently to the sermon, her partner had his head down, eyes fixed somewhere on the floor.

He hadn't seen the man before, but there was something instantly familiar about his profile. Logan had seen it before. Or seen one like it, at least.

Nudging Tyler, he pointed subtly in the direction of the couple. 'Son and daughter-in-law,' he whispered. 'Sure of it.'

Over on Logan's right, tucked in at the back corner, was a giant of a man. The DCI dwarfed most people, but this guy was bigger in every direction. It was as if someone had taken a man of Logan's build, and scaled him up by another fifteen percent.

He held a hymn book in his hands. The book was sizeable, but in the man's hands, it looked comically small. The man was listening intently to the minister, his lips moving as he silently repeated the words being spoken from the pulpit, like his mouth was helping his brain to process the information.

This had to be the 'big chap' Kevin Tillerson had mentioned. The one who'd received the tongue-bashing from Iona the night she'd died.

Logan was still sizing the guy up when, up front, Abraham ratcheted up his volume half a dozen notches.

'And speaking on sin…' he boomed, his beady eyes darting across the congregation.

They'd all been sitting silently until that point, but now they went a few steps further. They froze, held their breath, unmoving. This was it. This was what they'd all been waiting for.

'You will all now have heard the news of the death of Iona Wallace.'

Logan felt that one on the victim's behalf.

Iona Wallace.

That was what he called her. Not 'my daughter'. Not even 'Iona'.

Iona Wallace.

'Some of you, no doubt, will feel I have something of a vested interested in this news. Some sort of…' His nostrils flared, like the words disgusted him. '*Personal connection.*'

His gaze swept across them again. Not a hair moved. Not a breath was taken. Even the children, who'd been kicking their feet and twiddling their thumbs now sat quietly, not quite understanding what was going on, but knowing it was significant, somehow.

'And you would be correct. Of course, I have a personal connection. I stand here as a servant of God, and you are all— even Iona Wallace—God's children. Still, as the Bible tells us, "The body that is sown is perishable, it is raised imperishable; it is sown in dishonour, it is raised in glory; it is sown in weakness, it is raised in power; and it is sown a natural body, it is raised a spiritual body".'

He glanced up to the apex of the church's roof, and for a moment Logan thought there might have been a flicker of emotion on the old man's face. If there was, though, it didn't last long.

'We are all sinners, Iona Wallace perhaps more than most. We can only hope that the Lord, in His wisdom, will see fit to forgive her many, many transgressions.'

He reached for a hymn book and gave the nod to a stern-looking silver-haired woman who sat by an old cassette player. 'And now, we shall sing Hymn ninety-two, "Praise God, For He is Kind".'

The button of the tape machine clunked as it was pressed. The speaker had just started to crackle when a voice piped up from the centre of the middle row.

'*Kind*? What do you know about kind?'

A collective gasp went up. The cassette player was hurriedly clunked off again.

The families on either side of Roddy MacKay all shuffled sideways on their pews, making a show of distancing themselves from him as he jumped to his feet.

'You treated her like dirt. Like something on your shoe!' Roddy said, his voice trembling. He shot accusing looks at the congregation around him. 'You all did. Every last one of you.

She didn't need your bloody… judgement. She needed your support. She needed compassion. She needed help. And where were you all? Her neighbours. Where were any of you?'

He turned his attention back to the minister, who was peering at him like a buzzard eyeing up a juicy rabbit. 'And where were *you*? You were her father. You were supposed to watch out for her. To protect her. It's supposed to be your natural instinct. It's a… it's fucking *genetics*!'

'Hey now,' said a man in his fifties from the row in front. 'Settle down. There's kids present.'

'Good! They should hear this!' Roddy cried. He stabbed a finger up at the pulpit. 'They should know that *that*—him there—that's not what a parent should be like. A parent should love you. A parent should care. The only thing that bastard loves is the sound of his own voice. He's the reason Iona's dead. Him, and you, and you, and all of you!'

He leaned on the back of the bench in front, some of the fight going out of him. 'All of us,' he said, his voice cracking. 'Iona had her problems, but she was funny, and she was sad, and she was kind. She was one of us. And we let her down. We all let her down.'

The silence that followed was an uncomfortable one. It pressed down on the place, bending the necks of almost everyone in it, until their gazes pointed to the floor.

'Well, then, now that you've said your piece,' said Abraham, his voice calm and measured. He indicated the door with a single sharp nod of his head. 'Get out.'

For a moment, Roddy looked like he was going to protest, but then he began sidestepping past the family on his right, who were forced to half-stand, or turn their knees in to let him pass.

Roddy caught Logan's eye, but said nothing as he scurried past, his mouth drawn tight, his eyes shimmering.

'And if you're lucky,' bellowed the man of the cloth from up front, 'we'll consider saying a prayer for your soul.'

Logan leaned in closer to Tyler. 'Stay here. I'm going to go talk to him.'

'Aw, what? Can't I come?'

The DCI shook his head. 'Stick it out. See if anything else happens. Meet me outside after.'

He started to move, then turned back, 'Oh, and try to at least look like you're enjoying yourself.' He flicked his gaze upwards. 'The big man's got his eye on you.'

—

Logan caught up with Roddy halfway down the hill that led to the pub. Despite the detective calling after him, Roddy didn't stop until a hand like a twenty-ounce steak slapped down onto his shoulder.

'Mr MacKay?'

Roddy sighed below his breath, inhaled deeply through his nose, then turned, an attempt at a smile plastered in place. Logan was much taller than he was, and the angle of the hill didn't help matters. Roddy's smile wavered at the sight of the detective towering above him, but he did his best to hold it in place.

'Oh. Hello. Yes. Sorry. I wasn't... I was miles away.'

'Understandable,' Logan said. 'That was quite a speech you gave back there. I get the impression Mr Kerr doesn't often have anyone talk back to him.'

'Just Iona,' Roddy replied. 'And only if she'd been drinking.'

'You knew her well?'

Roddy's eyes darted down to the detective's chest, purposefully avoiding eye contact. He shrugged.

'Aye. I mean... we weren't close, but, she'd... we'd...'

He squeezed the bridge of his nose, shook his head, then tried again.

'Yes. We were friends. There. Iona and I were friends. OK?'

'Why wouldn't it be?' Logan asked.

'She wasn't like they all say. All of *them*,' Roddy said, his voice shaking like it had back in the church. 'They sit there every week and they go on about turning the other cheek, and loving thy neighbour, but they don't. None of them do. They all hated her, and they bloody well went out of their way to make sure she knew it.'

Logan followed Roddy's gaze back in the direction of the church, then motioned down the hill to the pub. 'Mind if I ask you a few questions inside?'

Roddy shifted his weight from foot to foot. He wrung his hands together. Logan could practically hear his brain whirring as he searched for an excuse.

'It'll only take a few minutes,' the detective said. He placed his hand on Roddy's shoulder again and guided him down the hill. 'And who knows? It might even help the both of us.'

Chapter 17

He wasn't saying she was an angel. Not by a long shot. He wanted to make that clear.

Logan had asked just one question in the past ten minutes—'Can you describe your relationship with Iona?'—and Roddy had taken it from there.

She'd been a customer to begin with. That was all. A regular, from the day that Roddy came to the island and reopened the long-dormant pub, right up to the day she died.

Over the years, Roddy had developed 'a soft spot' for her. Nothing romantic, he wanted to make that very clear, but he'd seen the way she was treated by most of the other people on the island, and he'd taken pity on her.

He'd given her a few shifts. Cleaning at first, then a few goes behind the bar. She wasn't half-bad, but nobody was keen on having her serve them, and so sales steadily dropped until he'd had no choice but to let her go.

Somewhere along the way, they'd become friends. It was mostly one way, Roddy was the first to admit. She took far more than she ever gave, borrowed money that he often didn't even have. But she was wild, and unpredictable, and fun to be around.

'No wonder the rest of the island hated her,' he concluded, before downing a gulp of the thick, stodgy-looking pint of real ale he'd levered from one of the bar taps. 'She was everything they're not.'

Logan asked his second question. It was a belter.

'Were you in love with her?'

He'd expected a quicker reaction. An incredulous shake of the head, maybe. A gasp and a raising of the eyebrows.

Instead, Roddy considered the question carefully, sucking the foamy head of his pint off the bottom half of his moustache.

'No. Not really. I mean, not in the way you're meaning,' he said, after a period of contemplation. 'Did I love her? Yes. Yes, I think so. I think I was probably the only one who did.'

'Were you ever involved in a sexual relationship?'

Roddy's flinch was there one moment, gone the next. Had Logan not been watching for a reaction, he'd have missed it.

'No. No, never. She wasn't interested in me in that way,' he said, then hurriedly clarified. 'And I wasn't interested in her in that way, either. That was mutual. We were friends, like I say. Just friends.'

He hadn't seen her the night she went missing, he said. He'd spent most of the evening upstairs in his flat, cashing up the weekend's takings. He'd only heard about the argument at the end of the night, when Bruce had filled him in on all the gory details.

'Don't suppose you've got any CCTV in here, have you?' Logan asked, gaze flitting around all the likely locations.

'No, never needed it. There's rarely any trouble,' Roddy replied. 'I mean, there are arguments, of course. Plenty of those. But nothing we'd need CCTV for.'

'Fair enough. Just thought I'd ask on the off-chance,' Logan said.

'There is the webcam, though.'

Logan blinked. His gaze gave the place another once-over. 'Webcam?'

'No, not in here. Sorry. I mean outside. It looks down from the shop out across to Rum. Runs on the Wi-Fi. It won't show in here, but it might show people coming and going.'

'Right. Got you,' said Logan, unable to fully hide his disappointment. 'But only up to ten o'clock?'

Roddy winced, then nodded. 'Yes. Good point. Only up to ten o'clock,' he confirmed. 'Still, Iona left before then, I think. Maybe it'll show something.'

'Maybe,' Logan said, making a note. 'I've come across a few of these sort of things before, though, and most of them don't record. They only... what's it called? Stream.'

'Oh no, this one records,' said Roddy. 'I helped them set it up when it was first being installed. It all gets backed up onto a server.'

Logan was more interested now. 'And who's responsible for the server?'

'Community Council. Joy. She made me walk her through the set-up step-by-step, then changed the passwords, so I don't have access. But yes, she'll be able to pull up the footage from the night Iona died. It should all be there.'

Logan wrote something else in his pad, then underlined it.

'That's useful to know, thank you. I have to go talk to her today, anyway. Do they have an office, do you know? The council?'

'Yes. Sort of. It's part of the school building,' Roddy said. 'It's not big—they hold any public meetings in the dinner hall—but yes. They have one.'

'Also useful to know,' said Logan, already relishing the thought of how Joy would react when he commandeered the place. It would be nice to have something to look forward to.

Logan checked the time, then pressed on with the interview. Roddy was fully forthcoming about Iona's relationship with her father, or what he knew of it, anyway.

He'd disowned her, apparently, in her thirties. Or she'd disowned him. One of the two. Either way, they'd rarely spoken since, and when they had, the words they'd exchanged weren't kind.

'She owed him money. A lot of money, I think,' Roddy said. 'She'd talk about it when she'd had too much to drink. Cried about it, sometimes. She was paying it back for a while, but she stopped a few weeks ago. She told me she'd had enough, that he wasn't getting another penny out of her. She wished she'd never started paying him back in the first place.'

'What did he give her the money for?' Logan asked.

Roddy shrugged. 'I don't know. She didn't say. I asked, but she always seemed… I don't know. Ashamed.'

'She never gave you any idea?'

'No. Although, she did once say she didn't owe him anything. That it "wasn't normal" for him to be asking her for it.'

Logan's pen paused above his pad. 'Wasn't normal?'

'That's what she said. She'd been drinking a lot, though. She wasn't making a lot of sense. I had to put her to bed upstairs in the end.'

Roddy's eyes widened, like he was suddenly worried he'd said too much. 'I slept on the couch. Nothing went on.'

'I understand,' Logan said. He made another note, which prompted the man opposite to take another big swig of his pint.

Roddy wasn't as keen to talk about Iona's son, beyond to confirm some basic details. His name was Isaac, he'd lived off the island for a number of years, before returning with his then-girlfriend, now fiancée, Louise.

Isaac had studied Economics at Glasgow University, but he and Louise now ran a small business making soaps and candles for customers all over the world.

'Iona was proud of him. So proud,' Roddy said. 'But he was mortified by her. You could see it whenever they crossed paths, he desperately wanted to be somewhere else. Somewhere she wasn't.'

'So why come back?' Logan asked. 'Big world out there, why settle back here?'

'I think his grandfather put up the money for the business,' Roddy said. 'Maybe there were conditions on it. Or maybe being here was good for branding. I honestly don't know.'

And that was about as far as Roddy would go into the relationship between mother and son. Best Logan asked Isaac about it himself, he suggested. It wasn't for him to say.

The impression Logan got was that Roddy was protecting Iona more than he was looking out for her son. It was like he didn't want to badmouth the lad, because he knew she wouldn't have approved.

Logan could've pressed, of course. Pressing was one of his strong points. Often, it involved the sole of his boot. But he elected not to, on this occasion. Roddy wasn't going anywhere. If he needed to come back and do some pressing, he wouldn't have far to go.

He stood up, flipped his notebook closed, and returned it to his pocket. 'Thanks for your time, Mr MacKay. I won't keep you any longer. For now.'

'Thanks. Aye. I should crack on and get set up. Think I'll be on my own today.'

Logan looked over at the empty space behind the bar. 'Not got your Ozzy on the night?'

Roddy blew out his cheeks. 'Your guess is as good as mine. Bugger didn't come back after his break last night.'

Something in Logan's gut stirred. 'He didn't?'

'No. Said he'd be fifteen minutes, then never came back.'

'And when was this, exactly?' Logan asked.

'Eight, maybe. Thereabouts,' Roddy said. 'He's staying in the wee flat out the back of the shop. I meant to go round there, but... other things on my mind.'

'I'll look into it,' Logan said.

'If you see him, kick his arse.'

'Will do. And, I must say, Mr MacKay, what you did back there? What you said at the church?'

Roddy looked up from his now almost empty pint glass. He appeared shrunken and cowed, like he was bracing himself for the worst.

'What about it?' he asked.

One corner of Logan's mouth turned up in a smirk. 'I reckon Iona would've loved every bloody minute of it.'

Chapter 18

The service was still dragging on when Logan returned to the church. Wee Free services tended to do that, if memory served. The prayers alone could go on for twenty minutes apiece— longer if the person leading them got sidetracked into slagging off Catholics, and denouncing the Pope as the Antichrist.

The rain was off—although, the colour and formation of the clouds suggested the respite was a temporary one—and so he took a wander a little further up the hill, and killed some time just looking out to sea.

He could see Skye rising from a bank of grey fog to the north, looking positively Jurassic from this angle.

To the east was Rum and, beyond that—though currently invisible—lay the mainland. Mallaig, Morar, and then a run down the A830 to Fort William, via Glenfinnan.

Out west, almost completely lost to the mist, lay... what? Another island, but which one? He tried to picture his place- ment on the map. Outer Hebrides. Barra, maybe, with its airport on the beach? South Uist? One or the other.

He breathed in. Deliberately. Growing up in Glasgow, this wasn't something he tended to do often, but this place practic- ally insisted on it. There was a freshness to the air that made him cough, like the years' worth of gunk built up in his lungs was protesting against the sudden intrusion.

And God, the place was quiet. Other than the faint rustling of the grass on the breeze, and the distant call of a sheep, there wasn't a sound beyond those he made himself. It was a world away from Glasgow, and a stark contrast to even Fort William or Inverness.

Hell, it was a stark contrast to the room in the B&B last night, which had probably endangered his hearing at points.

He'd always had a faint dislike for the islands. Or for the idea of them, maybe. Growing up in the city, they'd seemed snobbish, somehow. Their remoteness making them seem standoffish and aloof. He imagined them to have some sort of superiority complex, some greater claim to Scottishness than he, in his tenement block, had any right to.

And maybe they did, he thought, standing there at the top of the hill, looking out at the world through a veil of mist and fog. And maybe that was OK.

Or, maybe the claim they had wasn't greater or more authentic than his own, but just different. And maybe that was OK, too.

He enjoyed another big breath, really sucking this one down and letting it expand his chest. The freshness of it was flavoured with salt and *just* the faintest hint of sheep shit.

Since arriving on the island—and barring those few hours in the middle of the night—he'd felt calmer. More relaxed. He'd put it down to being out of phone range, beyond the reach of whoever had been plaguing him with all those mystery calls.

But what if it was something more than that? What if, God forbid, he actually *liked* the place?

He was just starting to come to terms with that possibility when he spotted the scarecrow. From where Logan stood, the hill dropped down before rising up again, forming a little gully of bracken and heather. The scarecrow was fixed in place near the top of the other slope, half-hidden by the shade of a large Scots pine.

It wasn't the same scarecrow as the one near Iona Wallace's house. Not unless it could move about and change its clothes. This one was fatter and squatter, with an old bowler hat fixed to the knotted ball of straw and canvas that made up its head.

Like the one at Iona's, there was no need for it. It made no sense. The point of a scarecrow was to protect crops, surely? Unless that tree was going to miraculously start sprouting fruit, there was no purpose for the thing being there.

Or none that was currently clear, at least.

Its ragged outfit fluttered in the breeze as it held Logan's gaze, its long, dark coat blowing around it like Dracula's cape. They stood there, eye to eye across the gully, and the world waited to see which would draw first.

The sound of the church's front door opening broke the spell. Thrusting his hands deep in his coat pockets, Logan turned his back on the scarecrow and trudged down the hill in time to meet DC Neish scurrying out of the church and onto the pavement, a conga-line of congregation members hot on his heels.

'Fuck's sake, boss. You got off lightly there,' Tyler grumbled.

Both men stood out of the way of the door as most of the rest of the island's population came filing out, all pulling on their jackets and shooting wary glances up to the sky.

'Anything interesting happen after I left?' Logan asked.

'Not a thing. Literally, not a thing,' Tyler said. He leaned in closer and dropped his voice to avoid anyone else hearing. 'Although I did come to the conclusion that God can be a bit of a prick when he wants to be. Or maybe that's just your man in there's interpretation of it.'

Logan shook his head. 'No. I hear he can be, right enough.'

He spotted a familiar face in the crowd and stepped past Tyler. 'Come here, this'll cheer you up,' he told the DC, pushing into the crowd. 'Mrs Bryden? Do you have a minute?'

Joy Bryden stopped, looked around for the source of the voice, then folded her arms across her chest when she spotted the detectives. Her face took on the look of someone who'd just sucked a whole lemon in through their teeth, and Logan felt a little surge of happiness that made it all the way to his face as a smile.

'Yes? Can I help you?' she asked, her expression making it abundantly clear that she'd much rather not.

'You can, actually,' Logan said. 'You've got an office, right? The Community Council, I mean?'

She eyed them both suspiciously. 'We do. Of course. Why?'

'We need it,' Logan said.

Joy's face didn't so much as twitch. 'I beg your pardon?'

'Your office. We're going to have to take it over,' Logan said.

'I'm sorry, no. You can't.'

'Oh, we can, Mrs Bryden.'

'*Ms*,' she corrected.

'Apologies. *Ms* Bryden. We're investigating a murder. But then, you already know that. In order to facilitate that investigation, we're commandeering your premises as of now.'

Truth be told, Logan had no idea what the legal position was on this. If DS McQuarrie had been here, she'd have known. She'd have been able to quote the exact law or regulation that gave him permission to take over the Community Council's premises.

But DS McQuarrie wasn't with him. She never would be. And DC Neish, despite his heart being more or less in the right place, was a poor substitute.

'You want to kick us out of our own office, so you can use it?' Joy said, her voice adopting a shriller tone.

'That's about the size of it, aye,' Logan confirmed.

'Under what authority?' she asked.

Logan groaned inwardly. This would be the sticking point. He didn't think intimidation would work on the woman, but he drew himself up to his full height, fixed a suitably disgruntled look on his face, and prepared to give it his best shot.

'*Under what authority?*' he growled.

'The Joint Services Co-ordination of Municipal Buildings Act, two-thousand-and-eleven.'

Logan and Joy both turned to Tyler. He beamed back at them. 'That's right, isn't it, boss?'

The DCI blinked, frowned, raised his eyebrows, then repeated this entire process again. Finally, he nodded. 'Oh. Aye. Exactly. Under that authority.'

He faced Joy again. There was a look of resigned indignation on her face that told him, without her having to say anything, that they'd won.

'So, do you have the keys handy? Or would you rather show us around in person?'

Joy heaved out an exaggerated sigh, then turned on her heels and started marching down the hill. 'Fine. I'll show you. But you had better not make a mess.'

Logan fell into step beside Tyler as they set off after Joy.

'Looks like someone's done his homework,' he remarked. 'Where'd you pull that one out of?'

'My arse, boss,' Tyler said.

Logan peered down at him. 'Eh?'

Tyler winked. 'Made it up. Sounded good though, eh?'

Logan nodded slowly, then gave just the tiniest and most begrudged of chuckles. 'Aye. Maybe there's hope for you yet, son,' he said, and then they hurried down the hill, closing the gap on the furious Joy Bryden.

—

The Canna Community Council office was small, sparse, and immaculately tidy. It was so tidy, in fact, that Logan had his doubts the place had ever been used for anything more than storing a couple of desks and a filing cabinet.

The only giveaway that anyone actually used the place on a regular basis was the A1-sized wall calendar, which displayed a number of past and upcoming events.

A printed sign above it read: 'COMMUNITY CALENDAR: IMPORTANT!!!!' and Logan was already making plans to Tipp-ex out those exclamation marks as a matter of priority.

A quick glance at the events on the calendar cast further doubt on their importance. There were six events listed—including two AGMs, for some reason—and none of them struck the DCI as particularly vital.

The other events ranged from a shore clean-up to 'duck tagging,' whatever that was.

Twice a month, there was a little red sticker stuck to the calendar—the first and third Wednesday of each month. The most recent was a few days ago, right after Iona Wallace had been murdered.

'What's all this?' Logan asked, pointing to the latest sticker.

DC Neish, who was standing in the corner scrolling through his phone, briefly looked up, before realising the question wasn't directed at him.

'Battery change. For the webcams,' explained Joy, grudging every word. She set the keys on the faded green padding that topped the larger of the two desks. 'Now, I'm going to leave you with these, but I want you to promise—'

'Webcams?' asked Logan, jumping on the remark.

Joy hesitated. 'Sorry?'

'You said "webcams". Plural. Is that right?'

The woman's expression tightened. Solidified. Fixed in place. 'Webcam. Singular. Slip of the tongue.'

Logan sat in the largest chair—her chair, he thought—not taking his eyes off her. 'Right. Easily done,' he said, after a lengthy pause. 'I meant to ask you about that, actually. I need the footage from Tuesday night. We believe it might show Iona Wallace leaving the pub.'

Joy threw her arms up and gave a heavy, emphatic sigh. This wound Logan up no end, and the next few words were out of him before he could stop them.

'I'm no' asking you to travel back in fucking time and fetch it for me,' he told her.

He took a moment to compose himself, lowered his voice a few decibels, then continued. 'It'll be backed up on the server, right? The one Roddy helped you set up. You can either get us the footage or you can give us some way to log in and get it ourselves. Up to you.'

'Fine. Fine, I'll get it looked out,' Joy snapped. 'Anything else you'd like me to get for you while I'm at it? Cup of tea? Home-made scone?'

'Only if you're making one,' Logan said, which earned him a fierce look.

'Kettle's in the bottom drawer of the cabinet,' she snapped. 'If you use any teabags, you'll replace them. Fair's fair. And leave the biscuits, they're diabetic.'

'Right. Well, they have my condolences,' Logan said, sitting forward in the chair.

He motioned for Tyler to open the door. The office building was attached to the school, but it had its own entrance out onto a small rectangle of tarmac that made up the playground.

'And when you've got that footage,' Logan began, as Tyler opened the door at Joy's back. 'Just drop it in here. At our office.'

Joy bristled at that, but said nothing. She caught the door handle on the way past Tyler and pulled it hard behind her. The effect was lessened somewhat by the slow-close hinge that prevented any impressive farewell slam.

Tyler only glanced up from his phone once the door had eventually eased itself shut. 'Bit harsh there, boss,' he said, before going right back to reading.

Behind the desk, the DCI shrugged. 'Good enough for the sour-faced cow,' he said, then he stood up, retrieved the keys from the desktop, and tossed them to DC Neish. 'Right, we're going to check out the shop. Bruce, the Australian fella from the pub? He didn't turn up for his shift last night. Seemingly, he rents the flat out back.'

Tyler said nothing. His lips moved silently as he continued to read.

'Sorry, am I keeping you from something?' Logan asked, his shadow falling over the junior officer.

'Hmm? Oh, sorry, boss,' Tyler said. 'It's just, have you seen the pathology report?'

'Didn't know it was in. Why?'

'It's just preliminaries so far. But it's Iona Wallace, boss…'

'Aye, well I should hope so. What about her?'

'The swabs. They found semen,' Tyler said. He turned his phone to show Logan the gory details of the report. 'Looks like she'd had intercourse the night she died.'

Chapter 19

Logan had knocked three times now, but had heard nothing from the other side of the door. He knocked again, a proper policeman's knock that shook the dimpled glass panel that ran the height of the door on one side.

'Bruce?' he called, having realised after the first knock that he had no idea what the Australian's surname was. 'You in there, son?'

He'd left Tyler talking to Hamza back at the newly commandeered office, and had taken a stroll across the street to check the flat at the back of the shop.

Part of him had thought he might find Bruce curled up under a blanket, loaded with the cold, but a much larger part had told him not to be so bloody stupid. The barman had upped and vanished shortly after the detectives had left the bar. Even if he believed in coincidences, Logan would have been highly sceptical of that one.

The door was flimsy. One good kick would do it. One good shove, maybe.

He contemplated it for a few moments, then decided to try the shop, on the off-chance they had a spare key.

The shop was essentially a *Spar* without the branding. It had the same limited selection of tinned and dry foods, a few racks of household products, and a fridge full of milk, cheese, yoghurts, and assorted soft drinks.

On the top shelf of the fridge sat a row of sad-looking sandwiches. They were all lined up like puppies at a dog pound, all sitting there side-by-side, hoping that today was the day they'd finally be chosen.

There was no one at the counter when Logan approached it. A door stood open behind it, and he could hear the rustling of someone moving about in there, and a tuneless mumble of whoever it was singing below their breath.

'Hello?' he called.

The singing came crashing to a halt. A small, wiry man in his late-seventies shuffled out, his coat hanging from one arm. His gaze went the length of Logan, top to bottom and back again. His expression was one of utter and total confusion, like he had no idea what he was looking at.

'We're not open,' he eventually said.

His voice was stronger than it had any right to be, given how withered the rest of him was. He didn't sound annoyed, exactly, more sort of bemused, like he couldn't get his head around how anyone could've made such a fundamental error of judgement.

Logan very slowly and deliberately regarded the shop around him before replying.

'Aren't you?' he asked.

'Sunday. We're not open for another half hour.'

'Right. But the door's open. You look open.'

'Looks can be deceiving. You'll have to come back.'

Logan almost let himself get drawn into a debate on the matter, then remembered what he was there for. He produced his warrant card, which went almost completely ignored.

'Do you own the flat out back?'

'Apartment.'

'Sorry?'

'It's not a flat. It's a self-contained apartment,' the shopkeeper said.

'Whatever it's called. Do you own it?'

The old man shook his head. Logan could've sworn he actually heard his neck creaking like dry wood. 'No.'

'Well, do you know who—'

'The business does,' the shopkeeper continued. 'And I own the business. I'm the shareholder. It's a limited company.'

Impressively, given his past form, Logan held it together.

'OK, so you're responsible for the fla—' He stopped himself just in time. 'For the apartment? And it's currently being rented to Bruce from the pub. That right?'

'That's correct.'

'Do you have Bruce's surname?' Logan asked, taking out his notepad.

'I do.'

Logan clicked the button on the end of his pen, flipped open his pad, and waited.

The old man said nothing.

'Can you tell me what it is?'

'Anderson.'

Logan wrote the name in the pad. 'When did you last see Mr Anderson?'

'How do you expect me to know that?'

By fucking remembering, Logan thought. He managed to avoid saying it out loud, and instead just gave the shopkeeper a hopeful, expectant sort of look.

'Wednesday, maybe? Thursday? He comes and goes. I come and go. We don't often come and go at the same time. He was in here doing his shopping one morning, though. I think it was Wednesday. I don't know. I can't be sure.' He waved a hand as if trying to swat away a particularly irritating fly. 'I think it was Wednesday.'

'Notice anything unusual about him?'

'Not really,' the shopkeeper said. 'I mean, I barely understand a word he says at the best of times. He's foreign.'

'Nothing strange about the transaction?'

'Strange? Like what? He wasn't standing on his head or wearing a dress, if that's what you mean.'

Logan counted to five in his head before continuing. 'Anything unusual about his purchases, I mean.'

The old man grunted gruffly. 'Right. I see. Well, yes, as it happens. There was.'

Logan raised his eyebrows. 'Oh?'

'Cleaning stuff.'

Logan's grip tightened on his pen. 'Cleaning stuff?'

'Whole basket of it. Bleach. Disinfectant. Cloths. That sort of thing. Shoe polish. Brown. Two wee things of it.'

'I see...'

'And a Twix,' the old man concluded. He placed his fore-fingers about eight inches apart. 'One of the jumbo ones.'

'And that was unusual?'

'Oh, no. Not unusual at all. He's partial to a Twix.'

'The cleaning stuff, I mean,' Logan said, who really should've seen that one coming a mile away. 'Would he normally be buying stuff like that?'

'No. Not at all.'

'You're sure?'

'Well, he's never bought it from me, and I'm the only bloody shop on the island, so you work it out.'

Logan jotted down a note as the shopkeeper continued. 'I remember I said to him, "What's all this for? You'd better not have made a mess of the place," I said. "Or you'll be out on your arse," I said.'

'What did he say?' Logan asked.

The old man shrugged. 'No idea. He's foreign. I can't for the life of me get to grips with the accent.'

Cleaning products. Wednesday morning. Hours after Iona Wallace was killed. And now he'd vanished, right after chatting to the two investigating officers.

'The flat—'

'Apartment.'

'The apartment,' Logan said. 'Don't suppose you've got a spare key?'

'Why do you ask?'

'It's just, we're having difficulty getting hold of Mr...' His eyes flicked to his pad. '...Anderson. He didn't show up for work last night, and now he's not answering the door.'

The old man gave Logan another look up and down, sniffed noisily, then pressed a button on the till that sat on the counter between them. The bottom drawer shot out with the force of a battering ram, ejecting a small pile of loose change onto the floor.

Muttering to himself, the shopkeeper fished around in the drawers, rattling the coins and rustling the notes.

After a good thirty to forty seconds of this, he finally produced a large copper-coloured key and held it out for the detective to take.

'Don't make a mess,' he instructed, as Logan took the offered key. 'And if he's in there, tell him he still owes me this month's rent.'

–

Logan entered the flat quietly, and stopped in a hallway no larger than a public toilet cubicle. Odours hung from the walls like paintings in a gallery. Cigarette smoke, cannabis, cheap beer, and sweat.

Whatever Bruce had bought the cleaning products for, it wasn't to tackle the hallway.

'Mr Anderson?' he called, projecting the greeting through the three closed doors that surrounded him. 'It's Detective Chief Inspector Jack Logan. We met yesterday. At the pub.'

Silence. Not a creak. Not a whisper. Nothing to suggest anyone was home.

Of course, Caitlyn probably thought the same thing back in Kinlochleven, right before Gillespie had shot her through the door.

One of the doors was half the width of the others. Storage cupboard. Had to be. He checked that first, tugging on the little brass doorknob with a rubber-gloved hand. It sprung open at the first pull, and he brought up an arm to deflect a flurry of movement from within.

The falling broom toppled as far as it could in the narrow hallway, then the handle clonked against the opposite wall. Logan retrieved it, had a quick squiz inside the narrow space behind the door, then returned the brush to its rightful place and pushed the cupboard closed.

That done, he turned to the door directly opposite, and gave the shoogly handle a downwards shove. The door opened into a small, messy bathroom. Toothpaste was flecked across a grimy mirror, and a bar of soap had all but dissolved in a basin of water.

The toilet was blocked, a gelatinous papier-mâché of bog roll and brown water filling it all the way up to the rim.

'Clarty bastard,' Logan muttered, burying his nose in the crook of his elbow and dropping the lid back into place.

He had a quick check behind the grim-looking plastic shower curtain, then quickly backed out of the room and closed the door behind him.

The other door led to an all-in-one living room, kitchen, and bedroom set-up. A bed seemed to have partially exploded out of the sofa, its curved metal legs not quite hitting the floor. There was a thin mattress on top, with a knot of bedclothes slung over to one side, and a couple of pillows so lacking in stuffing they barely made one good one between them.

The rest of the room was clean. Spotlessly clean, in fact. Logan pressed the pedal on the kitchen bin with the toe of his boot, flipping the lid to reveal a nest of disinfectant wipes and crumpled paper towels.

There was a smell of bleach that became more choking the closer he got to the small stainless steel sink. Like the rest of the kitchen, the sink had been scrubbed to a dull shine. A selection of half-empty bottles of cleaning products suggested Bruce had thrown everything at the place. And in a hurry, too, going by the way the bottles had been abandoned on the kitchen floor.

A theory began slotting itself together as Logan poked around the rest of the flat.

Bruce Anderson had had sexual intercourse with Iona on Tuesday night. Raped her? Possibly, although it could've been consensual.

After that, he'd killed her and left her body out of the way. Someone would find it, of course, but it'd take a few days. Time enough for him to clean the place up and remove any evidence of her having been in the flat.

He bought the cleaning products on Wednesday morning and set about scrubbing the place. He'd only cleaned the living area, which told Logan that he'd either run out of time, or he knew there was nothing incriminating in the bathroom. Maybe Iona hadn't gone in there.

The only thing was that Bruce had seemed perfectly calm when Logan and Tyler had spoken to him. Nothing he'd said or done had rung any alarm bells, and Logan prided himself on his ability to spot when someone was being a shifty bastard.

Still, his senses had occasionally failed him before, and Bruce's decision to pull a vanishing act almost the moment the detectives had left the bar was not helping to paint him in a particularly good light.

There wasn't much else of interest in the living area of the flat. The fridge was stocked with everything a young, single, Australian man would require—namely, several cans of cheap lager, a couple of microwave curries, and something that might once-upon-a-time have been a lettuce.

A quick finger-tip search of the bin produced nothing but the used cleaning products. Logan tied the bag off at the top and set it by the door to take away as evidence.

His hands were starting to sweat inside the rubber gloves he'd pulled on before entering the place. He'd never been able to bear the feel of the bloody things for long.

What else?

Standing in the doorway, he looked around the room, searching for anything out of place. Anything that shouldn't be there, or anything that should be, and wasn't.

Nothing jumped out at him. Nothing obvious.

Ducking, he took a look beneath the fold-out bed. At first, he thought there was nothing under there, but then he saw it, tucked away in the shadows at the back.

A box. A green plastic storage box.

Kneeling down, Logan reached into the gap until his fingers brushed against the smooth plastic. Catching the underside of the rim, he slid the box out, weaving it between the metal legs of the bed.

And then, he stared. For several long moments, he just knelt there, gazing blankly at the spaghetti of cables and wires that were spilling out of the box. Power cables. HDMI cables. Phone charging cables. All different lengths, all different thicknesses, all tangled together like some sort of diabolical Chinese puzzle.

'Well now,' Logan whispered. He poked around in the mass of wires. 'Isn't that interesting?'

Chapter 20

Tyler watched in silence as Logan deposited the black bag and the box of cables in the corner of the office, his mobile tucked into the crook of his neck, his fingers poised on the keyboard of his laptop.

'Who's that?' Logan asked, indicating the phone with a nod.

'It's Hamza, boss.'

'Get him to run a full search on Bruce Anderson.'

'The Ozzy?'

'I want a full background. Who he is, where he's been. Has he got any priors or warrants? If he's had a parking ticket, I want to know about it, and I want to know within the next half hour.'

Tyler spoke into the phone. 'Get all that, Ham? Aye. Bruce Anderson. Australian.'

He looked up at the DCI. 'Any other info to go on?'

'He's got good teeth,' Logan said. He scowled. 'No, I don't have any other info to go on, so tell him to get his finger out and get on with it.'

'Get your finger out and get on with it,' Tyler said. He grinned at the response. 'Want me to pass that on to the boss for you?' he asked. 'No. No, thought not. Keep in touch.'

He tapped the hang-up icon, then sat the phone on the desk.

'We got a suspect, boss?' Tyler asked.

'Aye. Maybe. Bruce Anderson bought a sizeable number of cleaning products on Wednesday morning. Bleach, Flash wipes, Dettol spray.'

'Could just be a neat freak,' Tyler suggested.

'You wouldn't be saying that if you'd seen the bastard's bath-room,' Logan replied. He pointed at the green plastic tub in the corner. 'Also found that little lot tucked under the bed.'

Tyler meerkatted up and peered over the top of his screen. 'Cables?' he said, initially confused, then quickly catching on. 'Oh. Right, aye. You think one of them's the murder weapon?'

Logan shook his head. 'I doubt he'd have strangled her with one of them, then put it back in the box. But we know he had access to the same sort of weapon used in the attack.'

'To be fair, boss, so does everyone.'

'I know. Neither one's much to go on on its own, but throw in the disappearing act and it gets a bit tastier.'

Tyler nodded. 'If there's something to find on him, Ham'll dig it up.'

'What else did he have for us?' Logan asked.

DC Neish looked down at the notes he'd taken during the call with his colleague back in Inverness.

'Couple of things. Body showed no sign of there having been a struggle, beyond the blow to the head and the strangulation. A few bruises, but day-to-day stuff. A bump on the shin and some light scrapes on both knees. No defensive injuries that would suggest she'd tried to fend off an attacker.'

'So it's not impossible that the sex could've been consensual,' said Logan.

'Nothing to suggest otherwise at the moment, boss,' Tyler said. 'I mean, other than her being murdered shortly afterwards, obviously.'

'What else did they get?'

'From a pathology point of view, not much. Something about gastric alcohol concentration levels—she was drunk, basically, but we knew that. Marijuana user, too. Long term, judging by the build-up. No DNA news on the semen sample yet.' Tyler scanned down the rest of the page. 'That's about it. More broadly, they found forty quid on the body. Two twenties.'

Logan stopped and straightened. 'Huh.'

Tyler raised an eyebrow. 'Something the matter, boss?'

'Kevin Tillerson—the other fella at the B&B—he said she was mooching about for drinks on Tuesday night. Very much gave the impression she was skint.'

'Maybe just tight,' Tyler suggested. 'Why spend your own money when you can get some other idiot to spend theirs?'

'Aye. Maybe,' Logan said. 'Or maybe she earned herself forty quid between the time she left the bar and the time she was murdered.'

'Earned?' said Tyler. 'How do...? Oh. You reckon she was on the game, boss?'

Logan let the thought percolate around for a few seconds, then gave a non-committal sort of shrug. 'I'm not ruling it out,' he said. 'Have we got anything else?'

Tyler flipped forward and back a page in his notes. 'That's about it, boss. Oh, although she had some scarring on her wrists. Old, though.'

'Suicide attempt,' Logan reasoned.

'That's the most likely explanation, aye,' Tyler agreed. 'DI Forde and Hamza are going to run her medical records, see if there's anything on there about it.'

'Right, good. But text him, and make sure he prioritises Bruce Anderson. He's our best lead.'

Tyler had picked up his phone halfway through the sentence, and his thumbs were already tapping on the screen.

'Done,' he announced, just a couple of seconds later. 'Oh. There was something else, boss. Not from Hamza, just...'

He stood up and crossed to the filing cabinet. 'It's probably nothing. Just a bit odd, is all. I was having a snoop around and found these.'

Tyler opened the top drawer of the cabinet, rifled through the paperwork for a moment, then took out a suspension folder.

'Meeting minutes. For the Neighbourhood Watch,' he said, handing Logan the folder.

The DCI opened it, revealing a neatly-typed set of minutes, dated a couple of weeks before. There was a stack beneath the top one, presumably from different meetings.

Logan scanned the page. It listed several incidents so mind-numbingly minor, he wasn't sure they should even be referred to as 'incidents' so much as just 'things that happened.'

A couple of teenagers had been observed milling around outside the pub one night. Part of a visiting family of wild campers. They'd tried to get a couple of people to buy them alcohol, but had been refused.

A woman—another visitor—had dropped her purse down near where the boat came in, but had found it again almost immediately.

A couple of locals had been seen smoking in the beer garden of the Canna Come Inn, despite the fact it was supposed to be a no-smoking zone.

That sort of thing.

'What's odd about this? Besides the fact anyone bothered their arse to write it down, I mean?' Logan asked.

'Look at the top, boss. "Members present".'

Logan's eyes flitted up the page. There was only one name listed. 'Joy Bryden,' he said. 'Just her? Quiet night.'

'Not just that night, boss,' Tyler said. 'Check the rest.'

Logan skimmed through the next few pages of minutes.

Members Present: Joy Bryden.

Joy Bryden.

Joy Bryden.

'She's the only member ever mentioned,' Tyler said. 'Like, ever. I went right back.'

'A one-woman Neighbourhood Watch,' Logan said. He shook his head and closed the folder. 'Still, if it was going to be anyone, it was going to be her. Struck me as a right bloody busybody.'

He passed Tyler the folder back. 'Odd, right enough,' he said. 'But each to their own. Now, we've got half an hour to kill before Hamza gets back to us. I think it's time you and I paid the Reverend Kerr a wee visit.'

Chapter 21

'Christ. He's no' short of a bob or two, is he?' Tyler whispered, as he and Logan waited in the hallway of the minister's house. It was attached to the back of the church, but overshadowed that building in every sense.

Logan's whole flat would've fit in that one room, and the oak and mahogany furniture was probably worth more than everything the DCI owned.

The floor was all exposed boards, carefully varnished and polished to a rich shine. Much of it was covered by a thick rug that would've carpeted several rooms of a normal-sized house, although the homeowners would have to be pretty desperate to put up with that pattern.

There were four large paintings, one on each wall. They each depicted famous moments from the Old Testament. There was Noah living it up on his boat while dozens of people flailed and thrashed in the water around him.

On the wall opposite, a pillar of salt looked back as Sodom burned. Flanking those on the other walls, choirs of angels slaughtered men, women, and children.

Aye, Tyler wasn't wrong, Logan thought. God could be a right prick when he wanted to be.

'Does the church pay for all this? No' exactly cheery, is it?' Tyler said, following Logan's gaze to the paintings. 'Quite impressive, mind you.'

'I'm more of a *dugs playing snooker* man, myself. Maybe a nice watercolour landscape,' Logan said. 'Babies getting rammed onto spikes isnae really my cup of tea.'

They'd been shown into the hall by a meek wee woman in her fifties, who might have been an employee, but might equally have been a particularly submissive spouse.

Iona's mother had never been on the scene from as far back as Logan could remember, but it was possible that Abraham had remarried. To a certain demographic of women—the God-fearing, self-hating, low self-esteem demographic—the vicious old bastard was probably quite the catch.

The wee woman appeared through a set of double doors at the far end of the hall, and practically curtsied as she addressed the detectives.

'The Reverend will see you now,' she announced, her head down as she studiously avoided meeting either man's eye. 'But he's asked me to inform you that he doesn't have long, so he's requested that you don't take up too much—'

'Aye, no' bother, pet,' Logan said, striding past her and into the room beyond.

'Cheers,' Tyler told her, smiling awkwardly as he followed Logan into a high-ceilinged study with wood panelling on the walls.

There was one desk, placed slap-bang in the middle of the room. This had the effect of making the person sitting behind the desk the focal point of anyone walking in. An effect, Logan thought, that was not accidental.

The Reverend Abraham Kerr sat forward in a luxuriously padded brown leather chair, his pointed elbows on the walnut desktop, his chicken-bone fingers interlocked as if in prayer.

His eyes blazed out from beneath eyebrows the colour of freshly driven snow. There were matching clumps of hair on his cheeks, too, like miniature mirror images of the eyebrows above. Given that the rest of him was clean-shaven, it was an odd choice on the facial hair front, Logan thought, but each to their own.

The minister said nothing, his hawk-like gaze inviting them to be the first to speak. *Daring* them, maybe.

Logan could never resist a dare.

'Mr Kerr?' he said, purposefully neglecting to address the man by his correct title.

'Reverend. But yes,' the minister replied. His voice was crisp and clipped. It wasn't booming with the righteous wrath of his sermon, but gave the impression it could head in that direction any time he chose. 'I am he. To whom am I speaking?'

Five seconds. That's how long it had taken. Five seconds, and Logan already felt rubbed up the wrong way by the bastard.

Granted, he hadn't been a fan of the man going in, but it had been a second-hand dislike of him, borrowed from the pages of Iona's diary. The near-instant contempt he'd felt when Kerr had opened his mouth was much more personal and authentic.

'Detective Chief Inspector Jack Logan, and Detective Constable Tyler Neish. Police Scotland Major Investigations Unit. We're investigating the death of Iona Wallace,' Logan explained, adding, 'your daughter,' in case the minister was having difficulty placing the name.

Kerr's fingers flexed to form a tent-shape, then locked together again. He peered at Logan over the top of his knuckles, his tongue licking drily across his puckered lips.

'Jack Logan?' he said. 'Not *the* Jack Logan? From Castlemilk?'

'The one and only,' Logan said.

'You've a nerve coming here.'

'I'm here to do my job, Mr Kerr,' Logan said.

'Reverend. And how can you investigate the death of Iona Wallace?' Kerr sneered. He shot Tyler the briefest of looks. 'They were in a relationship, you know? Back in the day.' He focused his attention on Logan again. 'How can you *possibly* be considered impartial?'

Logan wanted to say, *Because it wasn't a relationship, it was a twenty-second fumble up a darkened close,* but chose not to, more for Iona's sake than her father's.

'Aye, well, like it or not, I'm who they've sent,' was what he settled on, then he helped himself to one of the two chairs on the other side of the desk, and gestured for Tyler to take the other.

'I didn't invite you to sit,' Kerr said.

'Aye, we noticed,' Logan replied, making a show of getting himself comfortable. 'We'd like to ask you a few questions about Iona. Your daughter.'

Kerr gave a dry, mirthless chuckle. 'I'm sure you would,' he said. 'And how long will that take?'

Logan sucked in his bottom lip, then spat it out again. 'Oh, I don't know. How long will that take, DC Neish?'

'Suppose that's up to Mr Kerr, boss,' Tyler said. 'Depends on how forthcoming he is.'

'True,' said Logan, nodding sagely. 'Good point, well made, Detective Constable.'

He interlocked his fingers and leaned his elbows on the desk, mirroring the man opposite. 'Did you kill Iona?' he asked.

A little explosion of air escaped simultaneously through the minister's mouth and both nostrils. His expression was midway through a particularly impressive bit of contortion when Logan held up a hand to stop him.

'Sorry. Sorry,' he said. He held Kerr's gaze while addressing Tyler. 'Would you mind recording this interview, Detective Constable? Let's have an accurate record of what Mr Kerr here has to say.'

'No bother, boss,' Tyler said, producing his phone. He opened the voice recorder app, set the phone on the table, then spoke into it. 'Interview with the Reverend Abraham Kerr.'

Tyler checked his watch and recited the time and date, before continuing.

'Present are Detective Chief Inspector Jack Logan, and Detective Constable Tyler Neish.'

Logan hadn't taken his eyes off Kerr the whole time. The minister's face was stuck somewhere between 'shock' and 'outrage', but he was returning Logan's stare with interest. Even his eyebrows were joining forces in the middle in an attempt to muscle in on the action.

'That us recording?' Logan asked.

'That's us recording, boss,' Tyler confirmed.

The DCI lowered his clasped hands until they were resting on the desk in front of him. 'Did you murder your daughter, Mr Kerr?' he asked again, drawing another outraged exhalation from the man opposite.

'No, I did not! How dare you even suggest such a thing?' he blustered. 'How *dare* you? And it's *Reverend*. Reverend Kerr. I won't tell you again.'

'Your relationship was… difficult, was it not?' Logan pressed.

'Our relationship was non-existent. But that was as much her choice as it was mine, and it certainly did not mean I had any part to play in her death, Mr Logan.'

'It's *Detective Chief Inspector*,' Logan took pleasure in correcting. 'Iona owed you money.'

'She did.'

'How much?'

Kerr sniffed. 'I fail to see how that's relevant.'

'Well, how about you let us be the judge of that?' Logan suggested. 'How much did she owe you?'

'I don't have the exact figure to hand,' the minister said.

'Roughly, will be fine.'

Kerr's tongue moved from side to side in his mouth, like he was rolling the number around in there. 'Total, or still outstanding?'

'Let's go for outstanding,' Logan said.

'Eighty thousand pounds.'

'Bloody hell,' Tyler remarked. When the outburst drew a fiery look from the minister, he offered an apology, cleared his throat, and stared at his phone screen like it was the most fascinating thing in the world.

'Raising a child single-handed is not an inexpensive endeavour,' said Kerr. 'The costs soon mount up.'

Logan replayed the sentence in his head. Then, he replayed it again.

Surely not? Surely the man didn't mean what Logan thought he meant?

'What are you saying?' the DCI asked.

Across the desk, Reverend Kerr gave a curtly efficient little shrug. 'She said she was "disowning" me. Said she no longer considered us to be father and daughter—which, by the way, suited me just fine.'

He was. He bloody was. He was actually saying what Logan thought he was saying.

'So, you're saying you *billed* her? You billed her for the cost of bringing her up?'

'Precisely that,' Kerr confirmed. 'Why should I be left out of pocket for the sake of an ungrateful wretch like her?'

Logan and Tyler both sat mute and dumbstruck by the very idea of it.

'Iona brought nothing but shame and embarrassment on me, from the day she was born until the day she died. Drinking. Drugs. *Whoring* it around to anyone who'd have her,' the Reverend continued, his nostrils flaring and drawing further upwards with every word.

It was like even the mention of her name offended him. Like it had a stink to it that left a bad taste in his mouth and snagged at the back of his throat.

'I dedicated the best part of my life to that girl. Her brother, too. And did they appreciate any of it? Were either of them grateful? I gave them everything, and for what? How did they thank me?'

'Your son. Jacob. You hit him with a bill, too?' Logan asked.

Kerr barely skipped a beat. 'Jacob is dead.'

'Dead? Sorry, I didn't know. Since when?'

'Since he took his own life. Six years ago. Well, closer to seven now, I'd imagine. I don't keep count.'

He doesn't keep count, Logan thought. *What sort of heartless bloody husk of a human being wouldn't keep count?*

'I'm sorry to hear that,' Logan said.

Kerr's expression did nothing to suggest that he was. 'Yes. Well, it was unfortunate, but these things happen.'

These things happen. Jesus.

'The money Iona owed you,' Logan said, steering the conversation back on track. 'She'd stopped repaying it, hadn't she?'

The briefest suggestion of surprise went darting across the minister's face, then was gone. 'Who told you that?'

'A little birdie. Is it true?' Logan asked. 'And, not that I'd expect a man of your standing to lie to me, but we can check with the bank, so please answer honestly. Had she stopped her repayments?'

'She had. Yes.'

'And how did you react to that?'

'Not by killing her, if that's what you're driving at. It was all in the hands of my solicitor in Inverness. It's all documented and above board. She agreed to the monthly payments, and then she stopped making them, placing her in breach of contract. My intention was to settle it through legal means. Not violence.'

'But you've been violent before, haven't you?' asked Logan. 'Quick to anger, quicker with the belt.'

'Children need discipline. Mine more than most. Punishing a child for their transgressions is not the same as murdering one. I shouldn't even dignify your original question with a response, but I will reiterate. I did not kill Iona. I do not know who killed Iona. Her death, while hardly a surprise, is as much a mystery to me as it evidently is to you.'

He looked at his watch, sighed, then tapped it twice with a long, bony finger.

'Now, could we possibly hurry this up? I have an evening service to prepare for.'

'Evening service? We don't have to go twice, do we?' cried Tyler, practically spitting the words across the table in panic. 'The, uh, the congregation I mean. Surely they don't sit through that twice?'

'Many of them choose to, yes. Particularly at difficult times such as these. So, if we could draw this to a close...'

'Does it no' make you angry?' Logan asked, his stare boring deep into the minister, like he was trying to see inside his skull.

'Doesn't what make me angry?'

'You down here, nose to the grindstone, doing the work of the big man upstairs, and yet he goes and takes your kids from you. First your son, now your daughter, both gone before their time.'

Logan leaned forward, resting more of his weight on his forearms. 'I know I'd be raging. Putting in all them hours singing his praises, and then he goes and does something like that to you. How'd you feel about that, Detective Constable Neish?'

'I'd be fuming, boss,' Tyler replied.

'You and me both, son,' Logan said. 'And you, Mr Kerr? How does it make you feel knowing the God you've dedicated your life to could allow your children to end up the way they did? Doesn't that upset you?'

Kerr had only shown a single flicker of annoyance during Logan's latest line of questioning, when the detective had once again failed to address him by his correct title.

His reply, when it came, was calm and level, all but devoid of emotion.

'Why would it upset me? God gives life, and He takes life. Everyone who dies does so because God wills it.'

Logan started to respond, but the minister raised his voice to speak over him.

'Everyone acts like God owes them something. God owes us nothing. He rules and He governs, and everything He does is just and right and good.'

'Says who?' asked Logan.

'Says me. Says *Him*. If He does something, whatever that thing may be, then it's right. Then it's just. The Will of the Lord is infallible. We are only breathing, all of us, through His kindness and grace. If He kills us all tomorrow, He'll have done us no wrong. Our lives do not belong to us, they belong to Him. We *all* belong to Him.'

'And what about murder?' Logan asked. 'Your daughter was murdered. That's frowned upon, isn't it? It's in the Ten Commandments, if I remember rightly. "Thou shalt not kill". It's not acceptable to commit murder, is it?'

'Of course not. But, we are all just cogs in the Lord's great machinery. Even if we knew His plan, we're not equipped to understand it.'

He gave that a moment to bed in, then pushed his chair back from the desk and stood. 'Add to the fact that we're all sinners, mired down here in our own arrogance and filth, and it's a miracle that He tolerates our existence at all. No, *Mr* Logan, I am not angry at God for taking my children. If I were to be angry at Him for anything, it would be for inflicting them upon me in the first place.'

The minister checked his watch again, shook it, and briefly placed it to his ear before continuing in a tone that made it clear the interview was over.

'Now, unless I am under arrest, I'm afraid we'll have to reschedule the rest of this conversation for another time. At times like these, the community looks for guidance. And if I don't give it to them, then who will?'

He motioned with both hands for the men to rise. 'Helen will see you out,' he said, putting heavy emphasis on the name that Logan only realised wasn't for their benefit when the doors to the office were opened from the other side, revealing the woman who'd originally shown them in.

'Is Helen your wife?' Tyler asked.

'Good gracious, no,' Kerr replied, visibly appalled by the very thought. 'She's staff. If you wish to question her at any point, kindly arrange it for when she's off-duty. I don't pay her to sit around and chat.'

'We'll see what we can do,' said Logan, unconvincingly.

'A word of advice,' Kerr called after the detectives, as they headed for the door.

Logan and Tyler both stopped. Turned. Waited.

'The man who stood up in church today. Roddy Mac.'

'What about him?' asked Logan.

'I'd talk to him. He and Iona were… well, they *made videos*. Of a sinful nature, I believe. Together. I'll let your imagination do the rest. But, if I were you—if getting to the bottom of this were my concern—then I'd be starting with Roddy Mac.'

Chapter 22

Neither detective said a word as they trudged through the drizzle in the direction of the Community Council office. But by the time they were halfway, well out of earshot of anyone from the church, Tyler couldn't hold his tongue any longer.

'Jesus Christ, boss,' he remarked in an incredulous whisper. 'How's that for mental? You think he genuinely didn't give a shit about Iona's murder, or was he putting it on?'

'I don't think he could care less,' Logan said, as they opened the squeaky school gate and went striding along the side of the building, headed for the office door. 'Going by Iona's old diaries, he was always like that. Cold-hearted. Think he resented her from day one. The brother, too.'

'No wonder the poor bastard did away with himself,' said Tyler. 'Five more minutes in there and I'd have been giving it some serious consideration myself.'

'Aye. Charming fella,' Logan said, unlocking the office door and opening it. He ushered Tyler through, before following.

'We going to talk to that Roddy Mac guy from the pub again?' Tyler asked.

'That's him. And aye, we will,' Logan said. 'I'm in two minds about him. After speaking to him, I mean. I want to think he's being genuine. He says he and Iona weren't sexually involved, but it's very possible that he wanted to be, and she shut it down.'

'By all accounts, she'd shag anything with a pulse,' Tyler said.

'The fuck are you trying to say, Detective Constable?' Logan demanded.

Tyler's face fell. 'Shit. I mean… I didn't mean you, boss. On the island, I mean.'

Logan grunted. 'Aye, well. All the more reason for Roddy to get jealous. If he's been shooting porn with her, and has to watch her getting it from all and sundry, then it might just have tipped him over the edge.'

'We headed there now then, boss?'

Logan shook his head. 'Soon. But I want to put a call in back to base first for a catch-up. See what Hamza's dredged up on Bruce Anderson. But before that…'

Logan plucked a mug from a line of them hanging on hooks from the wall above a box of teabags. 'Is it no' high time you stuck the kettle on?'

–

DI Ben Forde peered along the length of his nose at Hamza's phone screen, and his own mirror-image peered back at him. 'That's no' Jack. I thought we were calling Jack?'

'We are, sir. Well, we're calling Tyler's phone, but they haven't picked up yet. Once they do, then they'll appear.'

'On the screen?' said Ben.

Hamza hesitated. To his credit, he resisted the urge to say, 'Naw, in person, like genies', or use any of the other sarcastic responses that had immediately popped into his head. 'Aye. On the screen.'

They sat side-by-side at Hamza's desk, the phone propped up against the base of the monitor. Ben took the opportunity to check himself out.

'Christ, you're looking old, Benjamin,' he muttered, running his hand down his face, then through his thinning hair. 'The scrapheap beckons.'

'Scrapheap's been beckoning you for years, ye old bugger,' boomed a voice from the phone, as Logan and Tyler material-ised on the main screen. 'Hasn't stopped you so far.'

'Hello, Jack,' said Ben, projecting his voice. 'Can you hear me?'

'Pretty sure I can hear you through the bloody window,' Logan replied. 'You don't have to shout. It's just like a phone.'

He turned to look off camera. 'That's right, isn't it? It's like a phone?'

'Pretty much, boss, aye. It's WhatsApp. Video calling.'

'All right, all right, I don't need the technical breakdown,' Logan said, then he faced front again. 'Hamza there?'

'Here, sir,' DC Khaled said, leaning into shot.

'Oh, look. There's us up the top,' said Ben, marvelling at the wee box in the top right corner of the screen that now held his and Hamza's image. He gave a little wave and chuckled as he waved back.

He was still waving when he realised that everyone else had fallen silent. He lowered his hand, quietly cleared his throat, then gave Logan a nod.

'Sorry. Got a bit over-excited,' he said. 'Hamza's been digging into Bruce Anderson, like you asked.'

'Good. We've just had quite the interesting conversation with Abraham Kerr, the victim's father,' Logan said.

Ben's eyebrows raised. 'Interesting how?'

'Interesting in that he's a fucking bampot,' the DCI replied. 'Basically, he reckons it's fair enough that his kids are both dead, because that's the way God wants it.'

'Sounds like a charmer,' said Ben. His eyes were flitting around the screen, like he wasn't quite sure where to look. 'Both kids?'

'Iona had a brother. Topped himself, apparently. Jacob, his name is. Can one of you look into it and make sure the story checks out?'

Hamza nodded, and jotted a note on his pad.

'He a suspect?' Ben asked. 'The father, I mean, no' the dead son.'

'That's the big question,' Logan replied. 'I'm undecided. I think he's an arsehole. I think he made those kids' lives hell. Depending on what's in the rest of Iona's diaries, I think we might be able to build a case for abuse. But did he kill her? I doubt it. Honestly? I think he'd tell us if he had. I think he'd say he was doing God's work and bloody revel in it.'

'Proper nutter, then?' Ben said.

'Bananas, boss,' Tyler chipped in. 'Proper heid the baw.'

'What did you get on Bruce Anderson?' Logan asked.

Ben shuffled aside a little, letting Hamza take centre stage. 'I haven't been able to look into him fully yet, but early signs are promising. Australian, as you know. Haven't been able to scare up any info from over there yet, but he's got an international arrest warrant out for him for a suspected sexual assault in Vietnam. Issued in July last year.'

'How did he get into the country with that?' Logan asked.

'He didn't, sir. Not officially, anyway,' Hamza explained. 'Must be here illegally.'

'Sounds like we might have our man, boss,' Tyler said.

'Aye, if we can find the bastard,' Logan said. 'Ben, what's the latest on getting us some reinforcements over here? We could do with some Uniform for the search. The island's no' exactly huge, but too big for the two of us.'

'We're hoping to get a chopper over to you later tonight. Ferries might start running tomorrow.'

'Hold them back as long as you can. At most, I want inbound only,' Logan instructed. 'Nobody gets off this island without my say-so. Anderson is our main target, but the victim wasn't winning any popularity contests around here, so there's no saying it was definitely him who killed her. Until we know more, I want this place as locked down as possible.'

'We'll get it sorted,' Ben said. 'Only slight problem is manpower. It's a big week.'

Logan frowned. 'How so?'

'Jesus, Jack. Royal visit this week, isn't it? Tomorrow, Her Majesty herself is gracing the good folk of Inverness with her presence.'

Logan stared blankly back at him from the screen.

'The Queen. It's been briefed for weeks. Two-day visit while she's up at Balmoral. I think she's opening something somewhere.'

'And?'

'And security's high. They're having to cancel all non-urgent leave as it is. We can get you some resource, but it'll be limited until she's been and gone.'

'Christ Almighty. Fine. Just get us who you can when you can. Hopefully, Anderson isn't going anywhere.'

Something caught the DCI's eye and he leaned closer to the camera. The tip of an enormous finger blocked half the screen as he pointed to something behind Ben and Hamza.

'What's that?'

The two men looked back over their shoulders. Ben's face had reddened slightly when he turned back to the phone.

'Oh, thought I'd have a go at doing a Big Board,' he explained. 'Haven't got Caitlyn's knack for it, though.'

Logan ejected a short exhalation through his nose. It wasn't quite a laugh, but it was in that neck of the woods.

'Aye, you can say that again,' he said. 'She'd a gift for the old Big Board.'

'Be better organised than that one, sir, that's for sure,' Hamza chimed in.

'She'd be raging, wouldn't she?' Ben laughed, shooting a glance back at the board again. 'She'd have taken one look at it, hauled everything down, and started again.'

'Aye, you can say that again, boss!' said Tyler. 'She'll be turning in her bloody grave.'

Everyone fell silent at that. Tyler wilted under the glare Logan shot his way. 'Bit fucking morbid.'

'Aye, come on, son. There's a line,' Ben said, shaking his head disapprovingly.

'Show some bloody respect,' Hamza scowled.

Tyler looked between them all. 'What? No! I wasn't being… I just meant…' he began, then he caught just the faintest smirk on Logan's face. 'Bastards!' he said, wheezing the word out in relief. 'You're all bastards.'

'Are you only just realising this now?' Logan asked. He checked his watch, then tapped the table with both hands, making the image on Hamza's phone screen shake. 'Right, places to go, people to harass. Get me them Uniforms, see what else you can find out about Mr Anderson, and let's talk again later tonight.'

'Right you are,' Ben said.

'Oh. And send us a picture of the Big Board.'

Ben looked back again. 'I was going to scrap it. You think we should keep it?'

Logan shrugged. 'Aye. Why not? DS McQuarrie would've, and that's good enough for me.'

Ben and Hamza both nodded their agreement. 'Aye. Good enough for me, too,' Ben said. On-screen, Tyler started reaching for the phone, but Ben jumped in quickly before the DC could end the call. 'Wait. Did Hoon get you, Jack?'

'Thankfully not,' Logan replied. 'He still on the warpath?'

'Like I've never seen before,' Ben said. 'He's bloody fizzing.'

'Aye, well, if I'm lucky, he might have a heart attack before he catches up with me. Tell him you passed the message on, and that I'm going to get back to him as a matter of urgency.'

'And are you?' Ben asked.

'What do you think?' Logan asked.

And then, with a nod from the DCI, Tyler's finger filled the screen, and the call came to an end.

'What do I think?' asked Ben. He sucked in his top lip and shot a wary glance at the Incident Room door. 'I think that daft big bugger's going to be the death of all of us.'

Tyler shoved his phone back into his pocket and rolled his chair away from the desk that Logan had claimed as his own.

'How come the Superintendent's gunning for you, boss?' he asked, positioning himself behind the room's second, far smaller desk. The 'Lesser Desk' as Logan had named it when they were sorting out the seating arrangements. *Desk Minor*.

'Who knows?' Logan asked. 'Probably nothing. Or maybe… you know Bosco, right?'

'Bosco Maximuke? The builder with the drug connections?' Tyler asked. 'Sorry, "alleged" drug connections,' he corrected, making quote marks in the air with his fingers. 'What about him?'

'I've got reason to believe he might have been supplying the Gillespies.'

'What reason's that, boss?'

'Because I know the crooked bastard,' Logan said. 'The shot that killed Caitlyn? I think it was meant for him. I think, if it wasn't for Bosco, DS McQuarrie would still be with us. 'Course, I've got no evidence to back that up. Nothing that would stand up in court, anyway.'

'So… what?' asked Tyler. 'Did you go round and accuse him?'

'In a manner of speaking, aye,' Logan said. 'In a way.'

'What way would that be, boss?'

'In a "leathered shite out of his henchman and burned his office to the ground" kind of a way.'

Tyler's eyes became two miniature globes of surprise. 'Fucking hell, boss! What were you thinking?'

'I was mostly thinking, "I'm going to burn this bastard's office to the ground", truth be told.' Logan clicked his tongue against the back of his teeth and shrugged. 'I didn't really think it through beyond that. Got a bit carried away in the heat of the moment.'

'Jesus, you didn't kill him, did you?' Tyler asked.

'Of course, I didn't kill him! Jesus Christ, son, what do you take me for?' Logan barked. He shifted his weight on his feet and shrugged. 'I mean, I can't say I wasn't tempted. But no.'

'That's something. But still, boss.' Tyler's eyes darted left and right, like he was seeing all the potential consequences of Logan's actions being played out before him. 'That could be career-ending. You could get your cards for that. You could get the bloody jail!'

Logan nodded slowly. Clearly, he'd come to the same conclusion some time ago. 'Aye. But I'll worry about that later. For now, while I still have one, we've got a job to do. There's still a lot of people to talk to, and Bruce Anderson isn't going to find himself. We get this done, we find out who killed Iona, and then Detective Superintendent Hoon, the PCC, and whoever else wants to throw their oar in can do what they need to do.'

He necked the last of his cold tea, pulled a face, then clonked the mug down on the desk. 'Right, you fit? Let's go see if Roddy MacKay'll gie's a swatch of his mucky videos.'

Chapter 23

They were outside the pub when they heard the shout from inside.

'Hey! What are you doing? Stop!'

Through the glass, they saw Bruce Anderson stuff his pockets with money from the till, then shoulder his way past Roddy, sending the pub's owner spiralling to the floor.

Anderson was out through the back door before either detective could react, already vanishing up the metal steps that led to the beer garden.

'Shite. Get after him,' Logan barked, practically throwing Tyler at the pub's front door.

The DC set off at a clip, powering through the pub, hurdling the fallen Roddy, and vanishing through the door, hot on Anderson's heels.

Logan offered up a hand as Roddy sprackled back to his feet, and pulled the man upright with a single jerk.

'You all right?' he asked, not waiting for an answer before adding, 'What happened? Where did he come from?'

'Robbed me,' Roddy wheezed, rubbing his chest with the heel of his hand. 'Nipped upstairs, then came down and caught the bastard with his hand in the till.'

He limped behind the bar and rummaged half-heartedly in the till drawer. 'He's got most of the float. All the notes, anyway. There was fifty quid there.'

Logan looked to the back door. The sound of footsteps had been lost to the soft rattle and clank of the rain falling on the metal staircase out back.

'Is there a way out past the beer garden?' he asked.

Roddy nodded breathlessly. 'Aye. Backs onto wilderness. Trees, bushes. Hills. Your man'll have to get a shift on, if he wants to catch him. Is he quick?'

'Depends in which sense you mean,' Logan sighed. 'Let's just keep our fingers crossed, eh?'

He pulled a chair out at one of the tables. 'Here. Take a seat. I'll get you a drink.'

Roddy looked across the optics, like he'd just remembered they were there, then emerged from behind the bar. He and Logan crossed paths as Roddy headed for the seat and the detective sidled in through the bar's narrow hatch.

'I'll have a wee Grouse,' Roddy said. 'Glasses are down below.'

Logan reached under the counter and found a suitable glass. He jammed the rim against the bottom of the optic and watched, transfixed, as a gurgle of golden liquid sloshed into the glass.

The smell of it was… something else. It transported him back to other places, other times. Better times.

And worse.

Something writhed and raged at the back of his brain, like a trapped animal hurling itself against the bars of its cage, demanding to be released, demanding to be set free.

'Everything all right?' Roddy asked, and Logan realised he'd been staring at the contents of the glass for several seconds.

'Fine. Aye,' he said, quickly turning. He joined Roddy at the table and deposited the glass in front of him without looking at it, then went to the back door and stepped out into the rain.

The metal steps were slippery as he stormed up them. The beer garden spread out in a semi-circle from the top step, a poorly-maintained wire fence the only thing separating it from the expanse of sweet-fuck-all that stretched out beyond it.

Logan could see two figures out there. One was a few hundred yards beyond the fence. The other was much closer.

At first glance, he assumed it must be Tyler and Anderson, but quickly realised that this wasn't the case. One of them was Tyler, right enough. He was the one furthest away, thundering across the uneven terrain, presumably in dogged pursuit of Anderson, although Logan couldn't see him.

The other figure stood crucified a relatively short distance away on the right. Another bloody scarecrow. How many was that now? Three? Four? Too many to make sense.

Firing another glance in the now much smaller DC Neish's direction, Logan thrust his hands in his coat pockets, and clumped his way back down the stairs.

—

Tyler ran.

He ran, despite his lungs burning, his knees aching, and the pervasive aroma of sheep shit playing havoc with the contents of his stomach.

He ran, despite his tightening chest, his inappropriate footwear, and the lingering sense that it was all a complete waste of time.

Bruce Anderson had been over the back fence of the beer garden and halfway to bloody nowhere when the DC had crested the top of the stairs. The Australian was solidly built, but the bugger was fast, too, and wasn't hindered by his choice of footwear.

Even as Tyler threw himself over the fence, he knew the chances of catching him were slim. If he could keep him in sight, then there was a chance Anderson would tire out first, but the area out back of the pub was dotted all over with trees and bushes, and the ground undulated in rolling dips and hills that offered ample opportunity for cover.

A little nagging voice at the back of Tyler's head told him he should probably just give up now. Another, much louder voice—one that sounded a lot like DCI Logan's, Tyler thought—warned him he had better not come back empty-handed.

And so, despite everything, Tyler ran.

And he kept on running.

—

He buried his face into the crook of his arm, trying to muffle the rasping of his breath, as he tucked himself into the undergrowth.

Stupid. *Stupid, stupid, stupid.*

He should've stayed away. Should've waited it out. Should've hidden until the boats started, then snuck aboard and got the fuck off the island at the first possible opportunity.

But he'd need money when he got to the mainland. He'd get nowhere without it. What choice did he have but to raid the till? Roddy had been upstairs. Why the fuck hadn't he stayed there?

The foliage around him was wet, the ground soaking him from below. A rock or a root—something bloody uncomfortable, anyway—was digging into his ribs, but the footsteps of that cop were coming closer, and he didn't dare move. Didn't dare give himself away. If he was caught, it was over.

If he was caught, he was fucked.

The footsteps slowed as they drew closer to the overgrown clump of heather and bracken that was hiding him.

No, no, no.

Shit, shit, shit.

He could hear the cop wheezing, sounding even more out of breath than himself. The footsteps swished through the grass, cautious now. Approaching steadily. Had he seen him? Was it already over? Was the game already up?

He slid his hand beneath him, cautiously feeling for the painful lump.

A rock. A sharp, pointed rock.

A weapon.

He wrestled it out from beneath him, keeping his movements slow and subtle. There had been no shout from the cop yet. No barked orders. No sudden weight on his back, or wrenching together of his wrists.

The cop hadn't seen him. Yet. But, it was only a matter of time. And that meant, it was only a matter of time before he was in a cell. Only a matter of time before he was standing before a jury, facing a life stretch.

No. Not going to happen. It couldn't. He wouldn't let it.

His hand tightened on the rock. The footsteps came closer, then stopped. The cop breathed deeply.

Down in the damp foliage, his heart thundered in his chest.

'Ah, bollocks to this,' said the cop.

And then, to his relief, the footsteps turned and walked away.

—

'What's with all the scarecrows?'

It was the first question Logan had asked as he'd plonked himself down in the seat across from Roddy, and it had evidently caught the bar-owner off guard.

'What? Oh. Them. I don't know. It's a thing.'

Logan waited until Roddy had drained the last of his whisky before pressing him on it further. 'A thing?'

'Like a… oh, I don't know. Gimmick. Dudley does them. For the kids and tourists mostly. The Tattiebogle Trail. Another of the Community Council's "great ideas".'

'Tattiebogle?'

'Another name for a scarecrow, seemingly,' Roddy explained. 'Old. Think it goes back a bit.'

'Right. Who's Dudley?'

'Dudley Broon. Well, Dudley Brown, but… you'll have seen him at church. Can't miss him. Great big lad.'

'Him. Aye. I clocked him, right enough,' Logan said. 'I'm told he and Iona had a bit of a set-to the night she died.'

Roddy shook his head, already anticipating the suggestion before Logan could propose it. 'Dudley wouldn't hurt a fly. He looks scary, sure, but he's a heart of gold in him. You'll find no one with a bad word to say about him.'

'Except Iona, by the sounds of it.'

Roddy picked up his glass, looked at it mournfully, then set it down again. 'She had a temper when she'd had too many. She'd have said things she didn't mean. She did that, but she always felt bad about it afterwards. Once she'd...'

'Sobered up.'

Roddy smiled, but it was a thin and unconvincing thing. 'Sobered up. Yes. Exactly.'

The more time Logan spent in Roddy's company, the more he found he liked the man. Despite everything currently going on, he had a down-to-earth air about him. Even now, he radiated a level of friendliness that made it abundantly clear why he'd ended up in the hospitality trade.

All that, however, just made what Logan had to do next all the more difficult.

'Tell me about the videos you made together,' he said, then he shut his mouth and took note of the reaction.

There was shock at first, a little widening of the eyes, a slight dropping of the bottom jaw.

Something like shame or embarrassment came next. The reddening of the cheeks. The darting of the eyes. The heavy swallow.

And then, to Logan's surprise, came amusement. The embarrassment was still written there across his face, but he was smiling, too. Laughing, almost.

'God. You heard about them, did you?'

Logan nodded.

'Who from? Was it Joy?' Roddy asked. 'Or, no. Wait. The minister. Reverend Kerr. It was him, wasn't it? What did he tell you they were?'

He stood up suddenly, still smiling but clearly annoyed. Not at Logan, the detective thought, but at whoever had told him about the footage.

'Fine. You want to see? You want to see the videos? I'll show you. They're upstairs. They're on my laptop.'

'One sec,' Logan said. He got up from the table, climbed the stairs out back, and saw Tyler trudging dejectedly back towards the beer garden.

Alone.

'Useless bastard,' the DCI grumbled, then he turned and clanked down the steps, and headed off with Roddy to watch some home-made porn.

Chapter 24

Logan sat at Roddy's kitchen table, eyes fixed on the laptop screen, watching Iona giein' it laldy.

He'd recognised her at once, not as the corpse he'd seen the previous day, but as the girl he remembered from years back. Sure, the years had taken its toll, and the booze had lent a hand, but it was still her behind the eyes. Still her in all those surprisingly energetic movements.

On-screen, Iona strutted around in the bar area, a microphone in her hand, belting out Cyndi Lauper's *Time After Time* to a backing track. She was performing as if to a full-house, but from the lack of response, it was clear that the pub was empty.

The video had been edited well, cutting to a tight close-up on the more emotional moments, when Iona would stop striding around and perform over-sincerely right down the camera lens.

Closing that window, Logan double-clicked another of the video files. In this one, Iona was earnestly murdering Tina Turner's *Simply the Best* while shuffling around the bar like a cowboy who'd lost his horse.

'She wanted to put them on YouTube,' Roddy explained. He was standing in the kitchen doorway, and Logan couldn't help but notice he wasn't watching the videos. The memory was too painful, maybe. Or too embarrassing.

'And did she?'

Roddy shook his head. 'Wanted to build up a bunch of them before she launched. A *portfolio*, she said. I've no clue how many she was aiming for. We did dozens, and she used to borrow the camera herself sometimes, so no idea how many she made on her own. Whatever it was, it clearly wasn't enough. She never got around to putting them up.'

'And that's it?' Logan asked. 'Just singing?'

'Just singing,' Roddy said.

'Never anything sexual?'

Roddy gestured to the laptop. 'You'll be taking it away anyway, won't you? Go through it yourself and see,' he said, his anger bubbling just below the surface. 'I know what the gossip was, but we never did anything like that. I wouldn't. It was just singing, that's all.'

Logan closed over the laptop lid and turned to the man in the doorway. 'When you say you "wouldn't". Does that mean she asked you?'

'No.'

'Never?'

'Never. No. Just singing. That's all she ever asked me to film, and that's all I ever did.'

Logan held his gaze for several seconds, giving Roddy the chance to change his story. The bar-owner stood his ground, though, and Logan eventually relented with a single nod of his head.

'Good. Well, we'll go through it and get it back to you as soon as we can,' he said, standing and drawing an evidence bag from his pocket.

Roddy watched, transfixed, as Logan placed the laptop in the bag and sealed it shut.

'Is that necessary?' he asked, his gaze flitting up to Logan's face and back again. 'I'm not... you don't think I did it, do you?'

'We're still at an early stage in the investigation, Mr MacKay,' Logan said, and the use of his title and surname made Roddy look even more worried. 'We can't rule anyone out yet.'

Logan tucked the bagged laptop under his arm. 'But, if it helps any... no, I don't think you did it.'

Roddy stepped aside as Logan headed for the front door of the flat. The detective stopped there and looked back, his features fixed in a grim smile. 'For your sake, I really hope you don't prove me wrong.'

'I... I won't. And thanks. For believing me.'

'Call 101. Get the robbery logged. If we can get you your money back, we will,' Logan said, and then he pulled open the door, and ducked down the narrow staircase that led to the pub corridor below.

'There you are, boss,' said Tyler, when Logan appeared through the door at the bottom of the steps. 'Bad news. I lost him.'

'Don't worry about it, son. I knew you would,' Logan said. 'To be honest, I just wanted you out from under my feet for five minutes.'

Tyler laughed, although he wasn't entirely convinced that the DCI was joking. His eyes went to the laptop tucked under Logan's arm.

'He show you the vids?'

'He did, aye,' Logan said.

'And?'

'And they were... eye-opening,' Logan said. He handed over the laptop, and Tyler's face practically lit-up. 'You can comb through them when we get back to the office.'

He checked his watch. After five. The day was slipping away from him, and while they had a solid suspect, they were no closer to catching Iona's killer.

'But before you get stuck into that, we're making a house-call,' he announced.

'That'll be a nice surprise for someone,' Tyler said. 'Who we dropping in on?'

Logan set off for the pub's front door. 'We've spoken to Iona's old man,' he said. 'Now, let's go see what her son has to say.'

'What the fuck do you want? Have you found him?'

Ben had made it just a third of the way through knocking on the door when Detective Superintendent Hoon pulled it open, leaving the DI swiping his knuckles at thin air.

As usual, Hoon's face was all rage and thunder. He still had one hand on the handle, like he was ready to slam the door in Ben's face at any moment. Perhaps repeatedly.

'Well?' he barked, before Ben had a chance to reply. 'I don't have the luxury of standing here all fucking day, Benjamin. Have you got him for me? Is he on the phone?'

'Uh, no, sir,' Ben said.

He stepped back as the door was slammed shut, and stood in awkward silence for several seconds while the man in the office gnashed and roared.

Eventually, the door opened again. 'What, then?'

'We, uh, we think the weather's going to improve. Looked like it'd be tonight, but forecast is now saying tomorrow morning. We want to fly Uniform in. To Canna, I mean. Back-up.'

'Back-up? You know what's got my fucking back up, Benjamin? That useless great cocksplash of a DCI we both have the misfortune of knowing.'

Ben wasn't quite sure how to react to that, so he gave a dry, slightly nervous chuckle.

This, it transpired, was a mistake.

'Something funny?' Hoon demanded. 'Eh? Are my elevated fucking stress levels amusing you, Detective Inspector? Is my mounting blood pressure proving to be enter-fucking-taining?'

Ben shook his head, but Hoon was off on one now. He gestured to the floor. 'Maybe I'll have a fucking heart attack, and give you a really good laugh, eh? Maybe I'll drop dead on the floor, and you can send it in to *You've Been* fucking *Framed*, so everyone can get in on the fucking joke.'

He glowered at the DI, his eyeballs bulging in that way they did, his lips moving as he swore repeatedly below his breath.

'One,' he said.

Ben blinked. 'Sorry, sir?'

'One. You can have one. Uniform.'

'One? But—'

'Take it or fucking leave it. We've got the bastard Queen coming. I can give you one officer, and you can fuck right off with the helicopter. Boat them in.'

'Ferries aren't running, sir,' Ben pointed out. 'And I'm not sure one is—'

'Did I say the word "ferry", Benjamin? Did you hear me mention a fucking ferry? Find a speedboat, or a yacht, or whittle sticks to make a fucking raft, I don't care,' Hoon snarled. 'In fact, you know what? Fuck it, pick a good swimmer and give them some goggles. I'm no' spunking money on a helicopter for one fucking Uniform.'

'Right. Aye. Fair enough,' said Ben. He cleared his throat. 'I just think, given the geographic area they have to cover, one is—'

'It's Canna, Benjamin. It's in the Small Isles. Key-fucking-word being "small". It's no' fucking... fucking...' He flailed a hand about, searching for a name. '*Botswana*. They can have one, and you're boating the bastard in. That clear?'

Ben stood up straight. There was no point in arguing. Not now. Not when he was like this.

Mind you, when was he ever not like this?

'Clear, sir,' he said, and the door was closed in his face before he'd even reached the second word.

Chapter 25

Isaac Young and his fiancée, Louise Beaton, were at their dinner when Logan and Tyler came knocking. They'd done a big roast chicken, and the smell of it cranked Logan's saliva glands into overdrive and set his stomach rumbling.

The detectives had offered to wait in the living room while they'd finished, but Isaac had waved the suggestion away, albeit with a certain level of irritation. He led the detectives through to the front room, while Louise stuck everything back in the oven to stay warm.

Up close, there was no mistaking Isaac's parentage. He had Iona's eyes. Nothing much else of hers, but the eyes were enough. They immediately marked him as Iona's son, and when Isaac looked at him, Logan felt a twinge of something like nostalgia.

'We're sorry to trouble you, Mr Young. We appreciate that this is a difficult time,' he said. 'I'm DCI Jack Logan. This is DC Tyler Neish.'

Logan gestured to Tyler, but the DC didn't immediately respond. He was peering up at the slightly taller Isaac, his eyebrows practically dancing up and down his forehead.

'Hmm? Oh. Aye. Sorry. DC Neish. Tyler,' he said, shaking Isaac's hand. 'Nice to meet you, Mr Young. Sorry about the circumstances.'

'Isaac's fine. And it is what it is,' he said. His accent was an odd one. A mix of a few different places, both north of the border and south.

'Do you have any ID on you?' Tyler asked.

'ID?' said both Logan and Isaac at the same time.

'Just, eh, for the notes,' Tyler said, as if this explained everything.

Shrugging, Isaac fished in his pocket, produced his wallet, and slid out the driving licence. Tyler took it, checked both sides, and handed it back.

'Perfect. Thanks.'

'Right. No problem,' said Isaac, returning the licence to the wallet. 'Please.'

He motioned to the couch and took a seat in a battered old leather armchair across from it, which looked even older than he did.

'Obviously, we're here about what happened to your mother,' Logan said.

'Aye, like she was ever much of that,' Isaac said. 'Our relationship was... well. It was barely a relationship at all.'

'You didn't get on?' Logan asked.

'Oh, she got on with me just fine. As soon as I was out fending for myself, I mean, and wasn't cramping her style. Once I was earning money, she was all over me. Before then?' He shrugged, one finger tracing a circle on the arm of the couch. 'I mean, technically we got on fine then, too. But only because I hardly saw her. She was young when she had me, though. I suppose I should cut her some slack.'

'What about your dad?' Tyler asked. Logan shot him a slightly quizzical look, but the DC was too fixated on Isaac to notice.

'Not much better. He left when I was, I don't know. Eight. We were living down south at the time. He stuck around for a while. I went between his place and Mum's, and then he got into some dodgy stuff and wound up inside. Drugs. He's out now, though. We keep in touch back and forth. Christmas. Birthdays.'

'Right. Right. Fair enough,' said Tyler, making a note in his pad.

Logan glared at him as if to ask if he could get back to his interview now, then continued with his own line of questioning. 'When did you last see your mum?'

'Tuesday,' Isaac said. 'In the pub. She was making an arse of herself. No surprise. Up to her usual trick.'

'Which was?'

'Trying to shag anyone who'd have her,' Isaac said. He spat the words out like they burned the inside of his mouth, and the way he flinched told Logan that, despite the issues he had with his mother, Isaac didn't like seeing her that way. 'It was like a ritual. As soon as a new bloke arrived on the island, she'd set out to have her wicked way with the poor bastard. It was a running joke.' He shook his head, his lips drawing back over his teeth in disgust. '*She* was a running joke.'

Louise came in from the kitchen then, drying her hands on an Edinburgh Castle tea towel. There were no other seats in the living room, so Tyler stood to give her his. Instead, she perched herself on the arm of Isaac's chair, and leaned her weight against him in a wordless show of support.

Tyler sat down again. He and Logan ran through their introductions, and then the conversation resumed.

'Was there anything unusual about Tuesday night?' Logan asked. 'Anything that struck you as strange, or out of the ordinary?'

Isaac stuck out his bottom lip and shook his head. 'No. Not really. I mean, I suppose it's a wee bit unusual for her to be in that state on a Tuesday night, but it's certainly not unheard of.'

'Every night's a weekend night for Iona,' Louise said, and the venom behind it made it clear there was no love lost between the two women. She shot her partner a look bordering on the apologetic. 'Was.'

'Aye, she had form for the weeknights,' Isaac admitted. 'In terms of her behaviour? Nothing out of the ordinary. She was pissed, tried to crack onto Bruce behind the bar and some tourist—practically put it on a plate for both of them—then she left when it was clear that nobody was going to buy her a drink.'

'And you left soon after. Is that right?' Logan asked. He looked from one to the other, studying their reactions. Confusion was all he saw.

'No,' said Isaac. 'I mean, not right away. We had a couple of drinks first.'

'Right. I see,' Logan said. 'It's just, a witness at the scene said you both left soon after Iona.'

'What witness?' Louise demanded. Her voice was suddenly shrill. Fingernails-down-a-blackboard stuff. 'And what do you mean? What are you getting at? Are you accusing us of something?'

Logan held up his hands for calm. 'Relax, Miss Beaton. Nobody's accusing you of anything. I'm just trying to build up a picture of the night Iona died. That's all. You say you didn't leave early? Fine. Can you tell me what time you did leave?'

Neither of them jumped in to volunteer a reply.

'Roughly?' said Logan.

'We didn't really keep track,' Isaac said, exchanging a fleeting look with his fiancée. 'Mum had… she'd thrown us. We weren't really paying attention to the time. We were upset.'

'Upset?' Logan said. 'Angry?'

'I mean—' Isaac began, but Louise took over.

'Yes, we were bloody angry. I mean, I know I was,' she spat. 'She'd mortified him. Both of us. *Again*. I was furious. But did we kill her? No, of course we bloody didn't.'

'To be clear again, nobody is saying you killed her,' Logan said, but Louise wasn't having it.

'But you're implying it, aren't you? That's what you're getting at.' She sat back against the armchair and took Isaac's hand in hers. 'We should have a solicitor. If they're trying to stitch us up, we should have a solicitor.'

'Miss Beaton…' Logan began, then he adjusted the severity of his tone, and tried again. 'Miss Beaton. Louise. You can get a solicitor. Of course. If that's what you want. But nobody is under arrest here. Neither of you was a suspect when we walked in that door, and I've heard nothing yet to change that fact. We're just trying to get a clear picture of what happened so we can clear all this up and get out of your hair.'

He smiled, first at Louise, then at Isaac. 'We're not here to stitch anyone up. We're here to catch a killer. Your mother's killer, Mr Young. Any help you can provide will be hugely appreciated.'

The couple exchanged glances again. Their interlocked fingers rubbed together. Time to seal the deal.

Logan sat forward on the couch. 'But if you'd rather we do it in a more official capacity, then that can be arranged. We don't have facilities here, obviously, but we can get you brought to the station in Mallaig, and arrange for a solicitor to meet us there. We can talk more... robustly.'

He produced a smile that everyone in the room understood wasn't really a smile, at all.

'It's up to you. Whatever suits.'

The couple sat in silence for a few moments, and then Isaac quietly cleared his throat. 'Here's fine,' he said. 'What do you need to know?'

Logan sat back. Tyler clicked the end of his pen.

'You said Iona had been trying to crack onto the barman. Bruce Anderson.'

Isaac sighed. 'Yes. Yes, she was. Not for the first time, either.'

Tyler made a note. Logan made an encouraging motion with one hand. 'Tell me, what do you know about Mr Anderson?'

'Bruce?' Isaac frowned. 'Not a lot, really. He arrived, what...?'

'Couple of months ago,' Louise suggested, although she didn't sound too confident. 'Australian, but he's been around a bit. He's travelling, apparently. Working his way around the world. Been at it for a couple of years.'

'Well, I don't know about all that,' said Isaac, shooting his fiancée a sideways glance that suggested he hadn't been aware of how chatty she and Anderson had been. 'But he seems friendly enough. Think he's staying out the back of the shop. That's where most of the staff Roddy gets in end up going. Have you spoken to Roddy, by the way? Him and my mum, they were close.'

'We have,' Logan said. 'But anything we should be aware of there?'

'I don't know,' Isaac said. 'She said he was a bit clingy, sometimes. I got the impression he wanted more than she was offering. Which was pretty rich. He must've been the only guy on the island who wasn't a blood relative that she hadn't tried it on with.'

'Were your parents married?' Tyler asked. The question came out of nowhere, and drew looks of confusion from the couple opposite, and a full-blown scowl from Logan.

'Do you mind?' he grunted, his expression making it very clear to the younger detective that they'd be discussing this later.

Logan held the look for a few emphatic seconds, then turned his attention back to Isaac.

'Sorry about that. He gets excited around new people. You were telling me about Iona's relationship with Roddy.'

'I don't know much about it, if I'm honest,' Isaac said. 'I tended to keep my distance from her as much as possible.'

'And yet, you've stuck to the same tiny island,' Logan said. 'You could've gone anywhere. You moved away, didn't you? If you were that keen to avoid her, you could've stayed away.'

'This is his home, too,' Louise said, jumping in again. 'He did most of his growing up here. His grandfather's here. He's as much right to be here as she has. Had. Whatever. More, even. People like him, which is more than I can say for her.'

'Louise.' There was a pleading tone to Isaac's voice. He may not have got on with his mother, but there was still feeling there. 'Please.'

'Well…' Louise sighed, but she took the sentence no further.

'We spoke to your grandfather earlier,' Logan said, changing tack. 'He seems like an interesting character.'

'He's that, all right,' Isaac replied, and there was something cagey about it, like he didn't want to say too much. 'Mum hated him.'

'And you?'

'He has his quirks, but he's always been good to us,' Isaac said. 'Even though, us living together… it's not ideal, as far as he's concerned. He's made that pretty clear. But he's been supportive. Of us. Of the business.'

'What is it you do again?' Logan asked.

'Soap. And candles,' Louise said. 'All handmade.'

Logan raised his eyebrows and nodded slowly. 'Right. Market for that, is there?'

'Not locally, really, but we send stuff all over the world,' she continued. 'Big demand for that sort of stuff worldwide, and the Scottish connection helps.'

She sniffed and wriggled upright on the arm of the chair.

'We're building a brand.'

'Right. Well… good for you,' Logan said. 'Well done.'

Isaac turned away for a moment, and Logan caught the longing look he fired in the direction of the kitchen.

'One final question, and we'll let you get back to your dinner,' he said. 'We were told that Iona got into an altercation with a man named Dudley Brown on the night she died. Would you know anything about that?'

Isaac snorted. 'Dudley Broon? Aye. She was having a go at Louise, effing and blinding. The usual. Dudley stood up and told her she should go, and she laid into him. Verbally, I mean. Called him a retard.'

'And is he?' asked Tyler, then his eyes instantly widened in horror at what he'd said. 'I mean, not a… not a… does Mr Brown suffer from any…' He gave a frantic wave of his pen, like he might be able to conjure up all the missing words he was looking for with it.

'Learning difficulties?' asked Isaac.

'Aye! Yes. Anything of that… nature,' said Tyler. He winced, gave the tiniest shake of his head, then looked back at his notebook again, all the while avoiding the glare from the DCI beside him.

'He's a good man,' Isaac said. 'Is he the sharpest knife in the drawer? No. And sure, maybe he's got some difficulties, but he's one of the good guys. His parents and grandparents both grew up here, so he's as local as they come. I've never seen him lose his temper. I don't think he's even capable of getting angry. So, if you're suggesting he killed my mum, I think you're barking up the wrong tree.'

'I've met a lot of people over the years, and in my experience, Mr Young, everyone has their breaking point,' Logan intoned. He slapped his hands on his thighs and smiled thinly. 'Still, there's a first time for everything, I suppose.'

He moved as if to stand, then stopped. 'Sorry, one final quick thing. The pub that night, who else was there?'

'Just the usual, really,' Isaac said. He rattled off a few names of locals, which Tyler scribbled down. 'They were still there after I left. Would've been there until closing, I'm sure. They'll be able to tell you at the pub.'

'Right. Thanks. Anyone else?'

'There was that tourist fella,' Louise said, nudging Isaac with her arm. 'In the corner.'

'Oh. Aye. I told you about him. Mum was offering it up to him. Poor bastard. He left pretty soon after. Can't say I blame him. He looked mortified.'

Logan felt a frown begin to form, but managed to put a stop to it. 'How soon after?'

'Twenty minutes, maybe,' Louise said. 'I don't think anyone really noticed. When I went to get another round, he was gone. That was about twenty minutes after Iona left.'

'So, he could've been gone for a while?'

The couple shrugged in near-perfect unison. 'Suppose so,' Isaac said.

'Could he have left at the same time as Iona?' Logan asked.

The headshake was immediate. 'No. I kept watching the door for a few minutes after she'd gone,' Isaac said. 'Kept thinking she'd come staggering back in. Thankfully, she didn't. I think your man probably just left after he'd finished his drink.'

'Aye, makes sense,' Logan agreed. He stood suddenly and jabbed a thumb in the direction of the kitchen. 'Now, away you go before your tea's ruined.'

Louise got up first, making room for Isaac to stand, too. 'Thanks,' he said. 'If there's anything else, just ask.'

Behind Logan, DC Neish flipped his notebook closed and got to his feet. Both detectives looked from Isaac to Louise and back again.

'We know where to find you,' Logan said, and the words sounded less of a statement and more of a threat.

After a quick glance around the room, Logan shoved his hands in his pockets. 'We'll see ourselves out,' he said, then he turned on his heels and marched for the door, with Tyler hurrying along behind him.

Chapter 26

'Kevin about?' Logan asked, as he and Tyler came trudging through into the lounge of the B&B. Norman was sitting by the window, gazing out at a sunset of pinks and oranges, lined with stringy strands of black and grey cloud.

'Hmm? Oh, sorry. Miles away,' Norman said, jumping to his feet. 'Stunning, isn't it? Never get tired of it.' He shook his head and smiled. 'Sorry. What did you say?'

'Kevin. From the other room,' Logan said. His eyes went to the ceiling for added emphasis. 'He around, do you know?'

'Uh, presumably, yes,' Norman said. 'I saw him earlier, but I'd imagine he's upstairs. Why? I mean, not that it's any of my...' He shook his head again. 'Sorry. Want me to get him for you?'

'No, it's fine,' Logan said. He gave Tyler the nod, and the younger detective retreated out of the room. His footsteps went thudding up the stairs as Norman continued the conversation.

'Have you eaten?' he asked.

'Eh, not in a while actually, no,' Logan admitted.

'Pat did a steak pie. There's some left. Can I tempt you?'

Logan's stomach answered for him, and Norman laughed.

'I'll take that as a "yes", shall I?'

'I wouldn't say no. Thank you. But, what about bawchops?' Logan asked, pointing with a thumb to the ceiling. 'DC Neish, I mean. There enough for him, too?'

Norman leaned in closer and put the back of his hand to his mouth, like he was revealing some big secret. 'There's enough for the whole island, and half of bloody Skye!' he chuckled. 'Pat cooks when she's anxious. It's her thing. And, well, I suppose all this murder business has got her wound up.'

The footsteps came clumping down the stairs again. Logan turned to the door just as Tyler appeared from the hallway. 'No answer, boss. Doesn't sound like he's in.'

Logan faced Norman again. 'Dinner would be lovely. Thank you. But before that… I don't suppose you've got a spare key to Mr Tillerson's room?'

Norman's face paled. 'Argh. No, actually.'

'No?' asked Logan. 'You don't have a spare key to one of the rooms in your own house?'

'We had a couple in last week. They went away with it. Supposed to be posting it back, but with the ferries being off…' Norman smiled apologetically. 'Kevin has the spare.'

Damn. That wasn't ideal. It would've been good to get a poke around in Tillerson's room, but all Logan had at the moment was some contradiction. Tillerson had said Isaac and Louise left early, and they'd said the opposite. Conflicting accounts by two parties who'd been drinking alcohol. Easy to lose track of time. Easy to get mixed up.

Probably nothing. Not worth putting the door in for, anyway.

He wanted another chat with Mr Tillerson, but it could wait. Right now, there was more pressing business to attend to.

'Right then, Norman,' Logan said. 'About that steak pie…'

–

Pat had dished them up their dinner at the same table where they'd eaten their breakfast earlier in the day. The plates had come out practically groaning under the weight of the scoff piled on top.

As well as the steak pie (with extra pastry) there were boiled tatties, roasties, carrots, and parsnips. There were also a couple of pieces of broccoli, which Logan immediately scraped to the side of the plate so they didn't contaminate the rest of the meal.

'Bloody hell. This is going above and beyond,' Logan had told her.

She'd smiled, a little embarrassed, and admitted that she'd made far too much, although she didn't directly mention the 'stress-cooking' thing that Norman had alluded to.

Once she was sure the detectives had everything they needed, Pat left them to it, before popping back in to tell them to leave room for dessert.

'Homemade banoffee pie. Best you've ever tasted,' she promised.

The first five minutes of the meal were spent in silence, other than the scraping of cutlery on plates, and the occasional expletive of enjoyment. Pat made an excellent steak pie, they agreed. It was so good, in fact, that Logan was even prepared to overlook the broccoli, which was just about the highest praise he could offer.

It was only when the worst of their hunger pangs were satisfied that the detectives moved on to discussing the day's developments.

Bruce Anderson was the big headline, of course. They still had an hour and a half before the internet cut off for the night, so time yet to follow up with Hamza on that. The worst of the weather had passed, so hopefully they'd get news about support arriving, too. That would make life easier.

They both agreed that the Reverend Abraham Kerr was a certifiable headcase, and that he seemed perfectly capable of committing murder. Assuming God tipped him the wink and okayed it.

Did they think he'd done it, though? There was no physical evidence to tie him to the scene—although, there was no physical evidence to tie anyone else to the scene, either—and Logan was still convinced that, had the minister killed his daughter, he'd have taken some perverse pleasure in owning up to it.

The son and his partner? There was clearly little love lost there, particularly on Louise's part. Still, it was a stretch to imagine they'd killed her. They agreed that they couldn't see Louise losing any sleep over her future mother-in-law's demise, though.

And there was that inconsistency between the accounts of who'd left when. That was something they were going to have to get to the bottom of, Logan had said, as he'd torn off a big chunk of puff pastry and dunked it in the pie's thick gravy.

It was around then that the conversation had taken an unexpected turn. Since they'd sat down, Tyler had been edging to say something, but had bottled it every time, until Logan eventually got fed up with waiting.

'Well? What is it?'

Tyler glanced up from his plate, where he was loading up his fork with a wee bit of everything.

'Boss?'

'You've clearly got something you're building up to saying. What?'

'Oh. No. It's, eh…' Tyler fished around inside his mouth with his tongue, then shook his head. 'It's nothing, boss.'

'Bollocks, it's nothing. What is it? Spit it out.'

Tyler brought the fork to his mouth, and held it there, ready. 'Isaac Young, boss.'

'What about him?'

'How old would you say he was?'

'I don't know. Late twenties?' Logan guessed. 'Why?'

'I wasn't sure either, boss,' Tyler said. He still had the forkful of food poised next to his mouth, ready to cram in. 'That's why I asked to get a look at his ID. Pin it down, sort of thing.'

'Aye, what the fuck was all that about?' Logan demanded. 'I meant to jar you about that when we left.'

'Like I say, boss, wanted to get his age. Thought it'd be a bit weird if I'd just come out with it and asked him.'

'Why'd you want his age?' Logan asked. 'What's his age got to do with anything?'

'Nothing. I didn't really. Want to know his age. I mean, I did, but...' Tyler began. He shot a longing look at his fork, clearly wishing he hadn't started this, and had just stuck to stuffing his face, instead.

'What are you talking about? You said you wanted to know his age, now you don't. Make your mind up, Tyler.'

'It was his date of birth,' the DC blurted out.

Logan blinked in surprise.

'His date of birth?'

'You're right. He is late-twenties, boss,' Tyler said. 'He's twenty-nine, in fact. Pushing thirty.'

Logan drew in a breath as if about to speak, but nothing came out.

'Born in August. Nineteen-ninety.'

Tyler shovelled his food into his mouth then, filling it before he could say any more. As he chewed, he watched the range of expressions that played across the face of the man sitting opposite. They each flitted by quickly, like the individual pages of a flipbook. The resulting animation was one of slowly dawning horror.

Logan placed first his fork, then his knife on the table.

He clasped his hands in front of his mouth and stared directly through Detective Constable Neish like he wasn't there.

'Oh,' he muttered. He bit down on his bottom lip, then spat it out again. 'Fuck.'

Chapter 27

He'd thought the lad had looked familiar. He'd put it down to him looking like Iona, but what if that wasn't it? Isaac had Iona's eyes, but that was about the lot. The facial structure... the profile... those could feasibly have been someone else's. They could easily have been...

'Christ Almighty,' Logan mumbled.

This particular 'Christ Almighty' was the fourth 'Christ Almighty' that had passed his lips in the last ten minutes. It was also, aside from a brief, 'Thanks,' aimed at Pat as she'd cleared the plates and brought dessert, the only words he'd spoken during that time.

He shovelled a big spoonful of banoffee pie in his mouth, hoping the sugar rush would take the edge off everything else he was currently feeling.

It didn't.

His head spun. His stomach churned. His heart alternated between racing like a humming-bird's and stopping completely.

A son. *His* son.

No. It couldn't be. Could it?

It could. He knew it could. The dates matched. He and Iona had gotten together after the Halloween Disco. Then, just a shade under ten months later, she'd had a bouncing baby boy.

And, God, Tyler was right. There was a similarity. It hadn't been immediately obvious to Logan, and you really had to look for it, but... maybe. Aye. Maybe.

'Christ Almighty,' he said, and a half-chewed lump of toffee-coated banana fell from his mouth and went thump on the tabletop.

Tyler was already scraping the last few remnants of the pie's biscuit base off his plate. While Logan had been spending half his time staring blankly at the wall, shaking his head, and *Christ Almightying* over and over, Tyler had devoted all his attention to eating.

He felt it was best not to get involved in the DCI's mini-meltdown any more than he already was, and stuffing his mouth with dessert was the best way he could think of to keep it from saying anything stupid.

A glance at his watch told him he had no choice but to speak up now, though. He dabbed at the corners of his mouth with the napkin Pat had set out for him, wiped his hands on it, then set it down on the table.

'If we're calling back to base, we'd better get a shift on, boss,' he said. 'Internet's going to go off shortly.'

'Hmm?' Logan stared uncomprehendingly at him for several long seconds, like the DC had just said something in Mandarin Chinese.

From another room, the cuckoo called nine. This seemed to kick Logan's brain back into gear, allowing Tyler's words to filter through. Blinking, Logan set his fork down on his plate, and wiped his mouth on the back of his hand. 'Shite. Aye.'

He stood up, the legs of his chair scuffing across the laminate flooring. 'Listen, do me a favour, will you?' he said. 'Not a word of this to the others. Not yet. Not until I know for sure.'

If Hoon found out, he'd be off the case before he could say *conflict of interest*. And maybe that was right. Maybe that was all well and good. But he wanted to find Iona's killer. He owed her that much.

Now, more than ever.

'Of course, boss. Mum's the word,' Tyler said. A smirk played at the corner of his mouth. 'Or Dad's the word, in this case.'

The force of Logan's look almost pushed the Detective Constable backwards out of his chair. He cleared his throat, the smile falling away. 'Sorry, boss,' he said. 'Too soon?'

—

They were at the bottom step when the doorbell rang. The door opened immediately, and Joy Bryden was ushered in by a sudden gust of wind that billowed the net curtain on the little hall window.

There was a brief flash of surprise when she saw both men standing at the bottom of the stairs, but then it was gone. To show surprise was to show weakness, Logan thought. At least, he guessed that's how the head of the Community Council would see it.

'Detectives,' she said. 'Just who I was looking for.'

'Hello?' said Norman, appearing from the lounge. His eyes were ringed with red, and he had the look of someone who'd just been woken up from a very deep, very enjoyable snooze.

When he spotted Joy he stiffened, practically standing to attention. His eyes, now wide and alert, tried to peer backwards through his own head in the direction of the kitchen.

'Patricia!' he called, and there was a hint of alarm in it. 'We've got a visitor!'

The way he said 'we've got a visitor' made Logan think that this was some sort of pre-arranged safe word, or warning. It was delivered in the same sort of tone as a sailor who'd just found a dirty great hole in their boat might sound a red alert.

Pat, sensibly enough, didn't answer. Joy waved Norman away before he could offer any words of welcome. Or possibly mutter any banishing curses.

'I'm not here to see you. I'm just here to show the officers this,' Joy said. She thrust an iPad into Logan's hands and gave the power button a prod. 'I was looking through the webcam footage, like you said. The night Iona…'

She turned to Norman, her face folding into a particularly sour look. 'Do you mind, Norman? This is police business.'

'Oh!' Norman said. 'Right. Sorry. Yes.'

He turned to his left, almost walked into the wall, then turned all the way around to the right until he was facing the kitchen. 'I'll just... right.'

Joy waited for him to scurry off, rolled her eyes at Logan as if expressing some shared pain, and turned her attention back to the screen. 'I looked through Tuesday's footage. There's not a lot. I mean, there's hours, obviously, but there's not a lot actually happens.'

Given the nature of life on the island, this did not come as a surprise to either detective.

'I can send you it all, but this bit... I thought you'd want to see,' Joy continued.

She leaned in so her head was briefly blocking Logan's view of the screen, then tapped the little triangle in the middle of an otherwise black rectangle.

It took a moment for the image to appear. When it did, it was immediately obvious what they were looking at. Most of the screen was still in darkness, with a few blobs of shapeless light dotted here and there.

'It's a bit blurry to start with,' Joy said. 'Give it a sec.'

They gave it a sec. Sure enough, the blobs of colour and expanses of darkness sharpened to form a view of the island's main street, looking down from by the shop, past the pub, and out across the water to Rum.

The water was a gently undulating carpet of black, with the occasional waves cresting as white horses here and there.

'What am I looking at?' Logan asked.

Joy tutted. 'Well, give it a minute,' she said in a conspiratorial whisper.

They gave it a minute. Or rather, half of one.

'There. See?' said Joy, her finger pouncing on a sudden movement on the screen. A woman in a tight dress stumbled

179

across the street from right to left, in and out of shot. It was hard to make out her face in much detail, but there was enough light to make a positive ID.

'That's Iona,' Logan said. Judging by the direction she'd staggered, she was heading towards the pub. 'When was this from? Earlier in the night?'

'No. Later. Shh,' Joy said. 'Watch.'

Logan watched. He hadn't stopped watching, in fact, since Joy had started the footage playing, but now no force on Earth could tear his eyes away from it.

Behind him, standing on the first step of the staircase, Tyler craned his neck to see the screen, too.

There was no sound, so when Iona appeared on screen from the left again, it came as a surprise. What came next was an even bigger one.

Iona was not alone. She was hanging off the arm of someone else. A man. The angle they were walking meant his face was hidden from the camera, but that didn't matter. Logan recognised the orange cagoule immediately.

Slowly, solemnly, Logan's eyes crept to the ceiling.

'DC Neish?' he said.

'Yes, boss?'

'Go and apologise to Pat and Norman, will you?'

Tyler frowned. 'What for?'

'We're about to kick one of their bedroom doors down.'

Chapter 28

The door to Kevin Tillerson's room was flimsy enough that one good dunt from Logan's shoulder did the trick. The DCI had been expecting more resistance, and swore loudly as he went freewheeling into the room, then almost broke his neck when he tripped over a rucksack.

'Everything all right?' called Pat from the bottom of the stairs.

She and Norman had assembled there after Tyler had told them the plan. Neither of them had looked particularly pleased at the thought of the door being forced open, but neither had voiced any strong objections, particularly once Logan had assured them that Police Scotland would cover the cost of the damage.

He didn't tell them it might very well take months to come through, of course. Some things, they were better off not knowing.

Joy had suggested she should probably stay, too, but Logan had sent her packing so she could email over the footage of Tillerson and Iona before the internet went down for the night.

He had hoped he could get her to keep the signal active after the usual ten o'clock shut-off, but she'd explained it was on a set schedule, and overriding it was a lengthy process involving calls to an IT support desk somewhere in India that she'd have to dig out the phone number for.

The room Logan now stood in didn't feel like it belonged with the rest of the house. There was no dated wallpaper, no horrible curtains with ancient, sagging pelmets. No chipped old furniture, or cracked switches.

There was just a lovely big bed with a driftwood frame, an ultra-thin wall-mounted TV, and a couple of nice scenic photographs to break up the crisp whiteness of the walls. The reason it felt like it didn't belong in the house was because this room, unlike the others, was genuinely nice.

'Modernised in here, all right. Eh, boss?' asked Tyler. He was standing out on the upstairs landing to reduce the risk of compromising any evidence that might be lying around.

'Yes, we couldn't put up with it any more,' called Pat from the bottom of the stairs. 'Please don't say anything.'

'Your secret's safe with us,' Tyler assured her, as Logan poked around in Tillerson's room.

Aside from the rucksack, which had been sat by the door, there wasn't a lot in the room that looked like it might belong to the guest. The built-in wardrobe was empty. The bedside table had nothing sitting on it.

There was a toothbrush and toothpaste in the small en-suite, both sitting on the sink. Remove those, though, and there was very little sign that the room was actually in use. Even the bed had been meticulously made-up. It didn't look like anyone had so much as sat on it all day.

'Bag packed by the door, ready to leave in a hurry,' Logan remarked. Squatting down, he pulled on a pair of blue vinyl gloves and had a rummage around in the bag's many compartments.

What was he looking for? He wasn't entirely sure. He didn't find it, though, whatever it was. All he found were a compass, map, and some camping cooking gear, a small multi-tool, a battered old pair of trainers, and a pile of neatly-folded clothes which, by the smell of them, had been recently laundered.

He vaguely recalled hearing the washing machine going when they'd been eating breakfast that morning. If Tillerson's clothes had all been washed and put through the tumble dryer, it almost certainly put the kybosh on getting any forensic evidence from them.

At the bottom of one of the side-compartments was a small hard-backed notebook. Logan didn't expect to find anything exciting written within, but was taken aback by just how right he was.

A good thirty or more pages of the notebook were full of detailed notes on what Logan guessed must be real ales and craft beers from across the UK. Each page was filled with phrases like 'hoppy and rich' or 'smooth, with bitter notes,' all written in the same fastidiously neat handwriting.

'Jesus Christ,' Logan muttered.

'Got something, boss?' asked Tyler, leaning into the room.

'No. Just... Jesus Christ, he's a boring bastard,' Logan said, returning the book to the bag, and zipping the pocket closed.

It was in the final section that he found something of interest. It was a small roll of cash, tucked into a Velcro pocket inside the main part of the bag. All twenties. All identical, aside from the serial numbers. Logan counted out eight notes—a hundred and sixty quid—then turned on his haunches and pointed to Tyler.

'Time?'

Tyler appeared momentarily confused, then checked his watch. 'Shite. Nearly ten, boss.'

'Phone Hamza.'

'WhatsApp,' Tyler said, before he could stop himself.

'Whatever! Just fucking get him. I need to know, the money found on Iona Wallace, what bank was it from?'

Tyler tapped Hamza's picture in the app, then touched the phone icon. He glanced at his watch again while he waited for the other DC to pick up.

'Cutting it fine,' he said, dancing from foot to foot. 'Come on, come on, come—' He stopped dancing. 'Hamza? Aye. No. Shut up. Boss needs to know something.'

He relayed Logan's question, and both detectives listened to the frantic tapping of keyboard keys coming over the speak-erphone.

Hamza's voice, when it came, was a rushed garble that crackled from the handset on a cushion of static.

'Bank of England. Why?'

Logan looked down at the notes in his hand. All twenties. All issued by the Bank of England.

'Kevin Tillerson,' Logan said, practically shouting the words at Tyler's phone. 'Look him up, get me what you can on...'

The phone gave a bleep as the internet connection went off. The cuckoo called from down the stairs.

Logan cursed below his breath. Then he cursed again, but louder. Finally, he stood and pointed past Tyler at the staircase beyond.

'Get down there. Use the landline, phone the office and tell Hamza to get digging.'

'Getting late, boss,' Tyler pointed out. 'Imagine they'll be knocking off soon, if they've been in all day.'

'Well, have him give it to someone else, then. Jesus, do I have to think of everything?' Logan spat. 'I want a full report on the bastard in my inbox for when the internet comes back on tomorrow morning. Got that?'

'Got it, boss,' Tyler said.

Logan waited for him to move. When it was clear he wasn't going to, the DCI ushered him along with a wave of his arms. 'Well, go on, then!'

While Tyler hurried down the stairs and asked Pat and Norman if he could use their phone, Logan took an evidence bag from his pocket and placed the money inside.

Then, after a moment's thought, he removed two of the notes, and placed those in another of the transparent bags.

He didn't have a bag big enough for Tillerson's rucksack, so he carried it carefully through to his and Tyler's room, and placed it out of sight between the beds.

That done, he shoved both the bundles of bagged money in his coat pocket and left the bedroom, locking the door behind him.

Logan was standing by the big window in the lounge when Tyler returned. The DCI acknowledged him with a nod, then went back to staring out at the water, and the sparse lights of Rum.

The rain had stopped, the wind had all but died away, and the sense of calm beyond the window was not one reflected within Logan himself.

'Hamza's going to find out what he can tonight, then get back in sharp in the morning,' Tyler announced. 'He did a quick search on HOLMES while I was on the phone. Nothing coming up on Tillerson, but it's not always the most up-to-date.'

Logan felt a twinge of disappointment. A nice juicy history of violence would've been handy when it came to the interview, although he wasn't entirely surprised. Tillerson hadn't struck him as violent. Certainly not as a killer.

But appearances, as he had learned the hard way, could be deceiving.

'Also, something that might be of interest, boss. Ham went through Iona's social media. Apparently, she'd been ripping into that Dudley fella—the big lad—for the past few weeks. Nothing too major, but lots of little digs about him. Pictures of Mr Potato Head with his face Photoshopped on. Petty stuff, but not nice. Quite a lot of comments from folk on the posts saying they're out of order, but she seemed to enjoy the attention.'

'Worth a word with him, then,' Logan said. 'Between that and the argument at the pub, he'd have motive.'

'Deffo, boss,' Tyler agreed. He shifted uncomfortably, glanced at the door as if contemplating making a run for it, then steeled himself. 'Hamza. I, eh… he's…'

The rest of the sentence died away like the wind outside.

'He's what?' Logan asked, meeting the DC's reflected gaze in the window.

'I thought—and I hope you don't mind, boss—but I got him to look into Isaac Young, too. Didn't tell him why, obviously, just thought it'd be good to have a bit more background. For, you know, for you to have a bit more background.'

Logan wanted to be furious at Tyler's interference. Annoyed, at least. Something. Instead, he just nodded, and pointed his gaze back out over the water again.

'Pretty mental stuff, boss,' Tyler remarked. He closed the lounge door, so Pat and Norman wouldn't hear. 'Your head must be spinning.'

'Aye. No' half,' Logan confirmed. 'Mind you, we don't know that he's definitely... that we're... that he and I are...'

Logan aborted the sentence there and then. Technically, he didn't know. Technically, Isaac could've been someone else's son. Someone else's boy.

Realistically, though?

The timing fitted. The face, too.

He exhaled through his nose, muttered another, 'Christ Almighty,' at his reflection, then went back to gazing out into the darkness.

The floorboards creaked as Tyler moved his weight from foot to foot, not quite sure what to do with himself, and even less sure of what to say.

Fortunately, Logan took it upon himself to do the talking.

'Always wanted a son. Back in the day. Aye, no' when I was fifteen. Later, I mean. When me and Vanessa got together.'

Tyler lowered himself into one of the wingback chairs and listened as the DCI continued.

'We had Maddie, of course,' Logan said. He was looking further than the lights of Rum now. Further, even than the mainland beyond. 'And she was bloody marvellous, if I say so myself. Funny. Smart. Kind.'

He tucked his hands behind his back, the fingers knotting together. It was the first time Tyler had seen the gaffer so ill-at-ease. He was used to Logan storming about, shouting his head off, or sitting quietly as a picture of calmness and control.

This, though? This was something new.

'I always thought kids made you vulnerable. Made you weak. And then, she came along. And, well… I realised that was a load of old bollocks.' He let out a little snort. 'I realised a lot of stuff that I used to believe was a load of old bollocks, in fact.

'I couldn't have loved her more. Couldn't have. Not possible,' Logan continued. 'But I still wanted a son. Complete the set, sort of thing. You know? Like a Panini sticker album.'

Both men smiled at that.

'Why didn't you?' Tyler ventured. The conversation was making him perhaps even more uncomfortable than Logan, but it felt like the DCI needed to off-load, and while Tyler very much doubted he'd be the boss's first choice, he was the only one around.

Logan looked deep into the eyes of his reflection in the window. When he spoke, his breath fogged the glass.

'Owen Petrie.'

'Mister Whisper?' asked Tyler. His forehead furrowed as he thought this through. 'I don't get it, boss.'

'Aye, you and me both, son,' Logan said, so quietly Tyler almost didn't hear it. Logan gave himself a shake, then carried on, louder this time. 'I wasn't much older than you when he was doing the rounds. When he started taking the kids. We didn't know then what he'd go on to do. What he'd become. He wasn't "Mister Whisper". No' then. No' yet. He was some random child-snatching bastard, and I was on the team that was meant to catch him.'

'And you did,' Tyler said. 'You got him.'

Logan grunted. 'Aye. Eventually. Years later,' he said. 'Years of following up on leads, acting on hunches, knocking on doors. Chasing bloody shadows.'

He swallowed. It sounded unnaturally loud in the near-silence.

'Consoling parents.'

'Couldn't have been easy, boss.'

Logan shook his head. 'No. No, it was not,' he admitted. 'But the bastard became an obsession. All-consuming. Not a minute of the day went by when I wasn't going over and over it all.'

Still facing the window, he pointed to the side of his head and slowly circled his finger around. 'Sitting at dinner, tick-tick-tick. School prize-giving, tick-tick-tick. Bloody… marriage counselling. Tick-tick-tick. Tick-tick-tick. *Tick-tick-tick*. Over and over. Non-stop. Only way I could stop it was through the drink.'

Logan sniffed and rocked back on his heels. His voice, when it came, was an admirable attempt at sounding nonchalant. 'She kicked me out in the end. Vanessa, I mean. My wife. Ex-wife. Don't blame her. The drinking was out of hand.' He ground his back teeth together, clenching and unclenching the muscles in his jaw. '*I* was out of hand.'

Neither man said anything for a while after that. Elsewhere in the house, the cuckoo clock called eleven.

'Still. Least you got him in the end, boss. At least you stopped him.'

'But for what? So he can sit in a hospital, staring out the window? Cushy wee number that, given what he did.'

'He's brain-damaged, isn't he? After the…' Tyler's hesitation was brief, but did not go unnoticed by the DCI. '…accident. After he fell.'

A tension knotted the muscles in Logan's shoulders and stiffened his neck.

'Aye.'

He thought back to all the silent phone calls over the past few weeks.

And all the whispered ones.

'Maybe.'

And then the spell was broken when a bright orange shape passed the window, waving at Logan as it came striding up the path.

The detective turned from the window just as the house's front door opened. The wistful, far-away look that had temporarily set up camp on his face was gone. In its place was a much more familiar grimace of grim determination that immediately set Tyler more at ease.

'Talk about timing,' he said, charging for the lounge door before the DC could scramble up out of the wingback. 'I'm just in the mood to ruin some bastard's night.'

Chapter 29

The dining room of the B&B stood in for the interview room of a police station. Tyler and Logan sat on one side, while Kevin Tillerson sat across from them.

Between them, a caddy of tomato sauce and other condiments sat ready for breakfast service in the morning. There had been cutlery set out, too, but Tyler had moved it all out of grabbing distance before he'd sat down.

Whose grabbing distance he was moving it out of, he wasn't entirely sure. There was always a chance that Tillerson would try something stupid, but Tyler reckoned the safe money was probably on Logan.

'Everything all right?' Tillerson asked, still wrestling himself out of his waterproof jacket.

He looked concerned. Not curious, like someone who had no idea what this was all about, but worried, like someone who did. And who knew what was almost certainly coming next.

'Just got a few questions, Mr Tillerson,' Logan said.

'Kevin, please,' Tillerson said, smiling so desperately it made Logan's stomach churn.

'Kevin. Right. We've just got a few questions. Some things we're hoping you can help us clear up.'

'Of course. No problem.'

'I warn you, this interview is being recorded.'

Logan paused momentarily, a silent signal for Tyler to take out his phone.

'For quality and training purposes?' Tillerson blurted, then he let out a panicky breathless cackle at his own joke, before momentarily looking like he might be about to burst into tears.

'Something like that,' Logan said. 'You're not under arrest, but if we decide to move to arrest, anything you say may be used in evidence against you in court. Is that clear?'

Tillerson nodded. He started to speak, but his voice became an unintelligible croak. He swallowed, inhaled slowly, then tried again.

'Should I have a solicitor?'

'That's up to you, Kevin. Although, obviously, that'll drag things out for you,' Logan said. 'My suggestion? Just answer honestly, we'll clear this whole thing up, and it'll never need to get to that stage. We're sure there's just been a misunderstanding. Aren't we, Detective Constable?'

'We're pretty confident, boss, aye.'

Logan raised his eyebrows, waiting for a response from Tillerson. Despite having shed his big jacket, Kevin was sweating profusely. When he nodded his head, a drop fell from his forehead and onto the table. He wiped it away with the sleeve of his fleece, then clasped his hands in an obvious attempt to stop himself fidgeting.

'Right. Yes. Let's get it sorted,' he croaked.

Logan clasped his own hands and leaned forward, mirroring Tillerson's body language. 'On the night Iona Wallace died, you said her son and daughter-in-law left soon after her. Is that right?'

'I, uh, yes. I think so. I'm pretty sure they did.'

'Pretty sure? How sure?' Logan asked.

Tillerson's face became an exaggerated picture of concentration. It gave him a cartoonish appearance, like his face was made of living rubber.

'Um. Let me think…' he said. 'Maybe… fifty percent?'

'Fifty percent?' Logan repeated.

'Maybe. Yes. Thereabouts.'

'Fifty percent isn't "pretty sure", Kevin. Fifty percent is, "I don't have a clue".'

'Is it?' Tillerson asked. 'Uh. Sixty, then? Sixty. Yes. About sixty, I'd say. I can't be certain.'

'You can't even be "fairly confident" at sixty percent, Kevin,' Logan countered. 'That's a vague hunch, at best. Would you agree, Detective Constable?'

'That's barely an inkling, boss,' Tyler said, neither detective taking their eyes off the other man.

'We spoke to the couple themselves, Kevin. They say they were in there much longer. They say they had a few drinks after Iona left.'

Tillerson exhaled with relief. 'Right. Well, my mistake then,' he said, clearly under the impression that the contradictory statements were the reason for the interview. 'Sorry. I wasn't paying too much attention. If they say they didn't, then they didn't. That's that. Apologies for the misinformation. Hopefully, no harm done.'

Logan smiled and tapped both hands on the table, one after the other. 'Well, glad we got all that cleared up. Thanks for your time, Kevin.'

'No problem! And, again, sorry for any confusion caused.'

'These things happen,' Logan said. He began to move as if he was about to stand up, then stopped. 'Oh. Just one other thing.'

'Yes?' asked Tillerson. He was beaming from ear to ear now, believing he was safely through the worst of it.

For a moment, Logan almost felt sorry for him.

It didn't last.

'Do you mind telling us what you were doing with Iona outside the pub shortly before she was murdered?'

Tillerson's face froze. Every line. Every crease. Every atom of it became rigidly fixed in place. His body, too. Not a part of him moved. It was like all his life-force had been diverted to the panic centres of his brain in an attempt to come up with an answer. An explanation. An excuse.

He failed. Dismally.

'Hmm?' he cheeped.

'Shortly before ten on Tuesday evening, you were seen crossing the street away from the pub with Iona Wallace,' Logan said.

'*With*?' Tillerson said. 'I don't… I can't… *with*? I did leave the pub around then, but, but, if she was there at the time, then it was coincidence. That's all. I wasn't *with* her. We may have just been, just been, just been… we weren't together. Is my point. If she was even…'

'She was hanging onto your arm, Kevin,' Logan said. 'Draped from it, some might say.'

'I'd say "draped", boss,' Tyler chipped in.

Tillerson's head tick-tocked between them. 'How did…? I don't…'

'When I said you were seen, I didn't mean by a witness, Kevin. I meant by the webcam,' Logan said. He is voice lightened, becoming chatty. 'Did you know there was a webcam? Looks along the street from up the hill, out over Rum to the mainland. It's nice. Nice view. And, well, the thing is, Kevin, they back-up all the footage. It all gets saved. Boats coming in. The weather changing. People coming and going.'

Kevin sat in a stunned, anxious silence. His brain was working overtime, trying to formulate a plan. Trying to work out what to say and how to say it, to make it all stop and go away.

He'd realise he should have his solicitor with him soon, Logan suspected, and so he pressed on before the thought had a chance to form in Tillerson's head.

'So, going by the footage, Iona walked in the direction of the pub at around nine fifty-three, visibly intoxicated. Roughly a minute later, she crossed the street in the opposite direction. With you, Kevin. Not at the same time as you. Not near you. *With* you. *With*.'

Logan's tone became markedly more serious again. 'Now, does that, or does that not, contradict your earlier statement?'

Tillerson swallowed several times, like he was fighting not to drown in his own saliva. 'I, uh… yes. Yes, it does,' he admitted, having no other routes available to him. 'I didn't kill her,' he blurted. 'I didn't. I swear. I swear to God.'

'I'll be honest, Kevin. From where I'm sitting? It looks very much like you did,' Logan said. 'How about from where you're sitting, Detective Constable?'

'View's much the same from this seat, boss,' Tyler replied. 'And it's not looking good for Mr Tillerson here.'

'Kevin,' Logan said.

'Oh. Aye. *Kevin*,' Tyler corrected, and the way he said it made it sound like a particularly nasty insult.

'So, if you've got another explanation—one that doesn't involve you raping and murdering Iona Wallace—now would be a good time to let us hear it,' Logan suggested.

Across the table, Tillerson's eyes filled with tears. He seemed to be shrinking before their eyes, his shoulders sagging, his back stooping until it was only his forearms on the table holding him up.

'We… we had sex,' he said. The words were a shameful whisper, sobbed more than spoken. 'But I didn't rape her. I didn't. She… she invited me. Everyone in the pub heard. And they heard me say "no!" I did! I said I wasn't interested, and… and… I wasn't. I'm married. I have a wife!'

'What changed?' Logan asked.

'Oh, I…' Tillerson closed his eyes, taking a moment to compose himself. 'I was going to come back here. I was only in the pub making plans for when I head to Skye. Checking maps. All that. When I was done, I left. I went outside.'

His eyes welled up again. A tear broke through and was quickly lost in the sweat-sheen on his cheek. 'And there she was. She'd been, I don't know, hanging around or wandering about, I suppose. She saw me, and she came over, and she… well, she… her hand, she put it down my… into my pants, and she… she… *manipulated* me. Down there.'

Tyler side-eyed the DCI. 'He saying she touched his cock, boss?'

'Aye. I think that's what he's saying,' Logan confirmed. 'Is that what you're saying, Kevin?'

'Yes! Yes. She... she touched my... down there,' he said, his face reddening at the very thought of it. 'And, well, I succumbed. I'd had a couple of drinks. She told me we could go back to her place, and...'

He buried his head in his hands, his shoulders heaving with big, breathless sobs. 'Oh, God. Oh, God, I knew I shouldn't have. I knew it was wrong!'

He straightened, and when his face re-emerged it was a deep crimson, and slick with sweat, tears, and snot.

'But she was so... so *insistent*. Kept telling me how good it would be. How much fun we'd have. And she wasn't unattractive, you understand? She wasn't half bad.'

'I'm sure she'd be delighted by that review,' Logan said. 'So she took you back to her house. What then?'

Tillerson shook his head. 'No. We didn't go.'

'I thought you said—'

'She invited me back, but we... we didn't make it. She said it was too far to walk, and so we went behind... the school, I think it was. It was dark, and she just... sort of... set about it. Doing it. She didn't mess around. We just got, I don't know, down to it, I suppose.'

'Did you use any sort of protection?' Logan asked.

Tillerson looked away, chewed on his bottom lip, and shook his head.

'Right. So, to be clear, you're saying that you and Iona Wallace had unprotected sexual intercourse behind the school building on the night she died?'

Tillerson let out another involuntary sob. 'Oh. God. When you say it like that... but, yes. Yes. We did. We did. But that was the last I saw of her. I swear. I *swear*. Once we were finished, she just sort of left.'

'She left? Just like that? Without saying a word?' Logan asked. 'Bit odd, that. Don't you think, Detective Constable?'

'Very unusual, boss,' Tyler agreed.

Logan reached into his coat pocket. He produced the evidence bag containing two twenty pound notes and slid it into the centre of the table without a word.

Tillerson's eyes swivelled down and fixed on the money. He gritted his teeth, like he was fighting back the urge to start crying again.

'Take your time,' Logan said.

Kevin continued to stare at the money on the table for a while, then tore his eyes from it and didn't look at it again for the rest of the interview. 'She, uh, she remarked on my performance. Not positively. She was... quite cruel. Rather damning, really.'

'And how did that make you feel, Kevin?' Logan asked, not unkindly.

'No more ashamed than I already felt. I just... Afterwards— right afterwards, I mean—I just wanted it over. I knew right away I'd made a mistake. That I shouldn't have done it. I was pulling up my trousers, and I felt sick. Properly sick, to my stomach. I just wanted her to go, to forget it ever happened, but she kept going at me. Laughing at me. Taunting me. Said it wasn't fair that I'd got something out of it, but that she hadn't.'

'Did that make you angry?' Logan asked.

'Angry? No. Just... humiliated. I tried to leave, but she followed. Kept asking what was in it for her? Kept going on about how I'd "got my jollies", but she hadn't. And that's when I realised.'

'When you realised what?'

'Money. That was what she wanted. Money,' Tillerson said, his voice little more than a whisper. 'That was what she was really after. I had forty pounds in my wallet. I offered her twenty.'

'Twenty?' said Tyler. 'Christ, he drives a hard bargain, eh, boss?'

'She got angry. She did, not me. Demanded all of it. Said she'd tell everyone what had happened. Told me she'd make sure it got back to my family. Blackmailed me,' Tillerson continued. 'So I gave it to her. I let her take it. Just to shut her up. Just to make it all stop. I gave her all of it.'

'All forty quid,' Logan said. 'Very big of you.'

'It wasn't a… a… *transaction*,' Tillerson protested. 'At least, I didn't think so when it… when we started. If I'd known she was a prostitute, I wouldn't have gone near her!'

For reasons Logan couldn't quite put his finger on, his heart skipped a beat.

'She wasn't a prostitute,' he said.

Tillerson let out a little cheep of nervous laughter. 'Well, she certainly seemed like one, from where I was standing.'

'And where was that? With your pants around your ankles and your cock hanging out?' Logan asked.

His tone was a dangerous one. The knuckles of his clasped fingers had turned almost all the way white. Tyler spotted this, and stole a quick glance at the neighbouring table, making sure he'd moved the cutlery far enough out of grabbing range.

'So what happened then?' the DC asked, taking the wheel while Logan wrestled his temper back under control. 'You paid her the forty quid. Then what?'

'Then she left. She stuffed it in her… down her cleavage, and she left. Said, "Cheers", winked at me, then left,' Tillerson said. 'That was it. That was the last I saw of her. I came back here. Got back before eleven.'

'And Pat and Norman can vouch for that?' Tyler asked.

'Yes. Well, Norman. I didn't see Pat, but Norman was up. He was watching television. *Newsnight*, I think. We chatted for a while, then I went to bed. Well, I had a shower.'

'What did you talk about?' Logan asked.

Tillerson puffed out his cheeks, drawing a blank. 'I'm not sure. Nothing. The weather. Ferries. Nothing substantial.'

'You didn't tell him about Iona?'

'Of course not!' Tillerson cried. 'I'm hardly going to mention that, am I? "How was your night?" "Oh, not bad. Just fucked a local prozzie round the back of the school. How has your evening been?"'

He winced, taken aback by his own tone, and sat back, wrapping his arms across his chest. 'Sorry. Sorry, that was… sorry. It's just… God, if my wife finds out. My kids.'

'I'd say that's the least of your worries right now, Kevin, wouldn't you?' Logan said. 'Your DNA has been found on the body of a murder victim. You've admitted to having sexual intercourse with her, and to then being coerced into paying her for the pleasure. We've got camera footage showing you together shortly before she died. At this stage, we've been unable to identify anyone else who saw or was in contact with Iona after you were seen with her… Do you see what I'm getting at here?'

Tillerson's face had been turning paler and paler while Logan laid out the situation as he saw it. By the time the DCI was finished, Kevin looked like a literal ghost of his former self.

'I didn't kill her. I didn't,' he whispered.

Logan leaned back in his chair and was about to reply when his phone rang. It was so unexpected, so out of the blue, that all three men sat exchanging looks of confusion, before Logan realised what was going on.

Reaching into his pocket, he pulled out the handset. The triangle of signal at the top showed one tiny bar tucked into the far-left corner.

Logan didn't notice this. Nor did he notice the notification at the top telling him he had new text messages.

All he saw were the green and red phone icons wobbling on the main part of the screen, and the text above it.

Unknown Number.

'Excuse me,' he said, snatching up the phone and getting up from the table.

He was out in the hall before he thumbed the green button and pressed the phone to his ear.

'Hello?'

There was no reply.

'Hello? Who is this?'

Nothing.

Taking the phone from his ear, Logan checked the screen. The single bar was still holding steady. The seconds on the call timer ticked up, suggesting everything was still connected.

'Petrie?' Logan hissed.

There was a sound—a snigger—soft and muffled down the line. It was followed by a beep.

When Logan checked the screen again, the signal triangle was empty. The line was dead.

'Everything all right, boss?'

The sudden appearance of Tyler behind him made Logan jump.

'Shite. What? Aye. Aye, fine,' he said. 'Fine.'

Tyler looked back over his shoulder into the kitchen. 'Want to get back to it?'

Logan was still staring at his phone, like he might be able to force it to reconnect through sheer force of will.

'Boss?'

'Eh, no. No. Let's turn him loose for now,' Logan said. 'Not like he can go far. We should have Uniform coming in tomorrow. We can start back on him again then.'

'Oh. Aye. About that,' Tyler said. 'Hoon's been a bit tight with resources.'

'How tight?' Logan asked. 'How many are we getting?'

'How many Uniforms?'

'What else would I be talking about? Aye. How many Uniforms?'

Tyler's lips moved silently, like he was doing some complex mathematical calculation in his head.

'One, boss.'

The bottom half of Logan's face remained completely impassive, almost like he hadn't heard the reply. His top half, though, from the forehead down to the bridge of his nose, made his displeasure very clear.

'One?' he said.

'Aye.'

'One? Fucking… one? He's sending one Uniform as support?'

'The DI tried to get him to up it, by all accounts, but he wasn't having it,' Tyler said. 'Also, he told Hamza to tell me to tell you that if you don't phone him soon, he's going to… well, I don't really want to repeat the words he used, boss, but it involves his foot and your… well… vagina.'

'Aye. I can imagine,' Logan said. He huffed out a big breath. 'Fucking *one*. Do we know who we're getting?'

'Not yet. Guess we'll find out.'

'One bloody Uniform,' Logan muttered. Then, he shook his head, ran his hand down his face, and pointed into the kitchen. 'Go tell him we're done for tonight, but we'll want to talk to him again in the morning. Then go get some rest.'

'Right, boss,' said Tyler. 'Fair enough. What about you?'

'I'm going to sit in the lounge and stare at some alcohol,' Logan said. He caught the concerned look on Tyler's face, and arranged his mouth into something close to a smile. 'I'll be fine. I'll be up soon.'

Tyler nodded. 'Right. If, eh, you want to talk, or whatever… about anything.'

'Thanks,' Logan said. He put a hand on the younger man's shoulder and drew himself up to his full, terrifying height. 'But I absolutely will not.'

Chapter 30

The lounge was in darkness when Logan wandered through. He clicked on the light, drawing a gasp from Pat, who was curled up on the couch nursing a large glass of red wine. She was wearing a pair of button-up pyjamas, the top two buttons undone.

'Shite. Sorry,' Logan said. 'Didn't think anyone was here.'

'It's fine. My fault. Guest lounge,' said Pat, uncurling her legs and making a move to stand.

Logan stopped her with a wave of his hand. 'It's fine. Don't be daft. It's your house.'

'Thanks,' said Pat, smiling. She reached over and tapped an ugly lamp on the table beside her. The light activated at her touch. 'Stick the big light off, then, will you? If you don't mind, I mean?'

As Pat moved, Logan caught a glimpse of a bruise where her shoulder met her neck. It was a pungent sort of blue, yellowing around the edges.

'What happened to your neck?' he asked, with typical levels of polis tact.

'Hmm? Oh, nothing, nothing,' Pat said, adjusting her pyjama top to cover the mark. 'Slipped in the shower, that's all.'

Logan nodded, but he wasn't buying it. He thought of Norman. Older. Stronger. He didn't seem the type, necessarily, but then they often didn't.

'You sure?' Logan pressed.

Pat mustered a smile. It was a sparse, paltry thing, and the sadness in her eyes betrayed the emptiness of it. 'I'm sure,' she said. 'Promise.'

She wasn't going to talk about it. Maybe later, but not right now. Not to him. Logan switched off the overhead light, and the stark brightness darkened to a dim, comforting glow.

'That's better. Hate that big light,' Pat said, relaxing a little in the gloom.

From elsewhere in the house, the cuckoo began to call twelve. Pat's lips thinned until they showed her teeth.

'Not as much as I hate that bloody clock, mind you,' she said, then she washed the words down with a swig from her wine glass.

'Thought you said you'd stopped hearing it?' Logan asked, taking a seat in one of the uncomfortable wingbacks.

Pat snorted. 'Yeah. That may have been a fib.'

She reached down the side of the couch, and there was a clinking of glass. Lifting a bottle, Pat gave it a shake, found it empty, then returned it and pulled out another. This one still had half the contents left in it. She sloshed it around, then offered it across to the DCI.

'Sorry. Manners. Wine?'

'I'm fine, thanks,' Logan said. 'Never really been a wine drinker.'

That wasn't quite true, of course. It had never been his drink of choice, but by God, he'd put his fair share away over the years.

'There's other stuff. Gin? Think there's some lager in the fridge. Belgian stuff in little bottles. I could get you a couple of those, if you like?'

Logan gave a polite but firm shake of his head. 'I'm fine. Thank you.'

'You don't mind if I do, do you?' Pat asked, refilling her glass with an unsteady hand.

'Not at all,' Logan said. He turned to the window, partly to admire the night-time view, but mostly to limit his exposure to the smell of the wine. It was cheap stuff. Supermarket own-brand. High alcohol content, low class.

Just his vintage.

'Quite a view you've got,' he remarked.

Pat finished filling her glass, deposited the bottle on the floor beside her, then shrugged. 'Suppose. It's like anything though, I suppose.'

Logan turned back to her and raised an inquisitive eyebrow.

'The novelty soon wears off,' Pat clarified. 'Especially when the weather turns and you're stuck here.'

'Aye. I'd imagine that takes some of the shine off it, right enough,' Logan said.

'Eighteen months we've been here. Shine wore off about a fortnight in. And then you've got Joy, with her beady eyes everywhere. That bitch sees bloody everything. Christ knows how. I swear the woman's bloody omniscient.'

She swirled the wine around in her glass, stared at her reflection in the darkened window for a moment, then blinked as if coming out of a trance. 'Sorry. Just moaning. Pretend you didn't hear all that. It's a lovely place. Really.'

'Just no' your cup of tea?' Logan asked.

It took a long time for Pat to pick her words. 'It's not what I hoped for. Put it that way.' She drew in a big breath, then fixed Logan with an intense stare. 'It's my own bloody fault, though. Me that pushed for it. Have you ever wanted something? *Really* wanted something, I mean, but then, once you get it, you realise the thing you wanted isn't actually the thing you wanted at all?'

Logan replayed the sentence in his head. 'Um, aye. Aye, I think so.'

'Right! Well, it's like that, I suppose,' Pat said. She pulled her legs up higher on the couch and motioned to the big window with her glass. 'We were so excited. Before we came, I mean. New start. New adventure. And then, once we were here...' She smiled, but there was nothing but sadness in it. 'The magic went. Poof. Gone. Just... gone.'

Logan didn't really know what to say, so settled for keeping his mouth shut. Sensing his awkwardness, Pat drew her sleeve across her eyes, cleared her throat, and switched her tone for one much more decisive, if not exactly upbeat.

'I think we'll sell up, ultimately. That's the plan. Or, we'll try to. It's not easy getting people to move out here, but if we're lucky we'll find someone.' She leaned in closer and whispered. 'I haven't told Norman any of this yet, though. So please keep it to yourself. He'll be bloody furious.'

Logan nodded his understanding. 'Well, best of luck, whatever you decide. And, if there's anything you want to tell me about Norman… anything you want to talk about?'

Pat's hand slipped to her shoulder where the bruise was now hidden by her pyjamas. 'Honestly, there's nothing. I promise. Just an accident. Norman is many things, but he isn't violent.'

'Right. Well, I'm very glad to hear it,' Logan said. He checked his watch, groaned quietly at the time, then stood up.

'You off to bed?' Pat asked. She picked up the wine bottle again and tilted it towards the detective. 'Sure I can't twist your arm? You look like you've got plenty on your mind. Might help.'

'Trust me, it won't,' Logan said. 'But thank you for the offer.'

'Was it him?' Pat asked, the words tumbling over each other in their rush to get out. 'Kevin. Mr Tillerson. Room one. Was it him?'

She watched the detective closely, silently appraising his response. Or his lack of one. 'If there's a murderer staying in this house, I should know.'

Logan's answer, when it came, was an honest one. 'I don't know. We're following up on a few different leads, and I'm afraid I can't say much more than that at this stage.'

'He fucked her, didn't he?' Patricia spat, and the venom of it took them both by surprise. 'Had sex with her, I mean. I overheard.'

Logan skirted around the question completely. 'He said he came back here before eleven on Tuesday. Do you know if that's right?'

'I don't know,' Pat said. 'I would've been in bed. Norman didn't mention anything, though.'

'I'll ask him in the morning,' Logan said.

He started to say his goodnights, but Pat wasn't finished yet.

'Probably shouldn't blame him too much. Kevin, I mean. For… you know. She had a reputation for it. Jumping on the tourists. "Fresh meat", she called them.'

'Aye. Well. Takes two to tango, I suppose,' Logan said.

Pat's eyes became two circles of surprise, then she gave a satisfied nod and raised her glass. 'Exactly! That's what I say,' she said, then she glugged down the rest of her glass and filled it from the bottle again.

Logan took that as his cue to leave. 'Well, goodnight. I, uh, I hope it all works out.'

'Thanks,' said Pat. She raised a glass and winked. Co-ordinating both these actions required quite a lot of concentration. 'You, too.'

–

Tyler was snorting and grunting like a pig in heat by the time Logan made it up to bed, and the DCI knew immediately that there'd be no sleeping through it. Not yet, at least. Not until exhaustion came creeping over him sometime in the wee small hours.

Instead, he rummaged in the box they'd taken from Iona's house until he found the diary from nineteen-ninety.

From the year Isaac was born.

Kicking off his shoes, Logan settled himself on top of the bed, and switched on the bedside lamp.

Tyler hissed and groaned in his sleep, like a vampire getting a face full of tanning lamp.

Muttering to himself, Logan switched the light off, then got up and checked in his coat until he found the small pocket torch he carried.

That done, he settled down to read, bracing himself for what he might find out.

It was the tail end of February when Iona realised she was pregnant. The date—the twenty-third—was marked by a full page filled from top to bottom with the words, 'Oh shit,' over and over again, in handwriting that became increasingly deranged as it continued down the paper.

The twenty-fourth was more of the same.

The twenty-fifth and twenty-sixth formed a double-page spread. On these, Iona had written an elongated, upper case version of the word 'fuck', with the letter U repeated forty or fifty times. In the bottom corner, she'd drawn a picture of a pregnant woman—herself, presumably—hanged from a tree, with her tongue sticking out and crosses where her eyes should be.

The rest of the week was blank. So was most of the following month, and the month after that, too. In fact, aside from a few scribbled pictures of freakish-looking babies with two heads and frog-like legs, and some low-level bitching about her father and brother, Iona didn't write much for the entire first half of the year.

Logan skipped on to August. Like July, the majority of the pages were empty. But then, he turned a page to reveal two short lines of text.

Isaac Donovan Kerr.

Seven pounds five ounces.

And below that, more telling than anything she could've written, was a neatly-drawn love heart that took up most of the page.

It was a few weeks later—the thirteenth of September, nineteen-ninety—when Iona first wrote about her plans to kill herself.

Chapter 31

Norman handled breakfast, explaining that Pat was having 'a bit of a lie-in.' The food wasn't to the same standard as the day before, but the effort was a valiant one. What it lacked in finesse, it more than made up for in quantity.

Tillerson didn't show face in the dining room, so Logan went back upstairs and made it very clear what would happen were he to attempt to get off the island before he'd been given permission. Tillerson listened with widening eyes, and then vowed on his mother's life that he'd stay in the house until further notice.

Logan chose to believe him, and arranged for Norman to lend the guest some clothes, as the detectives were holding onto his rucksack for the moment.

All that done, Logan gave Tyler the keys to the Land Rover, tasked him with finding and talking to Dudley Brown, then set off walking to the office.

Down at his side, Iona's diaries sat nestling in an evidence bag.

Logan reached the school building at just after nine. He was passing it, fishing the office key from his pocket, when a side door opened and a young man in an offensively yellow shirt sprang out in front of him.

'Hi! Are you… are you the policeman?' he asked. He had a strong Western Isles lilt to his voice. That sing-song quality you didn't get many other places.

'One of them,' Logan said. 'Why?'

The man shot a glance back into the building behind him, then stepped out and quietly closed the door.

'Fergus. McDougal. Fergus McDougal,' he said, giving a little wave. 'I'm the teacher here. At the school.' He winced. 'Obviously at the school. Where else would I be...?'

He caught the impatient look on Logan's face and got to the point.

'The kids... they're... with the murder. They've heard stories. They're really anxious.'

'Right,' said Logan. 'That's understandable. We're doing all we can.'

'Oh, I know. God, yes. No. I wasn't saying...' Fergus picked at the skin around his fingers and danced from foot to foot. If this guy was saying the kids were anxious, Logan thought, they must be in a hell of a state. 'I just thought, maybe, since you were here...'

Fergus's features screwed up and his shoulders raised, as if he was bracing himself for a haymaker straight to the face.

'I thought you might have a word. Settle them down a bit,' the teacher suggested. 'Two minutes. That's all it'll take. I swear. Two minutes.'

Logan groaned. His gaze went a few paces ahead of him to the door of the Community Council office. It was so close.

And yet, so far.

'Two minutes,' he grunted. 'That's your lot.'

–

Eleven minutes later, Logan stood in front of a whiteboard, completely dwarfing the six children sitting cross-legged on the floor in front of him.

They were of varying sizes and ages, all seven Primaries being taught by the one teacher in the same classroom. The little ones were down the front. They'd started a few feet from where Logan stood, but had shuffled incrementally closer while he spoke, so they were now gathered around him like lepers around Christ.

A couple of older kids—nine or ten, the DCI guessed— sat at the back, playing it marginally cooler than their younger classmates.

Most of the original two minutes Logan had promised had been taken up by the teacher introducing Logan to the class, then introducing the class to Logan, then encouraging the class to introduce themselves to Logan, then—for reasons Logan wasn't entirely sure of—getting them up out of their seats to sit on the floor.

After that, Fergus announced he was 'Just quickly going to do the register', and Logan stood in impatient silence while the teacher read out the names, and the children confirmed what was already perfectly clear—that they were in the room.

Talking to children had never really been one of DCI Jack Logan's strong points. Not really.

He liked kids. In general. Some of the wee bastards he'd met over the years, he'd have gladly throttled, but broadly speaking, he had nothing against them *in theory*. Children were great *as a concept*, and while he absolutely understood the importance of putting their minds at ease, he didn't really think he was the right man for the job.

And, all things considered, he was probably right.

While listening to the register being taken, he'd decided that he wasn't going to talk down to them. He was going to accurately explain the situation, albeit in simple layman's terms, and not make any false claims. He'd be honest, but reassuring. Calm, but accurate.

The next six minutes were spent listening to the younger children crying, as Fergus tried desperately to console them.

The two minutes after that were spent reassuring each of them in turn that no, they weren't going to be murdered, and no, their mummies and daddies weren't going to be murdered, and no, nobody was coming to kill their pets.

The following minute was spent listening to them listing the types of pets they had, and their names. It was round about this point that Logan started to think it was all starting to get away from him.

'Right, so... any questions?' he asked, looking down and around at the children.

Three hands went up near the front.

'That aren't about pets,' he clarified.

Three hands went back down.

'Well, then—' Logan began, then a tentative hand at the back slowly raised. It was attached to a girl who looked to be the oldest child in the class. The other kids around her whispered in anticipation of what she was about to say. Logan pointed to her and nodded. 'Yes?'

'Was it the Tattiebogle? Did the Tattiebogle do it?'

A worried murmur rippled through the small audience.

'The...? Oh. The scarecrow? No. I can definitely say—'

'There's a Tattiebogle near my house,' announced one of the younger boys. He was a particularly dishevelled-looking specimen, with a finger jammed up one nostril. 'Mrs Bryden says it's keeping an eye on me to make sure I behave. Will it kill me?'

'No, it—'

'Will it kill his mum?' asked a girl of around the same age. This suggestion made the boy yank his finger out of his nose with an audible pop.

'It'd better not try to kill ma mum. Or ma wee granny,' he announced. 'Or it'll get... boof!'

He mimed throwing a punch, which drew excited gasps from some of the other kids.

'Do you know the Tattiebogle song?' asked the oldest girl, raising her hand but not waiting for Logan to acknowledge her.

Logan shook his head. 'Um, I don't...'

'Great idea, Doris!' the teacher exclaimed, clapping his hands with barely constrained glee.

Doris, thought Logan. *Who the fuck calls a wean 'Doris' in this day and age?*

'Why don't we all sing the Tattiebogle song that Mrs Bryden taught us? I'm sure Mr Logan would love to hear it!'

Logan cleared his throat. 'Well, I mean, I'm not sure I—'

'And a-one, and a-two, and a-one, two, three, four...' chimed Fergus, waving his hands like a conductor and completely ignoring the DCI's protests.

The kids all launched into the song at the same time. Or approximately the same time, anyway. Logan felt he should offer a smile of encouragement as he stood listening, but the best he could do was a sort of fixed grimace that made him look as if he was suffering a minor stroke.

'Tattiebogle, Tattiebogle, standing on its own,' they sang. Or more chanted, really. 'Tattiebogle, Tattiebogle, waiting all alone. Tattiebogle watches, Tattiebogle sees.'

Their voices rose for the last part, getting steadily louder until they were practically shouting the words.

'Tattiebogle, Tattiebogle, don't take me!'

'Or ma wee granny,' the nose-picker down front added quietly.

'What about your big granny?' asked another.

'Ma big granny's deid,' the boy replied.

'How's she deid?' the girl beside him chipped in. 'Did she get killed by a killer?'

The nose-picker's brow furrowed. 'I don't know,' he said. He raised his eyes to Logan's again. 'Did ma big granny get killed?'

'How the f—' Logan began, then he caught himself in the nick of time. 'I doubt it. I'm sure she...'

'Was it cancer?' one of the other children asked. 'I bet it was cancer.'

'What's cancer?' enquired another.

They all gazed at Logan, expecting him to provide the answers. He shot a sideways look at Fergus, but the teacher was looking even more expectantly at him than the kids.

'It's, uh, it's a disease that people get,' Logan said.

'Old people?' piped up a voice from near the back.

'No. Anyone,' Logan replied. 'Anyone can get it.'

There were a couple of whispers from the audience.

'Even people who're the same age as us?' a boy asked.

'Uh, aye,' Logan said, although a nagging little voice in his head was starting to ask him questions of its own. 'Aye. Anyone can get it.'

The whispers became a concerned mumbling that rippled through the class. A few bottom lips started to go.

I told you, said the voice in Logan's head. *I tried to fucking warn you.*

'I don't want to get cancer and die like Michael's big granny,' a girl with a blue ribbon announced. Then she, and another girl beside her, simultaneously burst into tears.

'I miss ma big granny!' the nose-picker wailed, as the tears began to spread like a virus, infecting everyone from the front of the class to the back.

Logan regarded the crying children in silence for a few moments, then he turned to the teacher, puffed out his cheeks, and raised both eyebrows.

'Right, then,' he announced, jabbing a thumb in the direction of the classroom door. 'I'd best be shooting off.'

–

'Um, thanks for that,' said Fergus, stepping out after Logan and shutting the door so you really had to strain to hear the anguished wailing from within. 'That was… very helpful.'

'No bother. Any time,' Logan said, safe in the knowledge that there was no bloody way he was ever being invited back. 'Sorry if it went a bit… off-course.'

'My fault. Should've reined them in a bit. They just don't get many visitors, so they get a bit excited if it's not me or Joy.'

Logan looked down at the office key he now held in his hand again. 'Joy Bryden? Does she teach here?'

'Oh. No, no. Not officially. She just comes in and works with the kids. Neighbourhood Watch-type stuff. Security, safety...'

'Creepy scarecrows,' said Logan, adding to the list.

'Haha! Yes! She was behind the Tattiebogle Trail. You might have come across it?' Fergus said, then he shook his head. 'What am I saying? Of course you have. I think she made up the song to stop the kids messing about with them. Keep them at bay, sort of thing. Worked, too. They're blinking terrified of the things!'

'Aye, well—' Logan began, shooting a very deliberate look in the direction of the office, which went unnoticed.

'Surprised Joy hasn't told you who the killer is yet,' the teacher said.

Logan's eyebrows came together above his nose. 'Sorry?'

'Oh. Sorry. I don't mean she knows! I'm just surprised she doesn't,' Fergus said, quickly clarifying. 'She always knows what's been going on around the island. She's got eyes everywhere, that woman!'

Pat's words from the night before replayed themselves in Logan's head.

'*That bitch sees bloody everything,*' he muttered.

'Sorry?' said the teacher, taken aback.

Logan shook his head. 'Oh. No. Nothing. Just... something someone said.' He swung the key around his finger on its metal loop. 'I'd best get on. Good luck with that lot.'

'Thanks! I'll need it!' Fergus said, then the sounds of sobbing rose as he opened the door. 'Oh, and good luck. Iona had her differences with... well... everyone, but she didn't deserve that.'

'No. They very rarely do,' Logan said, then the teacher slipped back into the school and the door swung closed.

Logan was at the door of the office when he stopped, the key held poised in front of the lock.

That bitch sees bloody everything.

She's got eyes everywhere, that woman.

'Webcams,' Logan whispered.

She'd said, 'Webcams.'

Plural.

It had been raining. Pouring. *Pishin' doon*.

Had been for days.

Logan turned away from the door.

'So why was she watering the bloody plants?'

Chapter 32

This was the opening to a horror movie. Tyler was sure of it.

Dudley Brown lived alone, down near the water on the Skye-facing side of the island. The Land Rover had coughed and wheezed its way along the narrow single-track road, then struggled up something that might have been a driveway, could've been a footpath, but equally might have been none of the above.

Eventually, he'd arrived at a low white building with a corrugated iron roof that was surrounded by the decaying relics of old farming equipment. Bits of old tractor lay scattered around like dinosaur bones, lengths of fishing net draped between them in a way that made the DC think of giant cobwebs.

Knowing his luck, the giant spider who'd made them would be lurking somewhere nearby.

He cut the engine on a patch of vaguely flat ground around thirty feet from the building. The place didn't look like a house, exactly. It was more like a large garage or workshop, with a set of peeling wooden doors, and half a dozen high, narrow windows clustered around near the uneven roof.

Hamza had found the address, but it was possible he'd given him the wrong one. It certainly didn't look like anyone was home, but the boss would kill him if he didn't properly check it out.

'Mr Brown?' Tyler called, preferring to draw the man out, if he could. 'Dudley Brown? I'm Detective Constable Tyler Neish. I just need to ask you a couple of questions.'

There was silence from the house. The only sounds were the gentle crashing of water on rocks, and the strangled cries of the seabirds circling somewhere overhead.

'Mr Brown?' Tyler tried again. 'Dudley? Anyone home?' He listened for several seconds, before adding, 'Yoo-hoo', as much to calm his nerves as anything else.

The windows were too high for him to reach without a stepladder and a brass neck. Even if they hadn't been, they were too caked with dirt and grime to be able to look inside.

The double-doors were each the width of two normal-sized doors, side-by-side. Presumably, they would once have allowed tractors or animals through, but they had been fastened together by long straps of wood that were nailed across where they met in the middle.

It took another half a minute of exploring before Tyler discovered the other door tucked around the back of the building, on the water side. There was a wooden box fixed to the wall beside it with a hinged lid. The words 'Dudley Broon' had been painted on the top in white.

It was the right place, then. Tyler didn't know whether he should be happy about that or not. Had it belonged to someone else, he could've turned around and blamed Hamza for the mix-up.

As it was, though, he had no choice but to persevere. His arse would be out the window if he came back empty-handed again.

Tyler knocked on the door. 'Hello? Mr Brown? Police. We'd like a word.'

He gave it a minute.

Nothing.

'Oh, bloody hell,' he muttered, looking along the building in both directions.

This side was in an even worse state than the front, exposure to the wind and rain coming in off the water having taken more of a toll.

Tyler knocked again and gave the same spiel. Then, when he received no reply, he tried the door handle.

He'd have quite liked it to have been locked, if he was completely honest. He had no reason to kick it in, and no warrant permitting him to do so.

But an unlocked door? It wasn't exactly an invitation, but it wasn't a refusal, either.

What would the boss do? he wondered.

He didn't have to wonder for long. There was no doubt what Logan would do, were he here. No doubt, at all.

And so, with the waves crashing at his back, and the wind nudging him on, Tyler opened the door to the darkened building, and stepped inside.

—

Logan rummaged around in the hanging basket, pushing aside the plants and buckling their thin branches. It hadn't rained in hours, but the compost, or soil, or whatever the container was filled with, was still absolutely sodden. There would've been no reason for Joy to be watering it during the height of the storm, but Logan found nothing that might explain what else she could have been doing.

Plant food of some kind? That was a thing, wasn't it?

He'd have said she was just being a prying bastard and using watering the plants as an excuse to check out the new arrivals, but she'd been at it when they'd pulled up in the Land Rover. So, unless she was both nosy *and* psychic, that didn't explain it, either.

'Everything all right?'

Logan looked up and found himself face to face with Isaac Young.

Iona's son.

Isaac stood on the pavement right outside the pub, a small bundle of parcels all stacked up in a cardboard box that he was carrying on both forearms, and a quizzical look on his face.

'Lost something?'

Logan removed his hands from the basket, saw they were covered in wet muck, and quickly brushed it off.

'Eh, no. No, just... the baskets. Community Council, aye?'

'That's right,' Isaac said.

Logan nodded for a long time. Too long. 'Right. Right. Aye,' he said. 'And they're all over the island?'

'Just on the street here. Couple down at the dock. Why?'

'Nothing. Just interested, that's all,' Logan said. He gestured to the pub behind the other man. 'Listen, Isaac...' he began, but he couldn't find the end of the sentence.

'Listen to what?' Isaac asked.

'Have you got a few minutes?' Logan said. 'We could grab a coffee. There's something... it'd be good to talk to you.'

'I've told you what I know,' Isaac said, becoming defensive.

'No, I know. I know, it's not about... well, I mean, it *is* about...' He tutted, annoyed at himself, then pulled himself back together. 'Doesn't have to be now. But I think you and me should sit down for a chat once everything's settled down.'

Isaac's confusion was clearly written all over his face. He looked from the DCI's dirty hands to the hanging basket, then shrugged.

'Aye. Sure. Once it's all settled down,' he said. 'But for now, I need to go get this stuff posted off.'

'Of course. We'll talk soon,' Logan said.

From the corner of his eye, he watched Isaac continue along the street, then vanish inside the shop.

Then, he turned, scanned the street until he spotted the next hanging basket, and set off to investigate.

The second basket was closer to the school than the first, which was almost slap-bang level with the pub's front window. Like that one, this basket hung from a limb attached to a streetlight.

Unlike that one, there was something odd about it. On the inside wall of the plant pot there was a circle of sticky residue, roughly the size of a five pence piece. It was part of a foam pad—the kind of thing used to hang pictures when the landlord won't allow holes in his wall, or if you can't be arsed digging out a hammer.

Something had been stuck to the inside of the basket, pointed in the direction of the school window.

Backtracking down the street, Logan returned to the first hanging basket, and carefully checked around the inside of the plant pot contained within it.

It took him three runs around the pot before he felt a slightly raised circular outline. He tapped a finger on it. It wasn't particularly sticky, but there was a slight suggestion of tackiness there on the third and fourth tap.

There had been something in both baskets. Something stuck in place, which had now been removed. One facing the school window, the other pointing directly at the front of the pub

'Well, now,' Logan remarked. Then, he turned in the direction of the dock, shoved his hands in his pockets, and trudged down the hill.

–

The oval of light from Tyler's phone torch projected misshapen shadows onto the bare stone walls of the… what? It wasn't a house. It couldn't be. Surely, nobody lived here?

Workshop, then? Barn? Some sort of storage facility for old machine parts and long-past-its-best animal feed?

Whatever the place was, it reeked of mould and motor oil, and the scattering of straw strewn across the floor was home to lots of scurrying shapes that rustled around beyond the edges of the torchlight.

A face appeared from nowhere in the torch's beam. Its eyes were empty hollows, its mouth a twisted leer, and Tyler came dangerously close to soiling himself when he clapped eyes on it.

He gave the face a poke. Dried grass or straw rustled inside the hessian sack of the scarecrow's head. The whole thing teetered then, with a creak and a clack, the wooden frame supporting the figure hit the stone floor.

"'*Go talk to Dudley Brown, Tyler*",' he muttered, sweeping the light across a row of ancient metal shelving stacked with old paint cans and glass jars full of mysterious liquids. "'*See what you can find out*".'

He jumped and ejected a noise he was grateful nobody else was around to hear when he caught his reflection in a cracked mirror that stood propped against a wall.

'I found out I don't like creepy fucking buildings,' he grumbled. 'Does that count, I wonder?'

Tyler pressed on through the creepy fucking building as, behind him, a shape detached itself from the shadows.

–

Logan was poking around in the dockside hanging baskets when he heard the buzzing of an outboard motor that signalled an approaching boat.

He couldn't see the boat at first, and the open water made it difficult to pinpoint which direction the sound was coming from. He figured it out just as the prow of a manky old dinghy appeared around the curve of the island.

It was barely ten feet long, and dipped and rolled on the water, apparently at the full mercy of the waves cresting beneath it. It was made of rubber, dirty and scuffed, and its outboard motor stuttered and spluttered, and occasionally belched out balls of oily black smoke.

It was being steered by a man who, at this distance, appeared to be a hundred years old. He had a long grey beard that blew out behind him in the wind, and sat hunched over at the back of the boat. Up front, a uniformed officer clung to a narrow bench with both hands and, it seemed, tried not to throw up.

Logan finished checking the hanging baskets. By the time he'd determined that one of them had the same circle of sticky residue as the two up the hill, the boat was coughing and wheezing the last few feet to the dock.

'Well, Constable, you sure know how to travel in style,' the DCI remarked, turning to the new arrivals.

PC Sinead Bell—who was looking substantially greener than she had the last time Logan had seen her—attempted a shaky smile.

'It was this or swim, sir,' she said. The boat bumped to a violent stop against the dock, almost throwing her off the bench. She swore below her breath. 'On reflection, I might've made the wrong choice.'

Chapter 33

Tyler didn't know what hit him, only that it hit him hard, and fast, and came out of nowhere.

It was a shove, he thought. Or a shoulder. The impact sent the world into a sudden spinning lurch. He hit the shelves, grabbed for them, but his weight and momentum toppled them like dominoes.

His phone went bouncing across the hard floor—*crick-crack-clack*—the torchlight swinging wildly, sending shadows scurrying like spiders up the walls.

And then, darkness, as the torch went out, leaving only the faint light from the grime-encrusted windows to pick faint, silvery lines from the shadows.

Tyler twisted on the wreckage of the shelves, trying to get up, find his feet, get moving. A punch hit him like a sledgehammer, slamming him back down, and his mouth was filled with spit and copper.

A foot connected with his chest, hard and heavy, a battering ram with a rubber sole. The air left him in one sudden gasp. His lungs tightened, refusing to refill. Refusing to breathe. Refusing to respond.

He kicked out, weakly, pathetically, his foot skiffing the side of his attacker's leg. Doing nothing.

'S-stop,' he managed to wheeze, but then two hands were on his throat. Tightening. *Tightening*. Grip too strong. Wrists too thick.

His attacker's face swam in the dim light, his features blurred by blood and tears as, from all corners of Tyler's vision, a checkerboard of darkness came creeping in.

–

Once Sinead had clambered out of the boat and onto dry land—an undignified, shambolic process which had twice almost ended in soggy disaster—Logan had given the old fella in the boat a very clear, very concise set of instructions. These had started with 'Right, then' and finished with 'fuck off.'

The last thing he needed was a boat hanging around the place. Particularly with Bruce Anderson still on the loose somewhere. Nobody was getting off the island until Logan said so, which meant anything that could conceivably be used as a means of anyone doing so wasn't welcome.

They'd waited until the boat had chugged its way back around the headland, then set off up the hill towards the main street.

'Rough crossing?' Logan asked. Sinead's colour was marginally better, but she still had a wee touch of the living dead about her. She had a slight stagger, too, like she'd just got the hang of being on the water and was now finding it difficult to adjust to being back on dry land.

'You could say that, sir,' she replied. 'Still, at least the company was good.'

'Aye?' said Logan, stopping outside the front door of the pub.

'Not really. Crotchety old bugger didn't say two words the whole time.' She watched as Logan knocked on the pub's closed door. 'Bit early in the day for this, isn't it?'

'Hmm? Oh, aye. No. Just want to ask the landlord something,' Logan said. He glanced back at her. 'So, whose idea was it?'

'Whose idea was what?' Sinead asked.

'To send you? Yours or Ben's?'

Sinead smiled. 'Bit of both.'

'Aye, well. If I'm only getting one, might as well make it a good one,' he remarked, before knocking on the door again.

'Thanks, sir. Oh, and DI Forde asked me to tell you—'

'To phone Hoon. Aye, I'll get round to it,' Logan said. He stepped back, cupped his hands around his mouth, and shouted at the upstairs window. 'Mr MacKay? Roddy? It's DCI Logan. I need a quick word.'

A curtain twitched at the window. There was a creak as the window was opened. 'Sorry. Sorry, be right down,' Roddy said, and then the window closed over with a *thunk*.

'Nice place,' Sinead observed, looking around them.

'Has its moments, aye,' Logan said.

'Is that the school? It's tiny.'

'I was in there this morning, actually,' Logan said. 'Teacher asked me to have a word with the kids. Help set their minds at rest, sort of thing.'

'Oh. How did that go?'

Logan puffed out his cheeks. 'Well, they were all greeting their eyes out when I left, so it probably could've gone better.'

Sinead gave a chuckle. 'I'd have liked to have seen that,' she said. She skirted around the edges of the next question, before coming out with it. 'Tyler around?'

'That useless gobshite?' Logan grunted. 'He's following up on a lead. Should be back soon.'

There was the clunk of a bolt lock sliding across on the other side of the door, and it opened to reveal Roddy standing in a dressing-gown. His gaze flitted from Logan to Sinead and back again several times, getting more and more concerned each time.

'Hello. Um, hi. Morning,' he said, his throat dry. 'Is there... is everything all right?'

'Morning, Mr MacKay,' Logan said. 'This is my colleague, PC Sinead Bell.'

'Hi,' said Sinead, offering a brief wave.

'Hello,' Roddy said, managing a sort of half-smile. His eyes darted back to Logan. 'Was there...? Is there some sort of problem?'

Logan looked back over his shoulder at the closest hanging basket, then faced the pub landlord again. 'I think it'd be best if we discussed it inside.'

–

Tyler's brain screamed at him. His lungs burned, begging for air. His feet kicked out, but the weight of his attacker had him pinned in the wreckage of the shelving, the hands constricting around his throat like a boa constrictor.

He swung a punch. Again. Again. Each one made contact, but may as well not have for all the good they did. The hands kept squeezing. The weight kept pressing. The eyes of his attacker blazed down, and a thought slammed into Tyler harder than any shoulder, harder than any punch.

This was it. This. Now. This was the last sight he would ever see. Those eyes. These hands. This bastard.

Bollocks to that.

He grasped around him. His fingers found the handle of a paint pot. He swung it, and there was a satisfyingly solid thunk as it whanged off the skull of the man pinning him down.

His attacker sprawled sideways. Air—sweet, precious air— flooded Tyler's lungs. He coughed it back out in three big choking gulps, then kicked himself free of the shelves, the paint pot swinging for another direct hit.

'Ah! Ah!' squealed his attacker. 'Stop! Help! Murderer! Police! *Police!*'

'What the...? What are you...?' Tyler wheezed, the paint pot raised and ready to swing again. 'I am the fucking police!'

Down on the floor, his attacker cowered behind his raised hands. 'What?' he asked, after a moment's pause.

'I am the police!' Tyler repeated. He snatched up his phone and tapped at the cracked screen. The torchlight returned, drawing a hiss from the man on the floor.

Tyler recognised him as the giant they'd seen at the church the day before. The man he'd come looking for.

Dudley Brown's eyes were wide with shock and horror. His hulking great hands, which were raised in front of his face for protection, trembled as he lowered them. A trickle of blood ran from his hairline and was in the process of filling up an ear.

'You're the police?' he whimpered.

'Aye! And you, sunshine...' Tyler spat a wad of blood onto the floor between them. '...are bloody nicked.'

–

The flat above the pub was relatively spacious compared to most of the other living accommodation Logan had seen on the island. Roddy had led them up the stairs, through a good-sized, if sparsely-furnished living room, and into a kitchen–diner with a small circular table at one end, and a draining board teetering with dishes at the other.

They'd been offered a cup of tea. Logan had initially declined, but Sinead was quick to accept, so he decided he might as well join her.

He waited until the kettle had boiled and the mugs were placed down on the table, before throwing Roddy for a loop.

'I think you've lied to me, Mr MacKay.'

Roddy stood, his mug clutched in one hand, his face tight with worry.

'What? What do you mean? Lied? About what?'

Logan took a sip of his tea before replying. 'Tell me about the cameras.'

Roddy tried to sound like he didn't know what the detective was talking about. It was an admirable effort, but the rising inflection and the shake of the mug in his hand gave him away.

'Cameras? What... what cameras?'

Logan held his gaze over the rim of his mug.

'I don't... What cameras?' Roddy asked. He was practically sweating already. This wouldn't take long.

Logan took another sip of his tea. He smacked his lips together. He very slowly and deliberately set the mug on a coaster on the table.

'You know what cameras I mean, Roddy,' the DCI said. 'You're going to tell me sooner or later. Save us all a lot of bother and make it sooner, eh?'

Roddy's legs wobbled, and he flopped down into the chair across from Logan, sloshing tea up over his hand.

'She... she used to borrow them sometimes. Couple of cameras and a tripod. Microphone. One of my laptops. Basically, the set-up we used for her music videos.'

Logan frowned briefly, but chased it away before the other man could spot it.

'Go on,' he urged.

Beside him, without a word, Sinead took out her notebook and began to write.

'I don't... I don't know much more. She asked me to show them how they worked, how to transfer the footage to my laptop, and always brought the kit back next day.'

'Sorry,' said Sinead, looking up from her pad. 'Is this Iona we're talking about?'

Logan let Roddy do the confirming. 'Aye. That's right.'

Sinead smiled appreciatively and went back to writing.

'What was she doing with it?' Logan asked.

'She didn't tell me. But... I mean, it's not exactly a big leap of the imagination.' He shot a slightly embarrassed look in Sinead's direction and dropped his voice to a whisper. 'Sex stuff.'

'She was making pornography?' Logan asked.

Roddy recoiled at the word. 'Yes. I mean... yes. I think so. I didn't... I didn't *see* any of it, obviously. But there were a lot of... people talk, you know?'

'They do,' Logan agreed. 'Doesn't mean it's true, of course. Did she ever tell you that's what she was doing?'

'No, never.'

'And you never saw it for yourself?'

'No. I never saw it.'

'Did you know what she was doing with it? Was she uploading it somewhere? Storing it?'

'I don't know.'

'So, if you've never seen it, and you don't know what she was doing with it—' Logan began, before Roddy jumped in and cut him off.

'But I know Iona. Or… knew her. And, while I don't want to believe that's what she was doing, while I don't want to believe she was selling herself for money, or selling videos of herself doing things with men, or whatever it was she was doing… I do. I do believe it. What else could it have been? And she'd say things.'

'What sort of things?' Logan asked.

'Not… nothing specific. Little things. Or little looks she'd give when I asked what she was doing. "Nothing for you to worry about," she'd said. "Nothing you'd be interested in". But it was the way she said it.' Roddy shook his head. 'It's hard to explain.'

Logan nodded slowly. He took another drink of his tea, then smacked his lips together before continuing. 'How many laptops do you have, Mr MacKay?'

Roddy tried very hard not to let the impact of the question register on his face. He searched for a response, his tongue flicking across his lips, which were suddenly sandpaper dry.

'Sorry?' was the best he was able to come up with.

'You said she used to borrow one of your laptops. I took one away. How many others are there?'

Sinead's pencil stopped scratching on the pad. She joined the DCI in staring expectantly at the man sitting across from them.

'Um, two. My main one—that's the one you have—and a, and a backup. Which I'd loan Iona.' He cracked a smile, trying to lighten the moment. 'Wasn't that I didn't trust her with the main one, or anything, it was just… better safe than sorry.'

'Very wise,' Logan said. 'Is the other one here in the flat?'

Roddy's gaze flicked momentarily to the door leading into the living room. 'Uh…'

'Is it through there?' Logan asked. 'Mind if we have a look?'

'The, uh… I mean… No,' Roddy said. He shook his head. Or maybe it was shaking all on its own. 'Help yourself. I don't mind. I just…'

'Just what?' Logan asked.

Roddy swallowed. 'Nothing. It's in the bedroom, actually.' He began to stand. 'I'll go get it.'

'You're fine,' Logan said, stopping him with a raise of his hand. 'Constable Bell will go get it and take a look.'

Sinead pushed her chair back and stood. Logan kept his gaze fixed on the squirming Roddy Mac.

The DCI's eyes shone, like a cat that had found a mouse to play with. 'You and me can carry on our little chat.'

Chapter 34

Dudley Brown perched on a rickety wooden stool in the now brightly lit workshop, his hands fastened behind his back by a set of plastic zip-tie restraints, his eyes practically bulging out of their sockets in distress.

After securing the big bastard, Tyler had gone in search of something to clean himself up with, and had settled on a big stack of supermarket-brand toilet paper piled up at the back of a walk-in store cupboard.

He stood before Dudley now, dabbing gingerly at his bloodied face while trying to look suitably like he was in charge. The stool the other man was sitting on wasn't very big, but even seated, Dudley had a couple of inches height advantage over the DC.

'Right, then,' Tyler began. The vibrations of his voice made his nose ache sharply. 'Mind telling me what the bloody hell all that was about?'

'I thought you were the murderer,' Roddy said.

The direct simplicity of the answer, and the wide-eyed innocent way in which it was delivered told the detective to go easy. Duty of care, and all that. Although, he had to admit, he wasn't sure how that extended to his whanging the bastard with a paint pot.

'You broke in. I thought you were going to kill me like you killed Iona.'

'OK, first of all, I didn't kill Iona,' Tyler said. 'Like I said, I'm with the police. Detective Constable Neish.'

Dudley's brow furrowed, like he was struggling to store all these new details.

'You can call me Tyler.'

'Tyler,' said Dudley. He said it tentatively, like he was checking it for traps.

'That's right. And I didn't kill Iona. Also, I didn't break in. The door was unlocked.'

'Door's always unlocked,' Dudley said. 'That's the good thing about living out here. Everyone knows everyone. It's very friendly. You can leave your door open.'

The way he said it suggested he'd learned the sentences by rote. Tyler smiled and nodded, trying to further reassure the man that he wasn't the enemy.

'Aye. It's nice. Although, I'm not sure "very friendly" is how I'd describe the welcome I got.'

Dudley blushed and looked down at the floor. 'I thought you were—'

'The murderer. Aye. You mentioned,' Tyler said. He stepped in a little closer and indicated the red staining down the side of Dudley's face. 'How's the head?'

'Bit sore.'

'We'll get it looked at,' Tyler told him.

'Thank you. And we'll get you looked at, too,' Dudley said.

His smile was open and child-like. Tyler didn't reckon it was any sort of calculated attempt to get him on-side, but it had that effect.

'Some right hook you've got,' he said.

'Thank you very much,' Dudley said.

There was no point questioning him here. None of it would stand up. He'd need a support worker with him at the very least.

There was one thing Tyler had to know, though. He gestured to the scarecrow he'd knocked over earlier. When he'd found the switch and the lights had come up, three more of the things had been revealed propped against the far wall.

'What's with all the scarecrows?'

Dudley, who had been looking increasingly relaxed over the past couple of minutes, suddenly tensed again. His eyes widened. His mouth dropped open. There was a gasp as he sucked in a mouthful of air.

'Oh. No. I forgot!'

'Forgot what?' Tyler asked.

'No comment.'

Tyler blinked. 'Eh?'

'I'm supposed to say that. No comment.'

'Why are you supposed to say that? Who says?'

'Joy says. She said…' Dudley's face crumpled. He let out a low groan. 'No comment.'

'Joy? Joy Bryden?' Tyler asked.

'No comment.'

'From the Community Council?'

'No comment.'

Tyler approached the prisoner and flashed his most charming smile. Although, it had to be said, the swollen nose and the mask of dried blood that covered half his face took some of the appeal out of it.

'Dudley. Mate. I'm trying to help you here,' Tyler said. 'Why did Joy tell you not to talk to us? What is it she wants you to keep quiet about?'

Dudley shifted on his stool. His eyes darted in all directions, searching for somewhere to settle. His bottom lip grew fatter, like he was holding back tears.

'No comment,' he said in a whisper. 'No comment, no comment, no comment.'

'OK. OK,' Tyler said, keeping his voice measured and calm. Those restraints were tough, but they weren't unbreakable. The last thing he needed was for Dudley to Hulk-out on him and break free. Next time, he might not be able to reach the paint pot. 'Just you… just you sit there, all right?'

'No comment,' Dudley said.

'Aye, that wasn't really a question. You don't have to no comment that.'

'No comment.'

'Right. Fair enough,' Tyler sighed.

He turned his back on Dudley, decided that this might not be the best idea, and half-turned back. It had been the mention of the scarecrow that had turned him uncooperative, so Tyler sidled over to the one he'd knocked over and squatted next to it.

In the stark glow of the overhead lights, it wasn't nearly as terrifying as it had looked in the beam of the phone's torch. It just looked a bit... naff, in fact. A canvas bag packed with dried grass and sawdust, fastened to a skeleton made from a simple wooden cross.

It was dressed in a mishmash of old clothes—checked shirt, denim dungarees, and two boots that weren't even remotely similar, much less from the same pair.

The dungarees had a patch on one knee, and a few other holes had been repaired by some clumsy stitching.

There was a square pocket in the front of the denims, roughly the size of a cigarette packet. It bulged like there was something inside. Tyler started to reach for it, then stopped himself, found a pair of rubber gloves in his pocket, and tried again.

At first, he found himself fumbling with the pocket's shiny round button. It was only when he couldn't get it to unfasten, that he discovered it wasn't a button at all.

'Well now, Dudley,' Tyler said. He whistled through his teeth. 'What do we have here?'

–

PC Bell sat in Roddy MacKay's living room, tapping away at the laptop's keyboard. It was a clunky old thing, that whirred and chugged after every click and keystroke, and she was rapidly losing patience with it.

There was no email account set up on the machine, from what she could gather. No passwords stored in the browser. Nothing incriminating on the desktop, or any of the obvious folders. Nothing much of anything, really, incriminating or otherwise. It was all a bit of a blank canvas.

The only thing of obvious note was the desktop wallpaper, which showed Roddy with a woman in her forties. From the looks of her, she'd had her hair done nicely, but maybe thirty-six to forty-eight hours before, and she'd done very little with it since. Her burgundy lipstick was slightly smeared, and there was something about the leering grin on her face that suggested she wouldn't pass a breathalyser test.

The woman had her arm wrapped around Roddy's neck, pulling him in close to her chest. He was smiling. It was one of genuine warmth. Genuine happiness.

Sinead recognised Iona from the photo Hamza had shown her while she'd been reviewing the case back at base the previous night. She'd looked dour and trashy in that picture. She was still looking trashy in this picture, but there was a joyfulness about the desktop image that had been missing from the other one.

Sinead double-tapped the trackpad to open another folder. At first, the laptop audibly baulked at the idea, and the cursor arrow became a little spinning egg-timer. But then, with a real sense of begrudgement, the folder expanded to fill the whole screen.

Twenty or more other folders were revealed, all laid out in rows.

Sinead sighed. 'Balls to this,' she muttered, then she clicked the magnifying glass icon in the bottom left corner of the screen and began to type.

–

'What about the other cameras?' Logan asked, setting his mug down on the coaster again.

'Other cameras? What… I don't… What other cameras? I don't have any.'

'In the plant pots,' Logan said. 'I'm assuming Joy Bryden asked for your help to install them?'

'Plant pots?' Roddy parroted, and there was a real look of bewilderment on his face. 'What…?'

'Aye. You know. The cameras hidden in the hanging baskets. Keeping watch. Poking their noses in. You helped set those up, didn't you?'

'No!' Roddy protested. 'I didn't… I mean, *what*? Since when? She had cameras in the *hanging baskets*? I knew nothing about it. Let me see.'

'They're no longer there,' Logan said. 'But they were.'

'Well… how do you know?'

'I've a nose for that sort of thing,' Logan said, giving it a tap to emphasise the point. 'I think she removed them soon after we got here, so we didn't find them. But they were there, all right. Watching everything. Everyone. How did it make you feel, by the way?'

Roddy blinked. 'The cameras? I don't—'

'Iona. Doing those things. Other men,' Logan said. He paused momentarily. 'Not you.'

'What? No. She wasn't… she and I, we never…'

'I know. You said. And I believe you, Roddy. I do. You were friends. Just friends,' Logan said. 'But, I mean, come on. You must've thought of it, surely? Bachelor like yourself, all alone here. And her. No' bad for her age. You were close, too. It must've gone through your head once or twice. You must've thought about it.'

'I… no. No, that's not fair,' Roddy protested. 'We were… she was my friend. That was all.'

'You weren't jealous, then?' Logan asked. 'Of the other men? It didn't make you upset? Angry?'

'No!' Roddy yelped. A vein throbbed on the side of his forehead, getting more pronounced with every word he said. 'I mean... honestly? Did I like it? No. Because she was better than that. I hated that she felt the need to do it. To have that... that contact. With strangers. With people whose names she barely knew. Did it make me upset? Yes! Because she was worth more than everyone thought she was. More than *she* thought.'

He had been leaning further and further forward across the table during his speech, and now slowly sat back again, wringing his hands together in his lap.

'Come on, Roddy,' Logan said, eyeing the man across the table. One corner of his mouth pulled up into a boorish smirk. He winked. 'Don't tell me you never thought about it. You and her. Not once? Don't tell me the thought of her choosing to do those things with strangers—choose them over you, her friend—didn't get you riled up.'

The kitchen door opened before Roddy could reply.

'Uh, sir?' said Sinead. Her eyes went from Logan to Roddy. The pub landlord swallowed and shrunk further in his seat. 'There's something you really need to see.'

–

Logan sat on the couch, the laptop open in front of him, two naked bodies writhing and heaving on the screen. The sound had been on when Logan had first hit the play button, but the grunting and squealing and the *slap-slap-slap* of flesh on flesh had quickly led to him turning it down.

He looked over at Sinead, who stood in front of the kitchen door. She'd pulled it mostly all the way closed, but left it ajar just enough that she could listen out for Roddy doing anything stupid, like trying to climb out of the window, or slit his wrists with a bread knife.

'And there's a few of these?' Logan asked as, on-screen, arms and legs and assorted other body parts entangled.

'About a dozen, sir,' Sinead said. 'Maybe more. Obviously, I didn't sit and watch through them all.'

'No,' Logan grunted. 'You'd want to get settled in with popcorn for that, I suppose. And they're all the same?'

'Broadly similar, sir, aye,' Sinead confirmed. 'I mean, not always the same people, but you get the gist. There are photos, too. Pretty, eh, full-on. I can show you, if you like?'

'Tempting as you make that sound, Constable, I'll take your word for it,' Logan said.

He craned his neck so his head was sideways, his forehead furrowed into deep troughs of confusion. 'The hell's he planning to put...?' he wondered, then his eyes widened. 'Jesus. He's flexible. I'll give him that.'

Standing, Logan picked up the laptop and, with the video still playing, took it through to the kitchen. He plonked it on the table in front of Roddy, who was shaking from head to toe now, purposefully facing away from the screen.

'So then, Mr MacKay,' the DCI urged. 'You mind telling me what all this is about?'

Chapter 35

'Your car smells horrible,' complained the voice from the back seat.

'I told you, it's not my car,' Tyler said, chugging the Land Rover up the last hundred yards of the narrow dirt track, and onto a road that could, at best, be described as marginally less awful.

The surface of this one had been tarmacked at some point, but was so pockmarked with potholes it looked like it had recently come under heavy military assault.

They were halfway back to the main street area now. A couple of minutes of driving. That was all. Then, Tyler would take his prisoner into the office, and Logan could figure out what the hell to do about him.

A couple of minutes. That was all. A couple of minutes, and this was no longer his problem. Or not exclusively his problem, at least.

'I feel sick,' Dudley said.

'We're nearly there. We'll be stopping in a minute. You'll be fine,' Tyler told him.

'What if I'm sick?'

'Jesus. You won't be. We're nearly there,' Tyler said.

Dudley went quiet.

It was nice while it lasted.

'My hands are sore from sitting on them.'

Tyler sighed and looked at the man reflected in the rear-view mirror. 'Well, don't sit on them, then. Angle yourself sideways a bit.'

'Then my seatbelt might not work,' Dudley pointed out.

'Your seatbelt will still work.'

'It might not, though.'

Tyler's fingers tightened on the wheel, as he steered the Land Rover towards a tight, right-hand bend in the road.

'It will. And besides, we're in the middle of nowhere. It's not like we're going to crash, is it?'

'Look out!'

Tyler swore and swerved as the Land Rover rounded the bend to reveal a man crossing the road directly ahead of them. The brakes screeched. The suspension clunked. The tyres churned up a spray of loose chippings and gravel, which rattled around the inside of the wheel arch.

The vehicle thumped to a stop in a pot-hole just a few feet from the man outside.

The man carrying a rucksack on his back, a six-pack of toilet rolls under one arm, and a four-pack of beer in his hand.

The man with the blond hair and the surfer's tan.

Tyler stared at Bruce Anderson, who stood frozen like a rabbit in headlights.

Bruce Anderson stared back.

'Fuck me,' Tyler muttered. He unclipped his belt. He opened his door.

And with that, Bruce Anderson ran.

—

'What do you want me to say?' Roddy asked, the words coming out as a series of hoarse, throaty sobs. He looked from the detective to the uniformed constable and back again. 'What…? I don't know what you want me to say.'

Logan sat down across from the landlord. He tapped the pause button on the video currently playing on the laptop. On-screen, two glistening naked men froze, mid-thrust.

'So, I suppose that explains why you and Iona never got together,' Logan said.

Roddy blushed and looked down at his squirming hands. His shoulders were hunched over, his breathing was shaky, and he looked to be one wrong word away from a full-scale breakdown.

'You could've just told us, you know? It would've saved a lot of pointed fingers.'

'*Told you?*' Roddy asked, practically spitting the words out. His head snapped up, his eyes blazing with emotion. 'How could I have told you? What if it got out? What if everyone knew? Hmm? What then?'

'Would that be so bad?' Sinead asked.

Roddy snorted. 'Yes! Yes, of course! Maybe anything goes where you're from.'

'I'm from Fort William,' Sinead said. 'It's no' exactly Las Vegas.'

'But it's still better than here, I bet. Now. With this lot,' Roddy said, sweeping an arm in the direction of the window. 'I might as well tell them I'm a kiddie-fiddler.'

Panic flashed across his face. 'Which I'm not, by the way! It was… I was just making a point.'

'I know, Roddy. And I understand your concern. But I can assure you, nothing you tell us gets into the public domain. We're good at confidentiality. If you don't want anyone to find out…'

'Of course I don't!'

'…then they won't. Not from us. I give you my word on that,' Logan told him.

He caught Sinead's eye, then indicated Roddy's empty mug. Sinead nodded and clicked the kettle on.

'How long have you known?' Logan asked.

Roddy puffed out his cheeks. 'Forever. I've always known.'

'And Iona?' Logan asked. 'Did she know?'

The response took several seconds to come. When it did, it was in the form of a slow, weary nod. 'She did. Yes,' he admitted. 'I didn't… I didn't tell her. I didn't have to. She just knew somehow.'

'Did she maybe find all the videos of lads shagging each other on your laptop?' Logan asked.

For a moment, Roddy just stared back at him in horror, then he laughed. It wasn't big, or boisterous, or even particularly audible, but it was a laugh, all the same.

'I suppose it might've been that, right enough,' he admitted.

'Kind of gives the game away,' Logan agreed, and both men shared a thin smile.

'You really won't tell anyone?' Roddy asked.

Logan sniffed, looked up at the ceiling as if thinking it through, then shook his head. 'No. No, we won't tell anyone,' he said.

Sinead set a mug of coffee down in front of Roddy, and Logan took that as his cue to stand up.

'But I think you should,' the DCI said.

Roddy shook his head. 'People will… react.'

'Fuck them. Let them react,' Logan said. He pushed the chair in under the table and leaned on the back of it. 'I… we, PC Bell and I, we had a colleague. A friend. She was… something else. Miserable cow, most of the time, but she found someone. A partner. Female. And she was happy. It was a strange bloody sight, actually, but she was happy.'

Roddy reached for his coffee. 'That's… I'm very happy for her. But, again, though, she doesn't live here.'

'Doesn't live anywhere,' Logan said, his fingers flexing on the back of the chair. 'She died. In the line of duty. Came out of nowhere. Nothing anyone could've done.'

The muscles on his jaw tensed as he clenched his teeth, crushing the croak he could feel building at the back of his throat.

'And between you, us, and these four walls, Roddy, some nights I lie awake and I think… why didn't she find it sooner? Happiness, I mean. Why then? Why not years before? Decades before? Why just a few days before she…?'

Logan glanced down, just for a moment, composing himself.

'How is that in any way fair?' he asked.

He straightened, smoothed down his coat, then stuck his hands in the pockets. 'I'm not going to pretend to talk for her. For Caitlyn. She'd be able to say it all much better than I can.'

'She could do most things better than you can, sir, to be fair,' Sinead chipped in.

Logan didn't look at PC Bell, but he pointed in her direction. 'She's no' wrong,' he admitted. 'So I won't be able to do it justice, but if she was here, I think she'd be telling you to get your bloody finger out, Mr MacKay. None of us know how long we've got left on this side of the ground.'

He patted the seated man's shoulder. 'So what the bloody hell are you waiting for?'

–

'I feel sick! I feel sick!'

Tyler hissed through his teeth as the Land Rover's shock absorbers failed once again to absorb any of the shock that jolted up his arse and along the length of his spine.

'Jesus fucking Christ, Dudley, will you shut up?!' he bellowed, thundering the rust bucket across a series of bone-rattling dips and bumps. 'Just hold on!'

'I can't hold on! You've tied me up!' Dudley protested.

Tyler groaned. 'Aye. Fair point, right enough,' he conceded, then he jammed a foot to the floor and powered the Land Rover up an incline towards the peak that Bruce Anderson had just disappeared over.

The dashboard was a bonanza of warning lights. Some flickered. Others flashed. Most just stayed on. At last glance, he reckoned he needed another three for a full house. At the rate the terrain was slamming into the vehicle's underside, it was only a matter of time until…

'Bingo,' Tyler cried, as the Land Rover crested the hill to find Bruce Anderson stumbling off-balance down the other side. 'I've got you now, you bastard!'

From the back-seat came a loud 'hurp' as Dudley vomited. It came blasting from his mouth with not an unsurprising amount of force, given the size of him, splattered against the headrest in front, then cascaded down the back of Tyler's neck.

'What the fuck?!' the DC yelped, shoving his shoulders up to his ears in an attempt to stop the warm vomity sludge from oozing all the way down his back.

Dudley puked again. Tyler threw himself forward in the chair as the hot spray hit him for a second time.

'Jesus Christ! Stop it!'

'I told you!' Dudley sobbed. 'I told you I felt sick!'

Outside, Bruce Anderson hung a right across the wide-open wilderness, trying to dodge the pursuing four-by-four. Gagging at the stench of Dudley's spew, which was currently plastered all down his back, Tyler wrenched the wheel to the right and gunned the accelerator.

The Land Rover shot forward like a sprinter off the blocks.

There was a thud.

There was a scream.

And Bruce Anderson vanished, out of sight, beneath the front of the vehicle.

Chapter 36

Tyler slammed down on the brakes, but a gulley stopped the vehicle first, the front bumper smashing against the side and shearing off several centimetres of soil.

Driver and passenger were both flung forward. Dudley chose that moment—or perhaps the moment chose him—to empty the rest of his stomach contents in a predominantly forward direction, fully dousing the detective in front.

On the dashboard, the final few lights illuminated, like Tyler had just struck the jackpot.

Behind Tyler, Dudley gave a little groan. 'Oh. That feels a bit better,' he mumbled.

'Speak for yourself!' Tyler hissed, before ejecting a sentence made up entirely of swear words.

Gagging, dripping, and ever-so-slightly steaming, he hooked the door handle with a pinkie finger, prised it open, and almost fell out onto the hillside.

He waddled around to the front of the car like some sort of wind-up toy, desperately trying not to let any part of his body touch any other part, and wishing his vomit-caked clothes would levitate a couple of inches off his skin.

Tyler had no idea what sight would await him at the front of the vehicle. He'd wanted to catch Bruce Anderson, yes, but not to mash the poor bastard into a paste.

He was relieved, then, when Anderson subjected him to a torrent of abuse the moment he squelched around to the front.

'The fuck you think you're doing, you bloody maniac?' the Australian bellowed, his voice easily drowning out the chugging of the still-running engine. 'You could've flaming killed me!'

'Well, you shouldn't have run away then, should you?' Tyler snapped. 'Come out.'

'I can't come out, can I? Bloody stuck, ain't I?' Anderson protested.

Sure enough, while the Land Rover hadn't exploded his insides outside as Tyler feared it might've, the position the vehicle had stopped in meant Anderson's lower half was pinned between the front of the chassis and the ground below.

'Can't you jiggle sideways?' Tyler asked.

'Jiggle sideways? What are you talking about? If I could jiggle sideways I'd have jiggled bloody sideways and legged it, wouldn't I?' Anderson snapped. He shook his head. 'Jiggle sideways.'

'All right, all right,' Tyler muttered. He started to move in closer to investigate, but stopped when Anderson retched.

'Jesus fucking Christ, mate! Did you throw up on yourself, or something?' he demanded.

'No, I didn't throw up on myself,' said Tyler, witheringly. 'Someone else threw up on me.'

'Right, well... I mean, what? Well done, I guess,' Anderson said. 'Now hurry the hell up and get me out of here!'

Tyler reached a hand out. Anderson shrank back.

'Don't come near me! Christ! I don't want to get covered in puke, do I?'

'Well, what do you want me to do, then?' Tyler asked.

'I don't know. How about *not* hit me with a big bloody car?' Anderson suggested. 'Oh, wait. Scratch that. Bit fucking late!'

'Wait there,' Tyler told him.

'Good one. Funny,' Anderson replied, but Tyler was already penguin-walking back around to the driver's side of the Land Rover.

He recoiled at the smell as he reached the door. 'Fuck.'

Turning away, he raised his head like a werewolf howling at the moon, drew in a deep breath, and clambered into the driver's seat.

'Everything all right?' asked Dudley from the back.

Tyler gritted his teeth and crunched the gearbox into reverse. 'Just fucking peachy. Thanks for asking,' he said, then he depressed the accelerator and raised the clutch.

The engine died immediately. One moment, it was chugging and rattling away, the next there was nothing but silence. Something whined for a few seconds. Something else went *ping*, like metal cooling.

'Great,' Tyler groaned. 'Just... great.'

'What's wrong?' asked Dudley.

Tyler turned in his seat. He regretted this at once, as it gave him a close-up view of his headrest, which looked like the epicentre of some sort of gaseous swamp eruption. Smelled like it, too.

'What's *wrong*? What's fucking...' he began, then he shook his head in disbelief. 'What's *right*, Dudley? That's the real question here. What's bloody right?'

'Did you kill Bruce?' Dudley asked. His eyes shone, wide-eyed and innocent, through the mask of vomit that was currently plastered across his face.

'No. I didn't kill him. He's just... he's trapped under the front. I need to get him out.'

'How are you going to do that?'

Tyler said nothing.

'How are you going to get him out?'

'Jesus Christ, Dudley! I'm thinking,' Tyler barked.

In the back seat, the harsh tone of the DC's voice seemed to make Dudley shrink. He went from being a giant of a man to a slightly less gigantic man.

Tyler looked him up and down. Big. Strong. Caked in his own spew, right enough, but that was neither here nor there.

'Sorry, Dudley. I shouldn't have snapped,' Tyler said. 'Listen, you're a big lad. Fancy giving me a hand?'

Dudley looked unsure. 'If I say yes, can I get the handcuffs off?'

'Course you can.'

There was a snap and Dudley brought both hands out from behind his back. Tyler stared, struck dumb, as the big man rubbed the two bright red welts that marked his wrists.

'OK,' Dudley said, smiling cheerfully. 'What do you want me to do?'

–

It didn't take long to get Sinead up to speed on the case. It never did, which was why Logan had pegged her for a future career in plain clothes within minutes of meeting her.

After everything with Caitlyn, he'd offered Sinead a job— Detective Constable with the MIT. Perfect match for her, he'd said. Be right up her alley.

She'd said no. Aye, she'd been very grateful and respectful, and all that stuff. But she'd said no. It wasn't right for her current situation. Wasn't the right time. Wasn't the right choice.

Logan had rarely been more impressed with anyone in his life.

There had been no footage of Iona Wallace on Roddy's laptop. The only porn there had been of the man-on-man variety—or, occasionally, the men-on-man variety—and meant for his own personal consumption.

They'd had to take the laptop for further study, of course, and Logan was secretly looking forward to making Tyler comb through every last minute of the video content. All four-plus hours of it.

After leaving Roddy's flat, Logan and Sinead had headed out back to where the scarecrow stood watching over the beer garden. The DCI had hoped that he might find a camera tucked into the stuffing somewhere, but if there was one, then it was microscopic.

Still, he was sure there had been one, but that it had been removed. Joy Bryden, the one-woman Neighbourhood Watch, had reported people smoking in the beer garden in the latest meeting minutes.

Logan was sure that, if he went back through them, he'd find the locations of all her hidden cameras, and all the things they'd seen.

No wonder she was so keen to get wireless internet access for the whole island. Without it, she wouldn't have been able to spy on the place.

On the way back to the office, Logan had sent Sinead to borrow a whiteboard from the school. He'd have done it himself, he said, except he felt the kids might spontaneously combust through fear just at the very sight of him.

She'd come back ten minutes later with a flipchart on a rickety metal frame, which was the best the teacher had been able to rustle up. There was only one classroom, the teacher had pointed out, so they weren't exactly overflowing with spare equipment.

Logan had written while he'd explained, the Sharpie darting across the page as he'd told Sinead about Iona's background, her relationship with the other islanders, and filled her in on Bruce Anderson, Kevin Tillerson, Joy Bryden, and the 'utter fucking delight' that was the Reverend Abraham Kerr.

He'd made only the most basic reference to Isaac Young. He hadn't gone into any great detail. Not yet. It would all come out, soon enough, of course—the diaries would make sure of that—but now wasn't the time.

When he finished, they had three pages of A3 paper filled with barely decipherable scribbles. They found some tape, and stuck them to the wall of the office, side-by-side. It wasn't a Big Board, and, if Logan was being completely honest, it objectively made very little sense, but it would do the job.

They were discussing next steps over tea, when the office door opened. The smell of vomit came wafting in, followed a moment later by the source.

'Christ Almighty. What happened to you?' Logan asked, burying his nose in the crook of his arm.

'Sinead!' said Tyler, when he spotted the uniformed officer sitting across from the DCI. He opened his arms as if to move in for a hug, but was promptly told he could get that idea right out of his head.

'Is that… is that spew?' she asked, her nostrils clamping shut of their own accord. 'And what happened to your face? Is that blood?'

'Aye. It's been an eventful day. Had a wee…' Tyler began. He spun on his heels as a thought struck him, started in panic, then ran back outside. 'Shite!'

Logan and Sinead swapped glances across the desk. Sinead shrugged. There was something vaguely apologetic about it, like she felt the need to take some sort of responsibility.

'It's all right. I had him,' droned a voice from outside. Its deep resonance suggested a very large man, or perhaps a mid-sized bull. It was affable, too, though, and gave the impression that even if the owner of it was about to gore you to death with its horns, it'd be nothing personal. 'He wasn't going anywhere.'

'Cheers, Dudley,' Tyler said, then he reappeared sandwiched between two other men, both larger than he was.

Even with the vomit pebble-dash effect covering him from head to toe, Logan recognised Dudley Brown from the church service. It was the sight of the man Dudley was holding by the arm that got him up on his feet, though.

'Where the hell did you dig him up from?' Logan asked, looking Bruce Anderson up and down.

'From under the front wheels of the Land Rover, boss,' Tyler said.

Logan and Sinead both regarded him quizzically.

'Long story,' he said.

'He hit me with his fucking yute!' Anderson spat. His hands were behind his back, wrists bound together with another zip-tie.

Tyler shrugged. 'All right. Turns out it's not that long,' he said. 'Fortunately, no harm done. To him, I mean. Land Rover's knackered. Luckily, Dudley here was on hand to help me lift it enough to get him out.'

Anderson snorted. '*Help?* You did fuck all, mate. Dud lifted it, you just made groaning noises and went red in the face.'

'Shut up,' Tyler told him. 'I told you, anything you say can be used in evidence. This is all character stuff. I'd be careful what you say.'

'Stick it up your arse, you dickhead.'

Tyler patted his shirt pocket. The squelch it gave immediately made him regret this, but he tried not to let on. 'You want me to write that down? Because I will.'

'Ooh, you'll write it down? Shit, mate, you've got me on the bloody ropes now, all right.'

Tyler squared up to the much bigger Anderson. 'Look, pal, I'd be very careful what you say to me right now.'

'Why?' Anderson asked.

Tyler hesitated. His reply, when it eventually came, was disappointing for all involved. 'Just... because. All right?'

'Right, well, that told him,' Logan said. 'You've read them both their rights?'

Tyler stepped back from Anderson and nodded. 'Aye. Arrested this one on the suspected murder of Iona Wallace, and Dudley on assaulting a police officer. Although, that was a misunderstanding, and he's been a big help.'

Dudley straightened proudly. Tyler shot him a sideways look.

'Apart from no commenting me about the scarecrow stuff—on the orders of Joy Bryden, no less—and repeatedly vomiting on the back of my head.'

Tyler reached into one of his trouser pockets. 'Which reminds me. One of the scarecrows, it had—'

'A camera,' Logan said.

Tyler produced a plastic evidence bag with a flourish. He'd presumably been going for some big dramatic reveal, so the fact that Logan beat him to it caused him some visible disappointment.

'Right. Aye. A camera,' Tyler said. He handed over the evidence bag. 'Check the thickness of the wiring, boss. I'd say we've got a match for our murder weapon.'

'Check out Sherlock bloody Holmes,' Anderson sneered. 'Good job, mate. Pat on the head for you.'

Logan spoke before Tyler could open his mouth. 'PC Bell?' he said, fixing Bruce Anderson with a cool stare that just bordered on being mildly amused. He was going to very much enjoy interviewing this one.

'Sir?'

'Why don't you take DC Neish and Mr Brown here to get cleaned up? I'm sure Pat and Norman at the B&B will be able to help you out. DC Neish will show you the way. Get them cleaned up, then bring them back.'

'Ooh, can you clean me up, too, sweetheart?' Anderson asked, leering down at her. Tyler lunged, but Logan blocked his path with an arm like a steel girder.

'Go, Detective Constable,' he ordered. 'Now.'

Tyler's frustration was written all over his face, but he bit his tongue and followed Sinead when she stepped past him and headed for the door.

'Come on, Dudley,' the DC urged.

'Coming! Bye Bruce, bye... Mr Policeman,' he said. Then, with a clumsy wave, he turned and left with the others.

Bruce Anderson snorted and shook his head. 'Fucking cabbage,' he remarked, although he waited until the door was safely closed first.

He turned to find Logan standing very close to him. The mildly-amused expression was gone. In its place, a granite impassiveness had been chiselled into the lines of the DCI's face.

'Mr Anderson,' he said, indicating the chair tucked in behind Tyler's desk. 'Please, take a seat.'

'You going to make me?' Anderson asked.

Logan didn't move, yet he seemed to get closer to the other man. Anderson was tall, but he had nothing on the DCI.

'I can if you like, son,' he said. 'Middle of nowhere. No cameras watching. No one to dispute my account of you going mental on me, trying to escape.'

He clapped his slab–like hands together and rubbed them. The bang of them meeting made Anderson jump.

'So, if you want us to go down that road, just you go ahead and say the word.'

Logan could almost see Anderson's bravado seeping out of him, taking most of the colour in his face with it. There were no sarky comebacks. No snidey remarks. None of the cockiness that had previously been on display.

'Right then,' said Logan, indicating the chair again. 'How about you take a seat and we can talk this over like grown-ups?'

Chapter 37

Pat's voice was the first thing Tyler, Sinead, and Dudley heard when they arrived at the Bed and Breakfast. It was impossible not to hear it, in fact, the way it shrieked out through the ancient windows.

'No, *you* piss off, Norman! *You* piss off! I've had it up to bloody here, with—'

'Look, I said I'm sorry, all right?' That was Norman's voice. Angry, yes, but cowed, too. Whatever the argument was about, he knew he'd already lost it. 'It was a mistake. A stupid mistake.'

'A *mistake*?' Pat yelped. Tyler could see her through the net curtains, throwing her arms up as she turned away from her husband. 'You ruined my life, Norman! You ruined my bloody—'

She stopped when she saw the three figures standing frozen in the middle of the path. Tyler gave her an awkward wave. She returned it as a nod, then turned her back on the window and hurried away from it.

'That the owners?' asked Sinead.

'Pat and Norman. Aye,' Tyler confirmed, leading the way up the path. 'They're usually less... shouty.'

The door opened before they reached it. Pat was flushed red, either with anger or embarrassment. She shot Tyler an uncomfortable smile as way of an apology.

'Sorry about that,' she said. 'We were just...'

'It's fine,' Tyler said. He stopped on the step and looked past her into the house. 'Everything OK, though?'

'What? Oh. Yes. Fine. Just a domestic,' Pat said. 'I mean, not in that sense… just an argument.'

'About what?' Tyler asked, his polis instincts spitting out the question before he could stop himself.

Pat shifted her weight from one foot to the other. 'Uh…'

'Sorry. Force of habit,' Tyler said, smiling at her. 'None of my business.'

'No. It's fine,' Pat said. 'We were just arguing about this place, actually. About coming here. All Norman's idea. Can't believe I went along with it. That was all.'

She gave herself a shake, then looked the group up and down. She gave Sinead a welcoming nod.

'Hi. I'm Sinead.'

'Hello, Sinead. Nice to meet you,' Pat said. She turned her attention to the big man looming behind the officers. 'Dudley.'

'Hello, Pat,' Dudley said. 'Sorry you had an argument.'

Pat started to smile, but then her nostrils flared as the breeze brought the smell inside.

'Jesus, what's that? Is that… is that spew?'

'Aye, afraid so,' Tyler confirmed. 'Dudley had… an accident.'

'I was sick on him,' Dudley said.

'Yes, that pretty much—'

'And on myself.'

'She can see that, Dudley,' Tyler sighed. He half-rolled his eyes for Pat's benefit, then smiled. 'We were hoping we could…'

Pat stepped aside. 'You can use the one in your room, and Dudley can use the shower room downstairs.'

'Cheers, Pat,' Tyler said. 'You're a lifesaver.'

–

Logan sat in silence, reading over his notes. He hadn't been able to figure out how to connect to the office's printer, so he'd hastily jotted much of the information down longhand from Hamza's emails, then added his own thoughts and observations below.

Bruce Anderson was sitting in Tyler's chair, wedged in between the desk and the wall. The only way out of the room was through Logan, and they both knew that there was no way that was happening.

Logan's phone sat between them, the voice recorder app open and running. It had been going for almost five minutes so far, but had recorded nothing but the sound of pages turning, the occasional clearing of the DCI's throat, and an angry, 'Can we get on with it?' from Anderson.

That last one had resulted in a long, oppressive glare from Logan, and a promise that they'd get on with it when he was good and bloody ready.

And now, the time had come. He was ready.

Good and bloody.

'Sorry to keep you there, Bruce,' he said, flipping back to the first page of his notes.

'I'd prefer you to address me as "Mr Anderson",' the man on the other side of the desk sneered.

'Aye, well, I'd prefer you no' to be a thieving smart-arse, Brucie. Looks like we're both going to be disappointed,' Logan replied. He continued before Anderson had a chance to object. 'You saw Iona Wallace the night she died. Correct?'

Anderson shrugged.

'What was that?' Logan asked. 'Yes or no, son? It's not a difficult question. Did you, or did you not—'

'Yes. I was working,' Anderson spat. 'She was in the pub. She left. I didn't see her again. Happy?'

'Ecstatic,' Logan told him, although his face offered nothing to back that statement up. 'What time, exactly, did you last see her?'

'I don't bloody know. What am I, her fucking biographer, or something? She had a few drinks, got into a fight with… well, everyone, then she left. What happened to her after that? How the hell should I know?'

'You'd had sex with her before though, yes?' Logan asked. It was a stretch, but he said it with enough authority to make it sound like he knew more than he did.

As it turned out, Anderson didn't need the truth teased out of him. He looked positively gleeful as he spilled the beans.

'Course I did. Show me anyone between the age of twenty and fifty who hasn't.' He snorted, amused at the thought. 'Listen, mate, if shagging her's enough to get you found guilty, you'd better lock up most of the men on this island, and half the flaming visitors who come here every year. You'll need to build a whole new prison just to hold us all.'

'Yes. Thank you,' said Logan. 'I get the point. When did you sleep with her?'

'Which time?' Bruce asked. He grinned at the brief flicker of surprise that flitted across the detective's face. 'Island's dull as shit. You got to take your jollies where you can. Know what I'm saying?'

Logan slid a blank sheet of paper across the desk and placed a pen on top of it.

'Write the dates.'

'Dates? You expect me to remember the dates? I got no idea. Last time was about, maybe, what? Four weeks ago? Five? There were two times before that. Two nights in the same week.'

'When?' Logan asked.

'Christ, I don't know. Two weeks before, maybe? Maybe a couple of months ago, in total. Not like I kept a diary.'

'Iona did,' Logan said. 'Maybe you'll be in there.'

'Ha! Maybe I will,' Anderson said, but the way he shifted in his seat suggested he sincerely hoped he wasn't.

'How did it end between you?' Logan asked.

Anderson laughed. Properly, this time. 'Will you listen to yourself? Nothing ended, mate, because nothing started. It was sex. That was all. She knew it, I knew it. Just sex.'

'Did you pay her?' Logan asked.

Anderson's hesitation was fleeting but telling. 'Not like that. I mean, it wasn't a bloody *transaction*, if that's what you mean. She just… she was broke. I gave her a tenner to help her out.'

'Each time?'

'Fuck off. I'm not made of money! A tenner. Total.'

Logan felt his insides sink a little. He had a little flashback of Iona Wallace in her school uniform, bold and brassy, and taking no shite from anyone. What an ending to her story. *Three Rides for a Tenner,* like a big wheel or a roller-coaster at a funfair. A one-woman *Irn Bru Carnival.*

'What was with the cleaning gear?' Logan asked.

'What cleaning gear?'

'You bought a load of cleaning supplies from the shop the day after Iona Wallace was murdered. Why?'

'Because I was told to,' Anderson replied.

'Told to? By who?'

'By Roddy. In the pub?' Anderson said. It sounded like a question—both sentences did, in fact—but then, so did most things the Australian said.

Stupid bloody accent.

'You bought the cleaning supplies for the pub?' Logan asked.

'Yeah. Paid for out of the petty cash. I put the receipt in, and everything.'

'Very conscientious of you,' Logan said, his voice if not dripping, then at least moist with sarcasm. 'Used them on your own place first, though.'

'Perks of the job. Landlord's been bitching at me for weeks to get it cleaned up. Figured I might as well do it on Roddy's tab.'

'Again,' said Logan. 'How very conscientious of you.'

'Hey, I'm a bloody good member of staff, I'll have you know.'

'That why you had your hands in the till, is it?' Logan asked. 'Hardly screams "Employee of the Month" that, does it?'

'I was just taking my wages,' Anderson said. 'I'd earned it. That money was mine, fair and square.'

'I don't run a business, so I can't be sure, but I'm pretty confident that's no' how the payroll system works,' Logan said. 'You don't just grab a handful of notes and run. Roddy agrees with me, by the way. He says you nicked that money, no question about it.'

'Well, that's not how I see it,' Anderson said.

Logan pressed the tip of an index finger against the tabletop. 'Well, that's very much how I see it, Brucie, and I'm the one with the polis badge. I know a bad bastard when I see one, and I see one sitting in front of me right now.'

'Is that supposed to be scary?' Anderson asked.

'Scary? No. Not scary. Not yet,' Logan said. 'But how about I give it a try? I and a fellow officer both witnessed you stealing money from the pub till. As did the landlord. You attempted to evade arrest. You're in the country illegally, and you're wanted in a country that we will be *only* too happy to extradite you to. A country where the prison system isn't as jovial and carefree as our own. A country where, if you go down—and you will go down, Brucie—you don't get back up again.'

He spread his hands, palms upwards. 'In those circumstances? With what you're facing? Pretty boy like you? I'd be *wishing* I'd killed Iona Wallace, so I could spend the next fifteen years eating mince and tatties in a Scottish jail, instead of getting passed around in the showers of a prison in one of the... *less refined* nations, and coming out with an arsehole like the entrance to the Clyde Tunnel.'

Logan nodded down at the pad and pen that still sat, unused, in front of the prisoner. 'So, how about you go ahead and write your confession now?'

Anderson's eyes crept down to the paper and stayed there, but the rest of him made no move towards it.

'On you go. Don't overthink it,' Logan instructed. 'Doesn't have to be long or complicated, just write down the *what*s, the *when*s, and the *why*s, and we can make sure you do your time in this country, not in some underground Vietnamese dungeon.'

Anderson's fingers twitched. His gaze remained fixed on the pen and paper.

'I hear they're clamping down hard on sex offenders over there, Bruce. Really making an example of the bastards. Foreigners especially.'

He smiled thinly. 'How'd you reckon you'll cope with that? Being made an example of, I mean? I wonder just what that will entail? Nothing good, I'm sure. I'll tell you this, I don't bloody envy you, son.'

Bruce Anderson inhaled slowly through his nose, held it for several seconds, then exhaled through his mouth. He tore his eyes from the notepad just long enough to glance at the ceiling, then he was back to staring again.

'I'll be honest here. You're going to do time, Brucie. That's inevitable. But, do you do it here, or do you do it over there? Have you seen the conditions in some of these places? I wouldn't keep a bloody animal in them.' Logan's finger tapped the edge of the paper. 'Tell me how you killed Iona. Tell me *why*. And you can stay here. You'll serve your time in this country. I guarantee it.'

The DCI let out an incredulous laugh. 'They've even got Sky TV in the prisons now. Would you believe it? Sports package. Movies, I'm told. Over there, you'll be lucky to even catch a glimpse of the *actual* fucking sky ever again. Here? It'll be all catch-up, and Premier League, and HD On Demand. You'll be Live Pausing to your heart's content. Food's good too, these days. I mean, don't get me wrong, it's nothing spectacular. But it's no' bloody crickets, or grasshoppers, or whatever it is they make you eat in those Vietnamese places. It might no' be haute cuisine, but at least you can identify what's on your plate without a degree in entomology.'

Logan picked up the pen. He clicked the button on the end, extending the point, then he held it out for the other man. 'Go on, son. Get it off your chest. You'll feel better.'

Bruce reached a hand out. His fingers wrapped around the pen's plastic casing, and his eyes met Logan's. A nod of encouragement passed from detective to prisoner, and then Anderson took the pen and began to write in big, angry strokes.

It didn't take him long to finish. Not nearly long enough.

Once he was done, he held the pad up for Logan to see. On it were five words, written in the middle of the page in block caps:

I WANT A FUCKING LAWYER.

'Come on now, Bruce. You don't want to hold all this up any more than we have to, do you?' Logan asked.

'Cut the shit, mate,' Anderson said. He jabbed a finger against the notebook a few times, then waved it in Logan's face. 'And do as you're bloody told.'

Chapter 38

'Hello, Jack. It's yourself!'

DI Forde squinted at the screen of the phone propped up on his desk, tried his reading glasses on to see if that helped make it any clearer, then took them off again and shook his head.

'Is that Sinead with you? She arrived, then.'

'Aye, made it, sir,' Sinead said. 'Bumpy ride, but got here.'

She was sitting to the right of DCI Logan, the phone pushed back a bit to fit them both in. Sinead's head was down near the bottom of the screen, while everything of Logan's, from the eyebrows upwards, had been cut off at the top.

'What's the news?' Ben asked. He glanced up as Hamza sat a cup of tea next to him, and smiled appreciatively. 'Cheers, son.'

Hamza sat down and rolled his chair closer, so they could both see the screen.

'We've found Bruce Anderson,' Logan said. 'Well, I say "found". Tyler hit him with a Land Rover.'

'Jesus!' Ben exclaimed. 'Is he hurt?'

'Sadly not,' Logan said. 'Refusing to talk without a solicitor present, though. We're going to have to get him brought back to the mainland. Thought I'd get him up to Inverness for you two to take a crack at him.'

'Aye, be good to get our teeth into something,' Ben said. 'It's been a lot of internet and phone calls up this end, and I think we could both do with stretching our legs.'

'Watch your hips,' Logan suggested. 'Man of your age.'

'Don't you worry about me, Jack. I'm no' the heart attack waiting to happen,' Ben replied. 'I'm sure we can get a boat out to you from Mallaig today. Get a couple of Uniforms from Fort William to transport him.'

'Want me to arrange that, sir?' Hamza asked.

'Aye. Good. Thanks,' Logan said. 'We've got him locked in the storeroom at the shop. No windows, one door. Tyler's keeping an eye.'

'Nice bit of improvisation,' said Ben.

'Aye, well, the more temporary the better. I want him off the island and in an Interview Room by this afternoon.'

Ben nodded. 'No problem. I have to ask, though, Jack... if he's our main suspect, why are you no' coming to interview him yourself?'

Logan shifted his weight in the chair. 'I've a few things to tidy up here first. I'll send Sinead and Tyler back on the boat, so make sure there's enough room. I just need to...'

He thought of Isaac Young. He had to know the truth.

However hard that might be.

'...deal with a couple of outstanding issues.'

Ben smirked. 'Sure you're no' just hiding from Hoon, Jack?'

'I wish I was, Ben,' Logan replied, his voice one long, heavy sigh. 'I really wish that was it.'

–

The interview with Dudley Brown was slow going at first, but it helped when Tyler said they weren't going to charge him for leathering shite out of the detective.

There was still a lot of *no commenting* from the big man, but Logan had quickly realised that the only questions he replied with 'no comment' on were those that he would otherwise answer with 'yes.'

Ask him why he made scarecrows, and he'd recite his reasons at length—it was fun, he was good at it, it gave him something to do, the local children loved them. That sort of thing.

Ask him if someone had given him the cameras to hide in the scarecrows:

'No comment.'

Ask if that person was Roddy from the pub:

'Of course not! Why would Roddy want to put cameras in the Tattiebogles?'

Ask if that person was Joy Bryden:

'No comment.'

Within twenty minutes or so, Logan had got the whole thing worked out. Dudley was thanked for his time, warned to stay out of trouble, and then he and Tyler went off to find the big man a lift back home across the island.

After that, Logan had Sinead bring in Joy Bryden. He'd taken great pleasure in seeing the expression on her face when she'd been led into her own office to find him holding court from behind her desk. She looked like she had a mouth full of wasps, and was under strict orders not to let any of them escape.

'Joy. Nice to see you again,' he said. He gestured to the smaller, more rickety of the office's two seats. 'Please. Sit down.'

Joy regarded the seat with displeasure and distaste, then lowered herself onto it. She sat perched forward, like she thought she might catch something if she positioned herself too far back.

'Did PC Bell explain why I wanted to see you?'

Joy shook her head. 'No. Nothing. I asked, but she was *not* forthcoming,' she complained. 'I have to say, the timing was not good. I was in the middle of some important paperwork, which I'm having to do at home, I should add. Any idea yet when I'll be able to get my office back?'

'Oh, not long now,' Logan assured her. He pulled open one of the drawers of her desk and reached inside. 'Just got a few matters to clear up.'

There was a rustling sound and a soft thack as Logan placed an evidence bag on the desk between them. The beady eye of a camera gazed upwards from within a nest of wiring.

Logan sat back and folded his arms. 'I'm going to leave you to do the explaining,' he said.

Joy regarded the bag for a long, long time. She swallowed. She cleared her throat. She shook her head and had a stab at forming a nonplussed sort of smile.

'What's that?'

Logan's only reply was through his body language. It didn't change much—a slight adjustment of the shoulders, an incremental leaning forward of the head—but made it clear that he was not impressed by that answer. Not impressed, at all.

'Is it a camera, or something?' Joy asked.

'It is.'

'Right. Well, what does it have to do with me?' she asked.

'I know what you've been up to, Joy,' Logan said. 'Do us both a favour and stop wasting my bloody time.'

Now, Joy did sit back. Her lips drew tightly together, saying nothing, but her gaze went skittering around the room, like she might find a plausible explanation or excuse tucked away in one of the corners.

'Look, tell you what I'll do, Joy. I'll make it easier for you,' Logan said. 'I've got a boat coming over. Couple of officers on it. You know what they'll be bringing with them? A warrant to enter and search your premises, and to seize all your computer equipment.'

He let that revelation sit there for a moment.

'So here's what I want you to do for me, Joy,' he continued. 'I want you to think about what's there in your house right now. What's on your computers. What's lying around. Picture it for me. Because that—all that stuff—will be gone over with a fine-tooth comb.

'You might think you've deleted everything, but let me promise you, you haven't. We've got teams that can work wonders with that stuff. I've seen them reconstruct files from hard drives that had been smashed to pieces. I've seen them dig out stuff deleted years back. Had convictions on it, in fact.'

He looked at his watch. 'By my reckoning, they'll be here within the hour,' he said, then he tapped the bag. 'If I were you, I'd start talking.'

Throughout the DCI's speech, Joy had tried valiantly to remain stoic and calm. By the time he reached the end of it, though, the effort of maintaining her composure was taking a visible toll, ageing her ten years in ten seconds.

'I was just… it was for the Neighbourhood Watch,' she said, the words blurting out of her despite her best efforts to keep them inside. 'It was for security!'

'You don't have a Neighbourhood Watch, Joy,' Logan said.

'We do! Me! I'm the Neighbourhood Watch!'

'You're not. You're a nosy bastard. That's not the same thing,' Logan told her. 'You know what the law says about spying on people, Joy?'

Joy shook her head.

'No, nor did I. I mean, I probably should've, but it's no' really my area of expertise,' Logan said. He tapped the screen of his phone. 'Luckily, I had a colleague look it up. Apparently, it's covered under general Human Rights laws. You know, everyone's basic right to privacy, that sort of thing?'

He scrolled for a moment, then tapped the screen again. 'Here we go.' He cleared his throat, then rattled through a few lines in quick succession. '"It is illegal to fit spy cameras to a business or residential property that you do not own or in which you don't have legal occupancy." That's one. "All CCTV systems recording in public must be registered with the Information Commissioner's Office, and must be accompanied by signs that alert members of the public that CCTV is in operation".'

Logan pointed at the screen. 'They're apparently quite strict on that one,' he said, before reading the final bullet-point in Hamza's email. 'And "it is illegal to use spy cameras in areas where subjects may have a reasonable expectation to privacy. For example, you may breach the Human Rights Act if your CCTV camera is pointing directly into a neighbour's bedroom".'

He set his phone down again and looked across the desk to the woman now practically cowering opposite. 'Or a school. That's another example for you.'

Joy's voice was trembling now. Her eyes were wide, imploring, tears welling up at the bottom. 'I was just keeping an eye on things. Making sure everything was safe!'

'Didn't keep Iona Wallace safe, did it?' Logan said. 'There was a camera in the scarecrow next to where the body was found, wasn't there, Joy?'

'It… it didn't see anything,' Joy said. 'It was late. Internet was down. It didn't see anything.'

'No. But you did,' Logan told her, and the breathless sob that forced its way out of her told him he was right. 'See, I don't really care too much about you sticking cameras around the place. I mean, it's out of order, obviously, but it's not my department. But here's what I do care about, Joy…'

He sat forward and picked up the evidence bag. 'Whoever killed Iona used the cable of one of these things to strangle her with. It wasn't this particular one, of course. I think, given the damage to the scarecrow itself, the killer spotted the protruding wire, grabbed it, and used it to finish Iona off. That's my theory.'

Joy said nothing, just sat sobbing hot, silent tears of guilt, or shame, or a flavour not dissimilar.

'But here's the thing, there was no trace of it at the scene. No sign at all. No camera, no wiring, no battery pack, nothing,' Logan said. 'And you think, aye, fair enough. Killer took it. Makes sense, right? Except… next day was Wednesday.'

Logan turned in his chair and indicated the calendar behind him, with all its little stickers. 'Battery change day. That's what you said. For the "webcams". Plural.'

He turned back, fixing the woman with a glare that could've punched a hole through concrete.

'You found her, didn't you?' he said. It was a question, yes, but it didn't sound like one. 'Either when you went to change the battery, or when you realised the camera feed was down.

You found her body, and instead of telling anyone, you removed all evidence of the camera having been there. Then, when that was done, you left her. Just left her there, in the mud. Dead. Didn't you, Joy?'

Joy continued to choke back her silent sobs. She and Sinead both jumped when Logan slammed a hand down on the desk and roared the question again.

'Didn't you? You left her!'

Joy's mouth formed the words, but her throat had tightened to the point it was almost impossible to hear them when they came out.

'Yes,' she wheezed. 'I'm sorry. I'm sorry.'

Logan nodded. 'Aye. I'm sure,' he said, standing up. 'Joy Bryden, I am arresting you on suspicion of attempting to defeat the ends of justice and on...' He glanced momentarily at his phone on the desk, realised there was no way he was going to remember the details, and gave a vague wave of his hand. '...various privacy-related breaches of the Human Rights Act still to be determined.'

'I didn't kill her. I didn't. You have to believe me,' Joy babbled. 'Please. I didn't. I didn't.'

'Aye, well, it'll all come out in the wash,' Logan said, motioning for Sinead to put her handcuffs to good use. 'It'll all come out in the wash.'

Chapter 39

Logan, Tyler, and Sinead stood on the dock, the engine of a motorboat chugging away in the water beside them.

Joy Bryden and Bruce Anderson were safely aboard, and now under the watch of two of Fort William's brightest and best uniformed officers. Or, the two who happened to be available, at least.

'You sure you're going to be all right, boss?' Tyler asked. 'We could hang off with you.'

Logan shook his head. His hands were deep in his pockets, and the breeze coming in off the water was swishing his coat around his knees.

'No. You two go. Get us underway with Anderson. He should have a solicitor waiting when you get him to Inverness. I want him singing by the time I get back.'

'When are you coming back, sir?' Sinead asked.

Logan glanced back up the hill. 'Soon. Just… got a matter to attend to.'

Tyler met his eye, and a look of understanding passed between them. 'Good luck with that, boss,' the DC said.

'Aye. Thanks,' Logan told him. 'Whatever happens, I'm just pleased I don't have to listen to your bloody snoring.'

'He says I snore,' Tyler told Sinead. 'I don't snore.'

Sinead blushed a little, then smiled. 'No comment.'

'Right, off you go,' Logan instructed. 'Tell the boat to come back in an hour.' He checked his watch. 'Make it two, actually.'

'And you're sure you don't want us to stay, boss?' Tyler asked.

Logan shook his head. 'No,' he said, sighing wearily. 'This one is all on me.'

'Right, well, if you head back to the B&B, you might want to wear a crash helmet,' Tyler said. 'Norman and Pat were having a right set-to earlier.'

Logan frowned. 'Aye? What about?' he asked. 'Wasn't violent, was it?'

'No. Nothing like that. Mostly Pat raging at him,' Tyler explained. 'Think she's angry that he dragged them out here. All his idea, apparently.'

'Was it? That's interesting,' Logan said, after a momentary pause to consider this information. 'Right. Well, I'll be sure to keep my head down.'

–

He'd arranged to meet Isaac in the pub in an hour. Iona's son had seemed cagey when Logan called, but the DCI had stressed the importance of it, and Isaac had eventually agreed.

Between then and now, Logan was at a bit of a loss. He'd sent most of the evidence they'd gathered off on the boat, then had returned to the B&B to tell Kevin Tillerson that, provided he didn't leave the country, he was free to head home on the first ferry that turned up.

That done, Logan said his goodbyes to Norman and Pat, assured them Police Scotland would be in touch to cover everything, then asked if he could sit in the lounge and wait for his meeting.

They readily agreed, of course, and provided tea and biscuits to help him while away the time.

He sat in one of the wingback chairs, a single evidence bag down on the floor beside him, mug in hand, plate of biscuits balanced on his lap.

The view, which had been mostly obscured since he'd arrived, was finally clear. And Christ, it was worth the wait. He sipped his tea and gazed out at the world, lost in the cresting of the waves, the glacial movements of the clouds, and the circling of the birds above the rocks.

If he squinted, he could just make out the motorboat chugging towards Mallaig in the distance. There'd be transport waiting to whisk Joy and Bruce to their respective destinations. Joy Bryden was being handed over to CID in Fort William, while Bruce would be taken to Inverness to be met by an eager DI Forde and DC Khaled.

Anderson would likely prove to be a tough nut to crack, but Ben could handle it, particularly with the threat of the international warrant and life in a Hanoi prison to barter with.

He went back to admiring the scenery. It was the kind of view you could get lost in. The sort of vista a man would never tire of just gazing at. Admiring. Drinking in.

Four minutes later, his tea finished and all the biscuits eaten, Logan had seen enough of it to last him a bloody lifetime.

He took out his phone and, on a whim, typed in the address of one of the bigger porn sites, then he thumbed Iona Wallace's name into the search box.

No results.

He shut down the browser, clicked the button that put the phone onto standby, then set the device on the armrest of the chair.

He drummed his fingers.

Outside, waves crested and birds circled.

Somewhere in the house, that bastard of a cuckoo clock called three.

He picked the phone up again.

He opened the browser and typed in the address for another porn site.

He searched 'Iona Wallace'.

Nothing.

He searched 'Iona'.

Thousands of results. A quick scan through the thumbnail images didn't reveal anyone who resembled the particular Iona he was looking for.

He shut down the browser.

He set down the phone.

He sighed and scowled at the scenery, like it was really starting to get on his tits.

Logan moved in the chair. His foot hit the evidence bag on the floor beside him.

A thought crept in—slowly, tentatively, like it might be startled off at any moment.

He unlocked his phone. Opened the browser. Went back to the first site he'd checked and tapped in the search box.

He could see the front of the diary through the clear plastic of the evidence bag. The name there, written all those years ago. Her nom de plume. Her alter ego.

Logan typed.

Desiree Shanelle.

He hit return. The page went blank for a moment, and then the results loaded.

And there, in all her glory, she was.

There were nine videos. The thumbnail images of each one showed Iona—Desiree—either fully naked or in a state of undress.

Logan clicked on the first. The title was simply 'Desiree Shanelle 9' which, he assumed, made it the most recent.

The screen changed to show a video window. Logan got up, closed the lounge door, then returned to his chair before hitting the play button.

It jumped straight into the action. Iona lay on her front on the bed, while a naked man ground against her from behind, groaning and wheezing like he was a horse on the final furlong at Aintree.

Disappointingly, his face had been blurred out, which would make identifying him difficult. There might be something the tech bods could do, but Logan wasn't going to hold his breath.

He didn't recognise the room, either. Quaint. Old-fashioned. Like most of the houses on the island.

He reached for the back-up button so he could check through the other videos on the list. Somewhere, the cuckoo called.

'Stupid bloody clock,' he muttered.

And there, in that moment, was when it all made sense.

Chapter 40

Logan found Norman in the garden shed at the back of the house. The detective knocked twice on the open door, then stepped back as Norman wheeled around in surprise.

'Mr Logan. Uh, hi. Sorry. I thought you were gone,' Norman said. He had a screwdriver in one hand, held low at his side. A long screw hung from one corner of his mouth, like a cigarette. It bounced up and down when he spoke. 'Is… is everything all right?'

'Could you come out here a moment please, Mr Dawson?' Logan asked.

A frown creased Norman's brow at this sudden use of formality. He moved to step out of the shed, but Logan indicated the screwdriver with a nod.

'Can you leave that, please?'

There was a pause as Norman looked down at the screwdriver, but then he set it down on the workbench and emerged onto the neatly-cropped lawn.

'Is everything all right?' he asked again, more tentatively this time.

'What was your relationship with Iona Wallace, Mr Dawson?'

Norman's Adam's Apple bobbed all the way to the bottom of his throat.

'Relationship? We didn't have… we didn't have a relationship.'

'But you'd had sex,' Logan said. Not a question. A statement of fact.

'What?' Norman half-laughed, his voice disintegrating around the edges. 'Why would you…? What makes you…?'

Logan held up his phone. The image on-screen was frozen and showed a naked man, his face blurred, with Iona Wallace's legs wrapped around him.

With a tap of a finger, Logan pressed play, and the figures began to writhe and moan.

'I'm not… I don't know what—' Norman began, but Logan held up a finger for silence.

They waited, the only sounds in the garden the twittering of birdsong and the grunting of the people in the video.

And then, it came. The call of the cuckoo clock they both knew all too well.

Logan paused the video and returned the phone to his pocket.

'That was uploaded ten days after you and Pat arrived on the island,' Logan said. 'I checked.'

He sighed, but seemed more annoyed with himself than with the other man. 'People have been telling me since I got here that she was quick to jump on any new arrivals. I thought that meant tourists. Didn't occur to me that you were a new arrival, too.'

Logan turned and looked at the upstairs windows of the house. The smallest window was open, the textured glass coated white with steam.

'I had a poke through the other rooms in the house. Except the bathroom. I think your wife's in there. Thought best not to disturb her until you and I had this wee chat. The décor in the video doesn't match anywhere. But that's because you redecorated, isn't it? The one room in the house you changed is the room you had sex in. The room you knew she had video footage of.'

Norman said nothing, but half-stepped, half-fell backwards until he thudded against the side of the shed. He leaned there, using it for support, his face melting into sorrow and shame.

'I was… I was drunk. I didn't know she'd filmed it until weeks later. She asked at the time, and I said no. Of course, I said no, but she must've… she…' He buried his face in his hands. 'Oh, God! How did you find it? She said she hadn't shared it. She promised me. It's not online, is it? Oh, God, it's not online? I paid her! She asked for money, and I paid her! What more did she bloody want?!'

So, she was blackmailing him, then. That was it.

'You wanted to keep her quiet. Newly arrived in the community, struggling to fit in, you want to make a good impression. Video footage of you rodgering Iona Wallace isn't going to help your case,' Logan said. 'You wanted to make sure she stayed quiet, so you killed her.'

Norman opened his mouth, but Logan spoke before he could.

'Except… you were home. Kevin Tillerson saw you. Spoke to you. The night Iona died. You were home,' Logan muttered.

'Yes! Exactly!' Norman confirmed. 'I was home. All night. I didn't kill her, I swear!'

'Shh. Shut up.' Logan's eyes widened. He took a big step closer to Norman, pinning him to the shed with the sheer weight of his presence alone. 'Pat. Did she know? About you and Iona? Did she know?'

'She wouldn't—'

'*Did she know, Norman?*' Logan demanded.

'Yes! Yes, Iona told her. But she didn't… she wouldn't…'

But Logan had already spun on his heels and was thundering across the grass. Behind him, Norman slid down the shed wall, the tears of shame he'd been holding back for months finally bubbling to the surface.

–

Steam was seeping from beneath the bathroom door when Logan arrived at it.

'Mrs Dawson?' he said, knocking. 'Pat? Can you come out, please?'

There was no sound from within besides the faint whirring of the extractor fan. Logan knocked again, making sure to rattle the door this time in a way that suggested it wouldn't hold him out for long.

'Mrs Dawson, I need you to get dressed and come out. We need to talk.'

A door creaked open along the hall. Kevin Tillerson poked his head out. 'Everything OK?'

'Get back in your room, Mr Tillerson,' Logan ordered.

Tillerson didn't need telling twice. The door closed again immediately, and was followed by the clack of a lock sliding into place.

Logan rattled the handle of the door. Locked, of course, but there was something oddly violating about a bathroom door handle being turned from the outside that tended to force those inside into some kind of action.

Sure enough, he heard movement. A creak. A sob. A faint rattling sound.

'Fuck,' he spat, then he drove a shoulder through the door, throwing it wide.

Pat stood naked in the corner, tears streaming down her face, blood oozing from raw, gaping gouges in her wrists.

Logan crossed the room in two big steps, wrenched the pill bottle from her hand, and tossed it into the bloodied water of the bath.

She tried to fight him off. Screamed as she slapped at him. Howled as she pushed, and shoved, and kicked with her bare, water-wrinkled feet.

'She was going to tell everyone,' Pat sobbed. Her legs gave out and Logan had to wrap his arms around her to keep her on her feet. Her weight pressed against him, hot and wet and shaking from head to toe.

The words that tumbled out of her were all tangled up in tears, and snot, and raw, throaty sobs.

'She ruined our marriage. She was going to ruin our lives! We gave her money, but it wasn't enough. It was never enough!'

Logan checked the woman's wrists. The gouges looked painful, but they hadn't gone deep enough to do any serious damage.

'She was evil!' Pat whispered. 'She was *evil*.'

'She wasn't evil. Just damaged,' Logan said. He listened to the muffled sobs of Pat as she buried her face against his chest. 'But then, aren't we all?'

Chapter 41

Logan sat in the Canna Come Inn, a tepid cup of coffee on the table in front of him.

The boat had been quick off the mark coming back over. One of the Uniforms from Fort William had been aboard, and Logan had handed Pat Dawson over into his custody, then given instructions to wait at the dock for him to return.

He hadn't managed to get the full story from Pat yet, but he'd pieced together enough. Iona had been blackmailing them for months, demanding more and more money to keep secret the fact that she and Norman had done the dirty deed.

She'd threatened to release the video. They hadn't known that it was already online, albeit with Norman's face blurred out. She'd said she was going to send it to the couple's parents. To their siblings. To their nieces and nephews.

The local community would've shunned them, Pat said. Everything they'd built would've been taken from them. They'd have been ruined, if she'd gone through with it.

It was Iona's fault, Pat had insisted. She had left Pat no option. Murder was the only road left open.

Any other details could wait for now. He had his killer. He'd nabbed two other bastards, into the bargain.

Aye, he might not still have a job by the time any of it came to trial, but he'd done it. He'd brought them in. He'd given Iona a justice that, he had to admit, she may not even have deserved.

But there was one injustice he could still put right. One that she did deserve.

Logan looked up from the coffee cup as Isaac Young arrived at the table.

'Sorry, I'm a bit late,' Isaac said. 'Got caught up with a few errands.'

'No bother at all,' Logan said. He indicated the seat across from him. 'Can I get you anything?'

Isaac shook his head as he sat. 'I'm fine, thanks. I don't have much time.'

'Right. Well,' Logan said, getting down to business. 'First up, I want you to know that we've arrested someone for your mother's murder.'

'I heard. Bruce. The barman from here.'

'Eh, no. There's been a new development,' Logan said. 'We've had a confession from Pat Dawson.'

Isaac blinked. 'What? At the Bed and Breakfast? *That* Pat?'

'Aye,' Logan said.

'Why?'

'It's a long story,' Logan said. 'And one that, to be honest, you'd be better off not knowing for as long as you possibly can. We don't have the full story yet ourselves. But we will. We'll get it.'

Isaac stared down at the table in front of him, like he was trying to will a stiff drink into existence.

'Bloody hell,' he muttered. 'That's… bloody hell.'

'Aye. Understandable reaction,' Logan said. He took a swig of his cold coffee, grimaced, then sat up straighter in his chair. 'There was… there was something else, too. Something I found in your mum's old diaries.'

Isaac looked up, frowning. 'Mum kept diaries?'

'Aye. Sometimes,' Logan said. He cleared his throat, not quite sure how to say what he needed to say. 'And, well… the thing is, Isaac…'

He inhaled, held it, then breathed out.

'It's about your dad.'

Isaac sat and listened in silence as Logan told him. Told him how his life had been a lie. Told him how the man he'd thought was his father was not. Told him, for the first time ever, the full truth.

And then, when it was all out in the open, Isaac Young fell forward onto the table, buried his head in his arm, and sobbed in anger and in shame.

–

'Is Isaac OK?' asked Roddy, glancing over at the younger man. He was still sitting at the table, now nursing a hot cup of tea which he'd shown no signs yet of drinking.

Logan stood by the bar with his wallet open, ready to settle the bill. He glanced back at Isaac, then gave a single shake of his head.

'No. No' really,' he admitted. 'What do I owe you?'

'Nothing. On me,' Roddy said.

Logan thought about protesting, but what was the point now?

'Thanks,' he said, returning the wallet to his pocket.

'No. Thank you, Mr Logan,' Roddy said. 'I've been thinking a lot about what you said. About happiness, and not knowing what's around the corner. About what happened to your friend. And... you're right. It's stupid. I've been stupid, hiding away, pretending I'm someone I'm not.'

He inhaled deeply through his nose, and his chest seemed to double in size. 'I'm going to do it. I'm going to tell them all,' he vowed. 'If they don't like it, tough. It's my pub. If they don't want to drink here, fine.'

'No' like they've got a wealth of other places to choose from,' Logan said.

Roddy laughed. It was a giggle of relief. 'Exactly! Yes! What else are they going to do? Go to the cinema? Go bowling?'

He looked around at the patrons of the bar. There were three of them, not counting Logan or Isaac, all sitting at different tables, reading, doing crosswords, or just staring blankly into space.

'I'm going to do it,' Roddy whispered. 'I'm going to bloody do it.'

'Good for you, Mr MacKay,' Logan said. 'You could even consider a name change for the pub.'

Roddy's smile remained in place, but a frown troubled his brow. 'Eh?'

'The "Canna Come Out?" has a nice ring to it,' Logan said. He reached across the bar, shook the landlord's hand. Then, with a final look at Isaac—a look filled with every different shade of sadness and regret—he turned to the door.

He'd just pushed it open when the bell behind the bar rang. Logan stepped through, but waited and listened as Roddy cleared his throat, then spoke in a loud, clear voice.

'Sorry, everyone. Sorry. It's not last orders, don't worry. I just wanted to tell you all something,' he said.

He drew in a breath. All eyes turned his way.

'I'm gay,' he announced.

There was silence. Lengthy. Pregnant. Contemplative.

'Oh,' said the man with the crossword. 'Right. Fair enough, then.'

And then, Logan let the door close, and headed for his final appointment of the day.

–

'Do you mind? We are in the middle of a reading.'

Logan stood in the doorway of the church, a dark silhouette against the pale blue sky.

The Reverend Abraham Kerr stood at the front, scowling up the short aisle. Four elderly parishioners sat on the front-most pews. They shuffled around, craning their necks to look in the direction of the door.

'No. Don't mind at all. You carry on,' Logan said, strolling into the church and letting the door swing closed with a thunk.

'What do you want, Mr Logan?' the minister asked.

'Detective Chief Inspector,' Logan reminded him. He arrived at the front, and looked down at an old woman perched near the end of the pew. 'Budge up, sweetheart,' he told her, and she and the skeletal man beside her both slid a few feet along the bench.

Logan flopped down onto it, folded his arms, then gave the minister a nod. 'Crack on, then.'

'This is a private Bible study group,' Kerr said. 'I'd appreciate it if you—'

'Do you do requests?' Logan asked.

Kerr's hawk-like features frowned. 'I beg your pardon.'

'Requests. Bible's greatest hits. Feeding of the five thousand. Water into wine. All that shite,' Logan said. 'Do you do requests?'

'What are—'

'Matthew, Chapter One, Verse Two,' Logan said. 'That's a favourite of mine. Love to hear it.'

Reverend Kerr did not reply. His features locked together in place, frozen and immobile.

'Come on. Out with it, then,' Logan urged. He waited for a response he knew wouldn't come, then shrugged. 'Well, fortunately, I memorised it on the way up here. Wasn't difficult. It's very short.'

He stood, drawing himself to his full height. 'Matthew, Chapter One, Verse Two,' he began. 'Abraham begat Isaac.'

There was some murmured confusion from the elderly parishioners, but there was no confusion on Kerr's face. The truth, he knew, was finally out.

'Abraham Kerr,' Logan said. 'I am arresting you on suspicion of the rape of your daughter, Iona Wallace.'

–

The boat journey to Mallaig was, Logan had to admit, an absolute belter. At one end, the Uniform from Fort William was trying his best to keep Pat Dawson from throwing herself overboard, while Logan sat at the back with Reverend Kerr, glaring at him whenever he tried to open his mouth.

They didn't need a confession. They had Iona's diaries and, more importantly, they'd get Isaac's DNA. No matter how much the minister wriggled and squirmed, it was concrete. The twisted bastard was going away.

Isaac had taken it hard, of course. No surprise there. He told Logan he'd suspected the man he thought of as his dad wasn't his actual father, but he'd clung to it because he wanted to believe it. He didn't want to believe the alternative, that his dad was some random teenage hook-up down a dark alley somewhere.

Although, given what he now knew, Isaac had wished, more than anything, that that were the case.

And Logan, to his surprise, had, too.

The DCI watched the foaming waters breaking past the starboard side, losing himself in the churning bubbles.

They'd passed Rum now, where he'd watched stags go darting along the beach, almost like they were challenging him to a race. Mallaig was a few minutes ahead. The mainland. Normality.

And all the consequences and complications it would bring.

Still, four collars in one day. Not a bad way to end it.

There were three polis cars waiting at the harbour at Mallaig. Uniforms had jumped out of two of them when the boat came in, their jackets zipped up against the unforgiving winds.

Pat and Abraham had been separated, one in one car, one in another.

'Mind if I cadge a lift back to the Fort off you, son?' Logan asked the constable who'd landed the job of driving the minister.

The DCI had already opened the passenger door when the other Uniform piped up from the next car over. The only one not to have a prisoner in the back seat.

'Actually, sir, I've been asked to take you,' he said. Logan spotted the sergeant stripes on the man's shoulder and closed the door with a soft thunk.

'Aye. Right. Makes sense,' he said. 'You want me in the back or the front?'

'Up to you, sir,' the sergeant replied.

'In that case, if you don't mind, I'll call shotgun,' Logan said, opening the front passenger door.

He looked out across the water, to the islands sitting out there by the horizon. He inhaled, breathing in the salt, and the fish, and the freedom.

'Right then,' he said, climbing into the car. 'Let's get this over with.'

–

The journey passed in silence. Logan's choice. The sergeant tried to strike up a conversation a couple of times, but the DCI wasn't in the mood.

The convoy of police vehicles slowed as it approached the roundabout next to the Fort William station. Logan watched the first two cars hanging a left, caught glimpses of Pat and Abraham through the side windows as they turned onto the station road.

But then, the car he was in continued straight across the roundabout without turning.

'We no' going in there?' Logan asked. 'They've not got you taking me all the way to Inverness, have they? Can I stop for a pee first?'

'Not to Inverness, sir, no. West End car park,' the sergeant replied.

'West End... why? What's at the West End car park?' Logan asked.

The sergeant shrugged. 'Dunno, sir. Just doing what I'm told.'

They cruised through the sparse, off-season traffic. Logan gazed out of the side window, watching familiar landmarks slide by. There was JJ's café. The High School. The bridge he'd raced across in Sinead's car the first time he'd met her, when they'd thought her brother was in danger.

Onwards, past the turn-off to the pizza shop that didn't take card payments.

Past the leisure centre, past the supermarket. The hotel he'd stayed at with Ben and the rest of the team was down there somewhere, hidden by the golden arches of the MacDonald's.

Caitlyn had been with them then. It was the first night Logan had seen her truly happy.

And the last.

A black BMW was waiting at the West End car park. The door opened as the polis car pulled in off the roundabout, and Logan saw the bulky frame of Detective Superintendent Hoon step down from inside.

'Fuck,' he muttered.

'Aye. Good luck, sir,' the sergeant said. He pulled them into a space directly across from the Beamer, keeping a safe distance. 'Think I'll just drop you here, if that's all right?'

'Don't blame you, son,' Logan said. 'Cheers for the lift.'

He unclipped his belt, puffed out his cheeks, then stepped out to face his fate.

'Well, well, look who it is. The one-man clusterfuck,' Hoon spat, when Logan approached.

Behind the DCI, the sergeant's car went speeding out of the car park. Probably trying to escape the blast radius, Logan thought.

'Sir,' Logan said. 'Wasn't expecting a personal visit.'

'My toe should be paying a personal fucking visit to the crack of your arse, sunshine,' Hoon told him. 'Where the fuck have you been?'

'Canna, sir, it—'

'Don't come the cunt wi' me, Jack. You know what I fucking-well mean!'

Logan flashed the DSup an apologetic smile. 'Aye. Sorry, sir.'

'I appreciate that being a smart-arse is a force of fucking habit, Detective Chief Inspector, but now's no' the time or the fucking place. Got it?' snapped Hoon.

Logan nodded. 'Got it.' He shoved his hands deep in his pockets and rocked on his heels. 'So, I'm guessing this is about what happened at Bosco's.'

'Bosco? That clown? Fuck me, Jack. What do you take me for? Only mistake you made there was no' tying the prick to a fucking chair before lighting the match,' Hoon said. 'Bosco? Fuck off. I don't give a flying fuck about that Russian bastard.'

Logan's brow furrowed into lines of confusion. 'What? So… what's this about, then?' he asked, gesturing around them.

Detective Superintendent Hoon rolled his tongue around in his mouth for a moment, like he was having to manhandle the words out.

'You were right, Jack,' he said, and it visibly pained him to say the sentence aloud. 'You were right.'

'Right? About what?' Logan asked.

There was something about the way Hoon was acting that made the fine hairs on the back of Logan's neck stand on end. The wind coming in off the loch beside them seemed colder than it should be.

'Sir?' Logan pressed. 'What am I right about?'

Hoon sighed. It was heavy and weary, full of trepidation about what had happened.

Or what was about to.

'It's Owen Petrie,' he said. 'It's Mister Whisper.'

Logan's heart fell into his stomach. He knew what was coming. He knew, beyond a shadow of a doubt, what the man standing across from him was about to say.

'He's free.'

Do you love crime fiction and are always on the lookout for brilliant authors?

Canelo Crime is home to some of the most exciting novels around. Thousands of readers are already enjoying our compulsive stories. Are you ready to find your new favourite writer?

Find out more and sign up to our newsletter at canelocrime.com